Clark, Mary Higgins

The Anastasia syndrome, and
  other stories

DATE	ISSUED TO

By Mary Higgins Clark

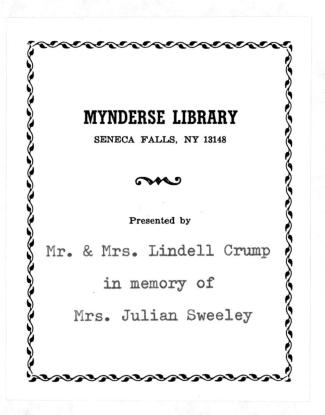

THE ANASTASIA SYNDROME

AND OTHER STORIES

Mary Higgins Clark

SIMON AND SCHUSTER

New York London Toronto Sydney Tokyo

Simon and Schuster
Simon & Schuster Building
Rockefeller Center
1230 Avenue of the Americas
New York, New York 10020

This book is a work of fiction. Names, characters, places
and incidents are either the product of the author's
imagination or are used fictitiously. Any resemblance to
actual events or locales or persons, living or dead,
is entirely coincidental.

Copyright © 1989 by Mary Higgins Clark

SIMON AND SCHUSTER and colophon are registered trademarks
of Simon & Schuster, Inc.

Designed by Levavi & Levavi
Manufactured in the United States of America

1   3   5   7   9   10   8   6   4   2

Library of Congress Cataloging in Publication data
Clark, Mary Higgins.
The Anastasia syndrome, and other stories / Mary Higgins Clark.
p. cm.
I. Title.
PS3553.L287A8   1989
813'.54—dc20   89–38841
CIP
ISBN 0-671-67367-X

"Lucky Day," copyright © 1986 by Mary Higgins Clark.
Originally published in *Murder in Manhattan*, edited by Bill Adler.

The following stories originally appeared in *Woman's Day*:

"Terror Stalks the Class Reunion," copyright © 1987 by Mares Enterprises.

"Double Vision," copyright © 1988 by Mares Enterprises.

"The Lost Angel" copyright © 1986 by Mary Higgins Clark.

CONTENTS

I saw their starved lips in the gloam
With horrid warning gapèd wide,
And I awoke and found me here
On the cold hill's side.

And this is why I sojourn here
Alone and palely loitering,
Though the sedge is withered from the lake,
And no birds sing.

John Keats
"La Belle Dame Sans Merci"

THE ANASTASIA SYNDROME

With a combination of reluctance and relief, Judith closed the book she had been studying and laid her pen on top of her thick notebook. She had been working steadily for hours, and her back felt cramped as she pushed back the old-fashioned swivel chair and got up from the desk. The day was overcast. Long ago, she had turned on the powerful desk light she had bought to replace the elaborately fringed Victorian lamp which belonged in this furnished rental flat in the Knightsbridge district of London.

Flexing her arms and shoulders, Judith walked over to the

window and looked down at Montpelier Street. At three-thirty, the grayness of the January day was already merging with the approaching dusk and the slight shudder of the windowpanes testified that the wind was still brisk.

Unconsciously she smiled, remembering the letter she had received in answer to her inquiry about this place:

> "Dear Judith Chase,
> The flat will be available from 1 September until 1 May. Your references are most satisfactory, and it is a comfort to me to know that you will be engaged in writing your new book. The Civil War in seventeenth-century England has proved marvelously fertile to romantic writers and it is gratifying that a serious historical writer of your stature has chosen it. The flat is unpretentious but spacious and I think you will find it adequate. The lift is frequently out of order; however, three flights of stairs are not too formidable, do you think? I personally climb them by choice."

The letter ended with a precise, spidery signature: *"Beatrice Ardsley."* Judith knew from mutual friends that Lady Ardsley was eighty-three.

Her fingertips touched the windowsill and she felt the cold, raw air forcing its way through the wooden frame. Shivering, Judith decided that she would have just enough time for a hot bath, if she hurried. Outside, the street was almost empty. The few pedestrians were scurrying along rapidly, their heads bent into their necks, coat collars rolled up. As she turned away, she saw a toddler running down the street just below her window. Horrified, Judith watched as the little girl tripped and fell into the road. If a car came around the corner, the driver wouldn't see her in time. There was an elderly man halfway down the street. She pulled at the window to scream for him to help, but then a young woman appeared from nowhere, darted into the road, scooped up the child and cradled it in her arms.

"Mummy, Mummy," Judith heard it cry.

[10

She closed her eyes and buried her face in her hands as she heard herself wailing aloud, "Mummy, Mummy." Oh God. Not again!

She forced herself to open her eyes. As she had expected, the woman and toddler had vanished. Only the old man was there, making his careful way along the sidewalk.

The phone rang as she was fastening a diamond pin to the jacket of her silk faille cocktail suit. It was Stephen.

"Darling, how did the writing go today?" he asked.

"Very well, I think." Judith felt her pulse quicken. Forty-six years old and her heart leaped like a schoolgirl's at the sound of Stephen's voice.

"Judith, there's a bloody emergency Cabinet meeting and it's running late. Do you mind terribly meeting me at Fiona's? I'll send the car."

"Don't do that. A taxi will be quicker. If you're late, it's state business. If I'm late, it's bad business."

Stephen laughed. "God, you do make my life easy!" His voice lowered. "I'm besotted with you, Judith. Let's only stay as long as we must at the party, then go off for a quiet dinner together."

"Perfect. Good-bye, Stephen. I love you."

Judith replaced the receiver, a smile playing on her lips. Two months ago, she had been seated at a dinner party next to Sir Stephen Hallett. "Quite the biggest catch in England," her hostess, Fiona Collins, confided. "Stunning looks. Charming. Brilliant. Home Secretary. It's common knowledge that he'll be the next Prime Minister. And darling Judith, best of all, he's *eligible*."

"I met Stephen Hallett once or twice in Washington years ago," Judith said. "Kenneth and I liked him very much. But I came to England to write a book, not to get involved with a man, charming or not."

"Oh nonsense," Fiona snapped. "You've been widowed for ten years. That's quite long enough. You've made your name as an important writer. Darling, it really is nice to have a man around the house, especially if the house turns out to be 10 Downing Street. My bones tell me that you and Stephen would be perfect together. Judith, you're a beautiful woman, but you always send out signals saying 'Stay away, I'm not interested.' Don't do that tonight, please."

She had not sent out those signals. And that night Stephen had escorted her home and come up for a nightcap. They had talked till nearly dawn. When he left, he had kissed her lightly on the lips. "If I have passed a more pleasant evening in my life, I don't remember it," he had whispered.

A taxi was not quite so simple to find as she had expected. Judith waited a chilly ten minutes before one finally came along. As she stood at the curb, she tried to avoid looking into the road. This was the exact spot where, from the window, she had seen the toddler fall. Or imagined it.

Fiona's home was a Regency house in Belgravia. A Member of Parliament, Fiona took glee in being compared to the acerbic Lady Astor. Her husband, Desmond, chairman of a worldwide publishing empire, was one of the most powerful men in England.

After leaving her coat in the cloakroom, Judith slipped into the adjoining powder room. Nervously she touched her lips with gloss and patted back the tendrils that the wind had scattered around her face. Her hair was still a natural dark brown; she had not yet begun to cover the occasional strands of silver. An interviewer had once described her eyes as sapphire blue and her porcelain complexion a constant reminder that she was believed to be of English birth and heritage.

It was time to go into the drawing room, to let Fiona drag

her from group to group. Fiona never failed to give an introduction that sounded like a sales pitch. "My dear, dear friend, Judith Chase. One of the most prestigious writers in America. Pulitzer prize. American Book Award. Why this beautiful creature specializes in revolutions when I could give her so much delicious gossip, I'll never know. Nevertheless, her books on the French Revolution and the American Revolution are simply brilliant and yet manage to read like novels. Now she's working on our Civil War, Charles the First, and Cromwell. Absolutely immersed in it. I'm so afraid she'll find some nasty secrets that some of us would just as soon not know about our ancestors."

Fiona would not stop the running commentary until she'd made sure everyone was aware of who Judith was, then, when Stephen arrived, she would rush around whispering that the Home Secretary and Judith had been dinner partners right here, in this house, and now . . . she would roll her eyes and leave the rest unsaid.

At the entrance to the drawing room Judith paused for a moment to take in the scene. Fifty or sixty people, she estimated quickly, at least half the faces familiar: government leaders, her own English publisher, Fiona's titled friends, a famous playwright . . . A fleeting thought crossed her mind that no matter how often she came into this room, she was struck by the exquisite simplicity of the muted fabrics on the antique sofas, the museum-quality paintings, the understated charm of the slender draperies that framed the French doors to the garden.

"Miss Chase, isn't it?"

"Yes." Judith accepted a glass of champagne from a waiter as she gave an impersonal smile to Harley Hutchinson, the columnist and television personality who was England's leading gossipmonger. Somewhere in his early forties, he was long and lean, with inquisitive hazel eyes and lank brown hair which fell forward on his forehead.

"May I say you're looking lovely tonight?"

"Thank you." Judith smiled briefly and began to move on.

"It is always a pleasure when a beautiful woman is also blessed with an exquisite sense of fashion. That's something we don't often see at high levels in this country. How is your book going? Do you find our little Cromwellian spat as interesting as writing about the French peasants and the American colonists?"

"Oh, I think your little spat is right up there with the others." Judith felt the anxiety that had been caused by the hallucination of the toddler begin to disappear. The thinly veiled sarcasm Hutchinson used as a weapon restored her equilibrium.

"Tell me, Miss Chase. Do you hug your manuscript to yourself until it's complete, or do you share it along the way? Some writers enjoy talking over the day's work. For example, how much does Sir Stephen know about your new book?"

Judith decided it was time to ignore him. "I haven't spoken to Fiona yet. Excuse me." She did not wait for Hutchinson's response as she walked across the room. Fiona's back was to her. When Judith greeted her, Fiona turned, quickly kissed her cheek, and murmured, "Darling, just one moment. I've finally cornered Dr. Patel and do want to hear what he has to say."

Dr. Reza Patel, the world-renowned psychiatrist and neurobiologist. Judith studied him intently. About fifty years old. Intense black eyes that burned from under heavy brows. A forehead that furrowed frequently as he spoke. A good head of dark hair framing his even-featured brown face. A well-cut gray pin-striped suit. Besides Fiona, there were four or five others clustered around him. Their expressions as they listened to him ranged from skepticism to awe. Judith knew that Patel's ability to regress patients under hypnosis to very early childhood and have them accurately describe traumatic experiences was considered the greatest breakthrough in psychoanalysis in a generation. She also knew that his new theory, which he called the Anastasia Syndrome, had both shocked and alarmed the scientific world.

"I do not expect that I will be able to prove my theory for quite a time to come," Patel was saying. "But after all, ten years ago many scoffed at my belief that a combination of benign medication and hypnosis could release the blocks that the mind throws up in self-protection. Now that theory is accepted and in general use. Why should any human being be forced to undergo years of analysis to find the reason for his or her problem, when it can be uncovered in a few brief visits?"

"But the Anastasia Syndrome is quite different, surely?" Fiona protested.

"Different, yet remarkably similar." Patel waved his hands. "Look at the people in this room. Typical of the crème de la crème of England. Intelligent. Knowledgeable. Proven leaders. Any one of them might be an appropriate vessel to bring back the great leaders of the centuries. Think how much better off the world would be if we could have the present counsel of Socrates, for example. Look, there is Sir Stephen Hallett. In my opinion, he will be a superb Prime Minister, but wouldn't it be comforting to know that Disraeli or Gladstone was offering him counsel? Was literally part of his being?"

Stephen! Judith turned quickly, then waited as Fiona darted to greet him. Realizing that Hutchinson was watching her, she deliberately stayed with Dr. Patel when the others drifted away. "Doctor, if I understand your theory, the woman Anna Anderson, who claimed she was Anastasia, was receiving treatment for a nervous breakdown. You believe that during a session when she was under hypnosis and had been treated with drugs, she was inadvertently regressed to that basement in Russia at the exact moment when the Grand Duchess Anastasia was murdered with the rest of the royal family."

Patel nodded. "That is exactly my theory. The spirit of the Grand Duchess as it left her body, instead of going on to the next world, entered the body of Anna Anderson. Their identities became fused. Anna Anderson in truth became the living embodiment of Anastasia, with her memories, her emotions, her intelligence."

"And what about Anna Anderson's personality?" Judith asked.

"There seems to have been no conflict. She was a very intelligent woman but willingly surrendered herself to her new position as the surviving heiress to the throne of Russia."

"But why Anastasia? Why not her mother, the Czarina, or one of her sisters?"

Patel raised his eyebrows. "A very shrewd question, Miss Chase, and by asking it you have put your finger squarely on the one problem of the Anastasia Syndrome. History tells us that Anastasia was by far the most strong-minded of the women in her family. Perhaps the others accepted their death with resignation and went on to the next plane. She was not willing to go, fought to stay in this time zone, and seized on the inadvertent presence of Anna Anderson to cling to life."

"Then you are saying that the only people you could in theory bring back would be those who died unwillingly, those who desperately wanted to live?"

[16

"Exactly. Which is why I mention Socrates who was forced to drink hemlock, as opposed to Aristotle who died of natural causes. That is the reason why I was truly being frivolous when I suggested Sir Stephen might be an appropriate vessel to absorb the essence of Disraeli. Disraeli died peacefully, but someday I shall also have the knowledge to recall the peaceful dead whose moral leadership is needed again. And now Sir Stephen is making his way to you." Patel smiled. "May I say I admire your books tremendously. Your scholarship is a pleasure."

"Thank you." She had to ask him. "Dr. Patel," she said hurriedly, "you have been able to help people retrieve memories of very early childhood, haven't you?"

"Yes." His expression became intent. "That is not an idle question."

"No, it isn't."

Patel reached into his pocket and handed her his card. "If you ever wish to talk to me, please call."

Judith felt a hand on her arm and looked up into Stephen's face. She tried to keep her voice impersonal. "Stephen, how good to see you. Do you know Dr. Patel?"

Stephen nodded curtly to Patel and linking her arm in his, steered her to the far end of the room. "Darling," he murmured, "why in the name of heaven are you wasting your breath on that charlatan?"

"He's not—" Judith stopped. Of all people, Stephen Hallett was the last man who could be expected to endorse Dr. Patel's theories. The newspapers had already printed Patel's suggestion that Stephen would be a likely candidate to become infused with the spirit of Disraeli. She smiled up at him, not caring for the moment that they were being observed by almost everyone in the room.

There was a stir as the Prime Minister was greeted at the door by her hostess. "I don't usually do many of these

17]

cocktail parties, but for your sake, my dear," she said to Fiona.

Stephen put his arm around Judith. "It's about time you met the Prime Minister, darling."

They went to Brown's Hotel for dinner. Over salad and sole Véronique, Stephen told her about his day. "Perhaps the most frustrating in at least a week. Damn it, Judith, the P.M. has got to end the speculation soon. The mood of the country demands an election. We need a mandate and she knows it. Labour knows it and we're at a stalemate. And yet I understand. If she doesn't stand for reelection, then of course that's it. When my time comes, I shall find it very hard to retire from public life."

Judith toyed with her salad. "Public life is your entire life, isn't it, Stephen?"

"Through all the years when Jane was ill, it was my salvation. It occupied my time and my mind and my energies. In the three years since her death, I can't tell you how many women I've been introduced to. I went out with a few of them, and I realized their faces and names all blended together. You want to know an interesting test of a woman? When she makes plans that include you, is she visibly annoyed when you're unavoidably late? Then one night, on a cold November evening, I met you at Fiona's, and life has been different. Now when the problems pile up, a quiet voice whispers, 'You'll be seeing Judith in a few hours.' "

His hand reached across the table and touched hers. "Now let me ask the question. You've created a very successful career. You've told me that sometimes you work through the night or hole up for days at a stretch when you have a deadline. I would respect your work as you respect mine, but there would be times, many times, when I'd need

[18

you to attend affairs with me or accompany me on trips abroad. Would that be a burden, Judith?"

Judith stared into her glass. In the ten years since Kenneth's death, she had managed to create a new life for herself. She'd been a journalist at the *Washington Post* when Kenneth, the White House correspondent of the Potomac Cable Network, was killed in a plane crash. She had enough insurance money to give up her job and begin the project that had been haunting her since the first time she had read a Barbara Tuchman book. She was determined to become a serious historical writer.

The thousands of hours of tedious research, the long nights at the typewriter, the rewriting and editing, had all paid off. Her first book, *The World Is Upside Down,* about the American Revolution, won a Pultizer prize and became a best-seller. Her second book, published two years ago, about the French Revolution, *Darkness at Versailles,* had been equally successful and received an American Book Award. Critics hailed her as "a spellbinding storyteller who writes with the scholarship of an Oxford don."

Judith looked directly at Stephen. The soft lighting from the shaded wall sconces and the glass-enclosed candle that flickered on the table softened the stern lines of his aristocratic features and emphasized the deep blue-gray tones of his eyes. "I think that like you, I've both loved my work and immersed myself in it to escape the fact that in the true sense of the word I haven't had a personal life since Kenneth died. There was a time when I could meet deadlines and still happily juggle all the commitments that come with being married to a White House correspondent. I think the rewards of being a woman as well as a writer are marvelous."

Stephen smiled and reached for her hand. "You see, we do think alike, don't we?"

Judith withdrew her hand. "Stephen, there's one thing you should consider. At fifty-four you're not too old to marry a woman who can give you a child. I'd always hoped to have a family and it simply didn't happen. At forty-six it certainly won't happen."

"My nephew is a splendid young man and has always loved Edge Barton Manor. I shall be glad for him to have it and the title when the time comes. My energies at this age simply do not extend to fatherhood."

Stephen came up to the flat for a brandy. They toasted each other solemnly as they agreed that neither one wanted to attract publicity about their personal life. Judith did not need the distraction of gossip columnists pestering her while she was writing her book. When the election came, Stephen wanted to answer questions about the issues, not about his courtship. "Although of course they'll love you," he commented. "Beautiful, talented, and a British war orphan. Can you imagine the field day they'll have when they connect us?"

She had a sudden vivid recollection of the incident this afternoon. The toddler, *"Mummy, Mummy!"* Last week, when she'd been near the Peter Pan statue in Kensington Gardens she had been torn by the haunting memory of having been there before. Ten days ago she had almost fainted in Waterloo station, sure that she'd heard the sound of an explosion, felt pieces of debris falling around her . . . "Stephen," she said, "there is *one* thing that *is* becoming very important to me. I know no one came forward to claim me when I was found in Salisbury, but I *was* well dressed, obviously had been well cared for. Is there any way I might be able to track down my birth family? Will you help me?"

She could feel Stephen's arms tense. "Good God, Judith, don't even think about it! You've told me every effort was made to trace your relatives and not one single clue was turned up. Your immediate family was probably wiped out in the raids. And even if it were possible, all we need is to unearth some obscure cousin who turns out to be a drug dealer or a terrorist. Please, for my sake, don't even consider it, at least not while I'm in public life. After that, I'll help you, I promise."

"Caesar's wife must be above reproach?"

He drew her to him. She felt the fine wool of his suit jacket against her cheek, felt the strength of his arms around her. His kiss, deep and demanding, quickened her senses, awoke in her feelings and desires she had resolutely put away when she lost Kenneth. But even so, she knew she could not wait indefinitely to search for her birth family.

It was she who broke the embrace. "You told me you have a very early meeting," she reminded him. "And I'm going to try to get another chapter written tonight."

Stephen's lips brushed her cheek. "Hoist on my own petard, I see. But you're right, at least for the immediate future."

Judith watched from the window as Stephen's chauffeur opened the door of the Rolls for him. An election was inevitable. In the near future, would she be riding in that Rolls as the wife of the Prime Minister of Great Britain? Sir Stephen and Lady Hallett . . .

She loved Stephen. Then why this anxiety? Impatiently she went into the bedroom, changed into a nightgown and warm wool robe, and went back to her desk. A few minutes later, she was deep in concentration as she wrote the next chapter of her book about the Civil War in England. She had completed the chapters about the causes of the conflict, the destructive taxes, the dissolved Parliament, the insistence on the divine right of kings, the execution of Charles I, the Cromwellian years, the restoration of the monarchy. Now she was ready to write about the fate of the regicides, those who had planned, signed, or carried out the death warrant of Charles I and were to know the swift justice of his son, Charles II.

Her first stop the next morning was the Public Records Office at Chancery Lane. Harold Wilcox, the Assistant Keeper of Records, willingly pulled out piles of aging documents. It seemed to Judith that centuries of dust had been assumed into their pages.

Wilcox thoroughly admired Charles II. "A lad of nearly sixteen when he first had to flee the country to escape his father's impending fate. A clever one he was. The Prince slipped through the Roundhead lines at Truro and sailed to Jersey and on to France. He came back to lead the Royalists, escaped again to France and remained there and in Holland until England came to its senses and begged his return."

"He stayed near Breda. I've been there," Judith remarked.

"An interesting place, isn't it? And if you look about, you'll see many in town with traces of the Stuart features. Charles the Second loved the women. It was at Breda that he signed the famous declaration promising amnesty to his father's executioners."

"He didn't keep his promise. In effect that declaration was a carefully-worded lie."

"What he wrote is that he extended mercy where it was *wanted* and *deserved*. But neither he nor his advisers believed that everyone deserved that mercy. Twenty-nine men were tried for regicide—the killing of a king. Others turned themselves in and were sent to prison. Those found guilty were hanged, drawn, and quartered."

Judith nodded. "Yes. But there was never a clear explanation for the fact that the King also attended the

[22

beheading of a woman, Lady Margaret Carew, who was married to one of the regicides. What crime did she commit?"

Harold Wilcox frowned. "There are always rumors that surround historical events," he said. "I do not deal in rumors."

The raw wintry cold of the past few days had given way to brilliant sunshine and an almost balmy breeze. When she left the Records Office Judith walked the mile to Cecil Court and spent the rest of the morning browsing through old bookshops in the area. The tourists were out in full force, and she decided that tourist season was now twelve months long. And then realized that in British eyes she too was a tourist.

Her arms filled with books, she decided to have a quick lunch in one of the little tea shops near Covent Garden. As she cut through the busy marketplace, she stopped to watch the jugglers and clog dancers, who seemed to be especially festive in the unexpected reprieve of the pleasant day.

And then it happened. The steady, piercing wail of the air raid sirens shattered the air. The bombs blotted out the sun, racing toward her; the building beyond the jugglers dissolved into a crumbled mass of broken bricks and fire. She was choking. The heat of the smoke was searing her face, closing her lungs. Her arms went limp and the books fell to the ground.

Frantically she reached out, groping for a hand. "Mummy," she whispered. "Mummy, I can't find you." A sob rose in her throat as the sirens receded, the sun returned, the smoke cleared away. As her eyes refocused, she realized she was clinging to the sleeve of a shabbily-dressed woman who was carrying a tray of plastic flowers. "You all right,

23]

luv?" the woman was asking. "Not going to faint, are you now?"

"No. No. I'll be fine." Somehow she managed to collect the books, to make her way to a tearoom. Not bothering with the menu the waitress offered, she ordered tea and toast. When the tea came, her hands were still trembling so violently she could barely hold the cup.

When she paid her bill, she extracted from her wallet the card Dr. Patel had given her at Fiona's party. She had noticed a phone box in Covent Garden. She would call him from there.

Let him be in, she prayed as she dialed the number.

The receptionist did not want to put her through. "Dr. Patel has just finished his last patient. He does not have afternoon hours. I can arrange an appointment for next week."

"Just give him my name. Tell him it's an emergency." Judith closed her eyes. The whine of the air raid sirens. It was going to happen again.

And then she heard Dr. Patel's voice. "You have my address, Miss Chase. Come over immediately."

By the time she reached his office on Welbeck Street, she had recovered some measure of control. A thin, fortyish woman, dressed in a white lab coat, her blond hair pulled back into a severe bun, admitted her. "I'm Rebecca Wadley," she said, "Dr. Patel's assistant. The doctor is waiting for you."

The reception room was small, his office quite large. Cherry-paneled, with a wall of books, a massive oak desk, several comfortable easy chairs, and an unobtrusive upholstered reclining couch in the corner, it felt like a scholar's study. There was nothing to suggest a clinical atmosphere.

Subconsciously Judith absorbed the details of the place

[24

as, at his invitation, she deposited her bags on a marble table near the reception-room door. Automatically she glanced in the mirror over the table and was startled to see that her face was deadly white, her lips ashen, the pupils of her eyes enormous.

"Yes, you look like someone who is just emerging from shock," Dr. Patel told her. "Come. Sit down. Tell me exactly what happened."

The somewhat genial attitude he had displayed at the party was gone. His eyes were serious, his expression grave, as he listened. Occasionally he interrupted her to clarify what she was telling him. "You were found as a toddler less than two years old wandering in Salisbury. You either had not yet begun to speak or were unable to speak because of shock. You were not wearing identification tags. To me that suggests you must have been traveling with an adult. Unfortunately, a mother or nurse would often carry a child's tags if they were traveling together."

"My dress and sweater were handmade," Judith said, "and I don't think that would suggest I was abandoned."

"I'm astonished that an adoption was permitted," Patel observed, "particularly to an American couple."

"My adoptive mother was the British Wren who found me. She was married to an American Naval officer. I was in the orphanage until I was nearly four before they were allowed to take me."

"You've been in England before?"

"A number of times. After the war, my adoptive father, Edward Chase, was in the diplomatic corps. We lived abroad in many countries until I went to college. We visited England and even went back to the orphanage. Oddly, I had no memory of it whatsoever. It seemed as though I'd always been with them, and I was never troubled about it. But now they've been gone for years

25]

and I've been living in England for five months, immersing myself in English history. It's as though all my English genes are churning about. I feel at home here. I belong here."

"And so whatever defensive blocks you built in your brain as a very small child are being attacked?" Patel sighed. "It happens. But I think there is more behind these hallucinatory incidents than you realize. Does Sir Stephen know you have come to see me?"

Judith shook her head. "No. In fact, he'd be very annoyed."

"I think 'charlatan' is his label for me, is it not?"

Judith did not answer. Her hands were still trembling. She clasped them firmly together in her lap.

"Never mind," Patel said. "I see three factors here. You are immersing yourself in English history—in a sense forcing your mind to go back to the past. Your adoptive parents are dead and you no longer feel a sense of disloyalty to them by searching out your birth family. And finally, living in London is accelerating these episodes. The Peter Pan statue in Kensington Gardens which you fantasized seeing a small child touch can probably be explained very easily. You may very well have played there as a child. The air raid sirens, the bombing. You may have experienced air raids, although that would not explain your being abandoned in Salisbury. And now you want me to help you?"

"Please. You said yesterday that you can regress people back to earliest childhood."

"Not always successfully. Strong-minded people, and I would certainly characterize you as one of them, fight hypnosis. They have a sense that hypnosis signifies the surrender of their will to another. That is why I would need your permission to use a mild drug if necessary to

[26

block that resistance. Think about it. Can you come back next week?"

"Next week?" Of course, she shouldn't have expected him to be able to treat her immediately. Judith tried to manage a smile. "I'll call your receptionist tomorrow morning for an appointment." She started to walk to the table where she'd left her shoulder bag and books.

And saw her. The same toddler. This time running from the room. So close that she could see the dress she was wearing. The sweater. The same outfit that *she* had been wearing when she was found in Salisbury, the outfit that was now packed in a closet in her Washington apartment.

She took a quick step forward, wanting to see the child's face, but the toddler, a mass of golden ringlets bobbing around her head, disappeared.

Judith fainted.

When she regained consciousness, she was lying on the chaise in Patel's office. Rebecca Wadley was holding a vial under her nostrils. The pungent odor of ammonia made Judith recoil. She pushed the vial away. "I'm all right," she said.

"Tell me what happened," Patel ordered. "What did you see?"

Haltingly Judith described the hallucination. "Am I going crazy?" she asked. "This just isn't *me*. Kenneth always said I had more common sense than the rest of Washington put together. What's happening?"

"What is happening is that you are close to a breakthrough, closer than I realized. Do you think you feel strong enough to begin treatment now? Will you sign the necessary permission forms?"

"Yes. Yes." Judith closed her eyes as Rebecca Wadley explained that she was going to open the collar of her blouse, remove her boots, and cover her with a light blanket. But Judith's hand was steady as she signed the forms Wadley gave her.

"All right, Miss Chase, the doctor will begin the procedure," Wadley said. "Are you quite comfortable?"

"Yes." Judith felt her sleeve being rolled up, a pad wrapped around her arm, the pinprick of a needle in her hand.

"Judith, open your eyes. Look at me. And then feel yourself begin to relax."

Stephen, Judith thought as she stared into Reza Patel's now shadowy face. Stephen . . .

The decorative mirror behind the chaise was actually a one-way glass that made observation and filming of hypnotic sessions possible from the laboratory without distracting the patient. Rebecca Wadley walked quickly into the laboratory. She switched on a video camera, the television screen, the intercom, and the machines that would monitor Judith's pulse and blood pressure. Carefully she observed the slowing heartbeat, the dropping pressure, as Judith began to succumb to Patel's efforts to hypnotize her.

Judith felt herself drifting, felt herself responding to Patel's gentle suggestions that she relax, fall into a restful sleep. No, she thought. No. She began to fight against the lulling drowsiness.

"Not responding. Fighting," Wadley said quietly.

Patel nodded and pushed the plunger attached to the hypodermic needle in Judith's hand, releasing a small amount of the drug into her system.

Judith wanted so to force her way to wakefulness. Her body was warning her not to let go. She struggled to open her eyes.

[28

Again Patel released fluid from the plunger into the hypodermic needle.

"You're at maximum dosage, Doctor. She won't allow herself to be hypnotized. She's coming out of it."

"Give me the vial of litencum," Patel ordered.

"Doctor, I don't think . . ."

Patel had used the drug litencum to get through psychological blockage in profoundly disturbed cases. It had the same characteristics as the substance used in the treatment of Anna Anderson, the woman who claimed to be the Grand Duchess Anastasia. It was the drug that, administered in quantity, Patel was sure would recreate the Anastasia Syndrome.

Rebecca Wadley, who worshiped Reza Patel as a genius and loved him as a man, was frightened. "Reza, don't," she pleaded.

Vaguely Judith heard their voices. The sleepy feeling was passing. She stirred.

"Give me the vial," Patel ordered.

Rebecca reached for it, opened it as she hurried from the lab back into the office, watched as Patel extracted a drop from it and injected it in Judith's vein.

Judith felt herself slipping away. The room faded. It was dark and warm and she was drifting again.

Wadley returned to the laboratory and consulted the monitors. Judith's heartbeat had once again slowed. Her blood pressure was dropping. "She's under."

The doctor nodded. "Judith, I'm going to ask you some questions. It will be easy to answer them. You won't experience discomfort or pain. You will feel warm and comfortable and as though you are floating. We will begin with this morning. Tell me about your new book. Weren't you doing research for it?"

29]

She was in the Records Office, talking to the Assistant Keeper, telling Patel about the restoration of the monarchy, about the fact that she had caught an incident in her primary research that fascinated her.

"What was that incident, Judith?"

"The King attended the beheading of a woman. Charles the Second was remarkably merciful. He was generous to Cromwell's widow, even forgave Cromwell's son who had become Lord Protector. He said that enough blood had been shed in England. The only executions he attended were for the men who signed his father's death warrant. Then why would he have been so angry at a woman that he chose to attend her execution?"

"That fascinates you?"

"Yes."

"And after you left the Records Office?"

"I went to Covent Garden."

Rebecca Wadley watched and listened as Dr. Patel brought Judith back in time to the day of her marriage to Kenneth, to her sixteenth birthday, her fifth birthday, the orphanage, her adoption.

Judith Chase was no ordinary woman, Wadley realized as she listened. The clarity of her memories was startling even as she regressed farther and farther into childhood. Wadley thought once again that no matter how many times she observed this procedure, she was endlessly awed to watch a mind open and reveal its secrets, to hear a self-assured, sophisticated adult speak with the soft, unclear speech pattern of a young child.

"Judith, before you were taken to the orphanage, before you were found in Salisbury—tell me what you remember."

Restlessly Judith shook her head from side to side. "No. No."

[30

The monitor showed that Judith's heartbeat was accelerating. "She's trying to block you," Wadley said quickly. Then, horrified, she watched as Patel released another drop from the vial into the plunger. "Doctor, don't."

"She's almost there. I can't stop now."

Wadley stared at the television screen. Judith's body was in a state of total relaxation. Her heartbeat was less than forty, her blood pressure seventy over fifty. Dangerous, Wadley thought, too dangerous. She knew that there was a zealot in Patel but had never seen him act so recklessly.

"Tell me what frightened you, Judith. Try."

Judith was breathing in soft, quick gasps. Now her sentences were fragmented, her voice the soft yet high-pitched tone of a very young child. They were going to go on a train. She was holding Mummy's hand. She began to scream, a child's frightened wail.

"What is happening? Tell me." Patel's voice was gentle.

Judith clutched at the blanket and in a childish cadence cried for her mother. "They're coming again, just like when we were playing. Mummy said, "Run, run!" Mummy won't hold my hand. It's so dark. . . . I'm running up the steps. The train is there. . . . Mummy said we're going to get on the train."

"Did you get on the train, Judith?"

"Yes. Yes."

"Did you talk to anyone?"

"Nobody was there. I was so tired. I wanted to go to sleep so that Mummy would be there when I woke up."

"When did you wake up?"

"The train stopped. It was light again. I went down the steps. . . . I don't remember after that."

"It's all right. Don't think about that anymore. You're a bright little girl. Can you tell me your name?"

31]

"Sarah Marrssh."

Marsh or Marrish, Rebecca thought. Now Judith's speech was that of a two-year-old.

"How old are you, Sarah?"

"Two."

"Do you know your birthday?"

"May fork."

Rebecca turned up the volume of the set, taking notes, straining to interpret the slurred, babyish words.

"Where do you live, Sarah?"

"Kent Court."

"Are you happy there?"

"Mummy cries so much. Molly and I play."

"Molly? Who is Molly, Sarah?"

"My sister. I want Mummy. I want my sister."

Judith began to weep.

Rebecca studied the monitor. "Pulse quickening. She's fighting you again."

"We'll stop now," Patel said. He touched Judith's hand. "Judith, you're going to wake up now. You'll feel rested and refreshed. You will remember everything you told me."

Rebecca sighed with relief. Thank God, she thought. She knew that Patel's desire to experiment with litencum was burning in him. She reached to turn off the television set and then stared as Judith's face convulsed in anguish, and she screamed, "Stop! Don't do that to her!"

The needles on the monitors were jumping erratically. "Heart fibrillating," Rebecca snapped.

Patel grasped Judith's hands. "Judith, listen to me. You must obey me."

But Judith could not hear him. She was standing on an executioner's block outside the Tower of London on the tenth of December, 1660 . . .

In horror she watched as a woman in a dark green gown and cape was led past the Tower gates through a jeering mob. The woman looked to be in her late forties. Her chestnut-brown hair was streaked with gray. She walked erectly, ignoring the guards who clustered around her. Her beautifully sculpted features were frozen in a mask of fury and hatred. Her hands were bound before her with thin wirelike strands that bit into her wrists. An angry red crescent-shaped scar at the base of her thumb glistened in the early morning light.

As Judith watched, the crowd separated to make way for dozens of soldiers, marching in orderly fashion toward a draped enclosure near the execution block. The ranks parted to allow a slender young man in a plumed hat, dark breeches, and embroidered jacket to step forth. The crowd cheered wildly as Charles II raised his hand in greeting.

As though in a nightmare, Judith saw the woman who was being led to the block stop before a long spike to which a human head was fixed. "Hurry along," a soldier ordered, pushing her forward.

"Do you deny me a wife's farewell?" The woman's tones were icy with contempt.

The soldiers hustled her to the place where the King was now seated. The dignitary standing next to him read from a scroll. "Lady Margaret Carew, His Majesty has deemed it indelicate that you be hanged, drawn, and quartered."

The people in the mob nearest the enclosure began to

33]

hoot. "Don't she have innards the same as me wife?"
one yelled.

The woman ignored them. "Simon Hallett," she said
bitterly, "you betrayed my husband. You betrayed me.
If I have to escape from hell, I'll find a way to punish
you and yours."

"That's enough from you." The captain of the guard
grabbed the woman and tried to hustle her toward the
platform where the executioner awaited. In one last
defiant gesture she turned her head and spat at the foot
of the King.

"Liar!" she screamed. "You promised mercy, liar. A
pity they didn't have your head when they took your
father's."

A soldier slapped her mouth and dragged her forward.
"This death is too good for you. I'd burn you at the
stake if I had the say."

Judith gasped as she saw that she and the prisoner bore
a striking resemblance to each other. Lady Margaret
was forced to her knees. "You'll not pull this off
again," a soldier sneered as he covered her hair with a
white cap.

The executioner raised the ax. It hovered for a moment
over the block. Lady Margaret turned her head. Her
eyes bored into Judith's, demanding, compelling. Ju-
dith screamed, "Stop! Don't do that to her!" rushed
across the platform, threw herself down, and embraced
the doomed woman as the ax fell.

Judith opened her eyes. Dr. Patel and Rebecca Wadley were standing over her. She smiled up at them. "Sarah," she said. "That's my real name, isn't it?"

"How much do you remember of what you told us, Judith?" Patel asked. His tone was guarded.

"Kent Court. That's the street I talked about, isn't it? I remember now. My mother. We were near the train station. She was holding my hand, my sister's hand. The doodles, I guess I meant doodlebugs, came. A drone like planes overhead. The sirens. The sound of the engines stopped. And then everywhere people screaming. Something hit my face. I couldn't find my mother. I ran and got on the train. And my name—Sarah, that's what I told you. And Marsh or Marrish." She got up and grasped Patel's hand. "How can I thank you? At least I have some place to start looking. Right here in London."

"What was the last thing you remember before I awakened you?"

"Molly. Doctor, I had a sister. Even if she died that day, if Mother died that day, I know something about them now. I'm going to search the birth records. I'm going to find the child I was."

Judith buttoned her collar, rolled down her sleeve, ran her fingers through her hair, bent down and reached for her boots. "If I can't trace my birth certificate, can you put me under again?" she asked.

"No," Patel said firmly. "At least not for some time."

After Judith left, Patel returned to Rebecca. "Show me the last few minutes of the tape."

Somberly they watched as Judith's expression changed from shock and horror to bitter anger, listened again to her shriek, "Stop! Don't do that to her!"

35]

"Do *what* to her?" Rebecca demanded. "What was Judith Chase experiencing?"

Patel's forehead was furrowed, his eyes sick with worry. "I have no idea. You were right, Rebecca. I never should have injected the litencum into her. But perhaps it is all right. She had no memory of whatever experience she had."

"We don't know that," Wadley told him. She put her hand on his shoulder. "Reza, I have tried to warn you. You must not experiment with our patients, no matter how much you want to help them. Judith Chase seems to be all right. Pray God that she is." Rebecca paused. "There's just one thing I noticed. Reza, did Judith have a faint crescent-shaped scar at the base of her right thumb when she got here today? When I was looking for the vein in her hand for the hypodermic, I absolutely did not see it. But look at that last frame before she woke up. She has one now."

Stephen Hallett did not notice the lovely English countryside, with its premature hint of spring in the sunny afternoon, as he was driven to Chequers, the Prime Minister's country estate. The Prime Minister had gone there after her brief appearance at Fiona's party. Her abrupt summons this morning could have only one meaning: At last she was going to tell him she intended to retire. She was going to indicate her preference as to her successor for party leadership.

Stephen knew that except for one blot on his record, he would have been the inevitable choice. How long would that terrible scandal of thirty years ago continue to haunt him? Had it spoiled his chances now? Was the Prime Minister being generous enough to tell him personally that she could not support him, or was she planning to announce her support?

His longtime chauffeur, Rory, and his Scotland Yard

Special Branch bodyguard, Carpenter, were keenly intelligent men, and he sensed their awareness of the importance of the meeting. When they stopped in front of the imposing mansion, Carpenter got out of the car and saluted him as Rory held open the car door.

The Prime Minister was in the library. Although the warmth of the sun flooded the handsome room, she was wearing a heavy cardigan, and the vital energy that had always characterized her was somehow missing. When she greeted him, even her voice had lost its usual vigor.

"Stephen, it's not good to lose the lust for battle. I was just scolding my psyche for betraying me so badly."

"Surely, Prime Minister!" Stephen stopped. He would not insult her with hollow sentiments. For months her obvious fatigue had been the subject of media speculation.

The Prime Minister waved him to a seat. "I have made a decision that is very difficult. I am going to retire to private life. Ten years in this office is enough for anyone. I also want to spend more time with my family. The country is ready for an election and a newly-elected party leader must head the campaign. Stephen, I believe you are my ideal successor. You've got what it takes."

Stephen waited. It seemed to him that the next word would be "but." He was wrong.

"There is no doubt that the press will rake up the old scandal. I've personally had it investigated again."

The old scandal. As a twenty-five-year-old solicitor Stephen had gone to work in his father-in-law's law firm. A year later his father-in-law, Reginald Harworth, was convicted of embezzling from his clients and sent to prison for five years.

"You were totally exonerated," the Prime Minister said, "but a nasty business like that has a way of bobbing up constantly. However, I don't think the country should be deprived of your abilities and services because of your unfortunate in-law."

Stephen realized that every muscle in his body was tense. The Prime Minister was about to endorse him.

Her face became stern. "I want a straight answer. Is there anything in your personal life that could embarrass the party, cost us the election?"

"There is not."

"None of those sluts who have a way of selling their life history to the newspapers? You are an attractive man and a widower."

"I resent the implication, Prime Minister."

"Don't. I need to know. Judith Chase. You introduced me to her last night. I met her father, her adoptive father I suppose, a number of times over the years. She seems above reproach."

Caesar's wife must be above reproach, Stephen thought. Wasn't that what Judith had said last night?

"I hope and expect to marry Judith. We have both agreed that we do not want personal publicity at this time."

"Very wise. Well, count your blessings. Her adoptive parents were top drawer, and she has the romance of being a British war orphan. She's one of ours." The Prime Minister smiled, a smile that warmed her entire being. "Stephen, congratulations. Labour will give us a run for it but we'll win. You'll be the next Prime Minister, and no one will be gladder than I to see you present yourself to Her Majesty. Now for God's sake, be a good fellow and pour us both a generous scotch. We need to plan carefully."

When she left Patel's office, Judith went directly to the apartment. In the taxi she realized she was whispering "Sarah Marsh, Sarah Marrish." I'm going to like my real name, she thought with delight. Tomorrow she would begin the search for her birth record. She could only hope that she had been born in London. If her recollections were accurate, knowing her name and birth date would make the search infinitely easier. No wonder they hadn't been able to trace her. If she had gotten on a train in London and wandered off it in Salisbury and then blocked out the memory of what had happened, it would explain why no one had claimed her. She was sure her mother and Molly must have died that day. But cousins, Judith thought. Who knows, I may have an extended family living right around the corner.

"We're here, Miss."

"Oh." Judith fumbled for her billfold. "I'm woolgathering, I guess."

In the flat she made a cup of tea and resolutely went straight to her desk. Yes, tomorrow would be time enough to begin the search for Sarah Marrish. Today she had better stick to being Judith Chase and get back to writing her book. She studied the notes she had made at the Records Office and wondered once again about the woman, Lady Margaret Carew, who had been executed in the presence of the King, and what her crime had been.

It was nearly six o'clock when Stephen phoned. The harsh ring of the telephone, so different from the ones in America, startled Judith from the total concentration she experienced when she was writing. Astonished at how much time had passed, she realized that except for the desk light the apartment was dark. She fumbled for the phone. "Hello."

"Darling, is anything wrong? You sound troubled." Stephen's voice was concerned.

"Oh Lord, no. It's just that when I'm writing, I'm in another world. Takes me a minute or two to come back to earth."

"That's why you're such a good writer. Dinner tonight at my place? I have rather interesting news."

"And I have interesting news for you. What time?"

"Is eight o'clock all right? I'll send the car."

"Eight is fine."

She replaced the receiver, smiling. She knew Stephen hated to waste time on the phone, and yet he always managed to be brief without seeming abrupt. Deciding that she had worked enough for one day, she turned on the lamps as she walked through the living room and down the narrow hallway toward the bedroom.

That's something else terribly English about me, she thought a few minutes later as she relaxed in steaming, scented water. I love these long claw-footed cast-iron tubs.

She had time for a brief rest, no, a "lie-down," she thought as she pulled the quilt over her. What was Stephen's news? He'd sounded almost noncommittal, so it couldn't have to do with the election, could it? No, of course not. Even he didn't have that much sangfroid.

When she dressed, Judith chose a silk print she'd bought in Italy. She'd always thought that the vivid colors were not unlike the effect of paints poured indiscriminately over a palette. It was a dress to brighten the now overcast January night. It was a dress in which to give bright news. "Stephen, do you like the name Sarah?"

She let her hair fall loose, just skimming the collar of the dress. The strand of pearls that had been her mother's, her *adoptive* mother's. The pearl and diamond earrings, the narrow diamond bracelet. A festive evening. And you don't look your age, she assured her image. And then thought, I've been two years old today. Maybe that helps bring a touch of youth back. Smiling at the possibility, she looked down at her hands, trying to decide which rings to wear.

And then noticed it. The faint outline of the crescent scar at the base of her thumb. Frowning, she tried to remember how long it had been there. When she was a teenager, she'd caught her hand in a car door and it had been badly cut and bruised. It had taken a long time for the scars from the plastic surgery to fade.

And now one of them is coming back, she thought. Great!

It was five of eight. She knew the car would be downstairs waiting. Rory was always early.

Stephen's town house was on Lord North Street. He refused to tell her his news until after they had dined and were settled on the deep, high-backed sofa in the library. A fire was blazing and a bottle of Dom Perignon was chilling in a silver wine cooler. He had dismissed the servants and closed the library doors. Solemnly he got up, opened the champagne, filled the glasses, and handed one to her. "A toast."

"To what?"

"A general election. The Prime Minister's assurance that she will support me to become her successor as party leader."

Judith jumped up. "Stephen, oh my God, Stephen." She touched her glass to his. "Britain is very lucky."

Their lips met and clung. Then he warned, "Darling, not a hint of this to anyone. The plan is that for the next three weeks or so, I'll be busy preparing a campaign strategy, making political broadcasts, becoming highly visible in the EEC conferences on terrorism and quietly gathering support."

"In Washington it's called developing a high profile." Judith's lips grazed his forehead. "God, I'm so proud of you, Stephen."

He laughed. "A high profile is exactly the goal. Then the

41]

Prime Minister will announce her decision not to stand for her seat again. The first battle will be when the party chooses a new leader. There's competition but with her backing it should be all right. Once I'm elected party leader, the P.M. will go to the Queen and ask for Parliament to be dissolved. The general election follows about a month later."

He put his arm around her. "And if our party wins the election and I become Prime Minister, I can't tell you what it will mean to know that you're here at the end of the day. Darling, I never realized how alone I'd been all those years when Jane was so ill until that night at Fiona's when I met you. So exquisitely dressed. So witty and beautiful. And your eyes with that hint of sadness."

"They're not sad now."

They settled back on the sofa, his long legs stretched on the leather cocktail table, she curled beside him. "Tell me every single detail of your meeting with the Prime Minister," she demanded.

"Well, I assure you, in the early moments I was certain she was about to let me down as gently as possible. I don't think I've ever told you about my father-in-law."

As Judith listened to Stephen's account of the scandal, and of his fears that it might have cost him the support of the Prime Minister, she realized that she could not tell him about her visit to Dr. Patel, could not ask for his help in uncovering her background. No wonder he had so vehemently opposed her desire to find her natural family. And that would be all the newspapers would need, to learn that the future wife of the Prime Minister was consulting the controversial Reza Patel.

"And now for your news," Stephen said. "You said you had good news."

Judith smiled and touched her hand to his face. "I remember when Fiona informed me she was placing me next

[42

to you at dinner. She said you were absolutely stunning. She was right. My news pales after hearing yours. I was going to tell you about a tremendously interesting chat with the Assistant Keeper of the Records Office. He seemed to love the fact that Charles the Second had an eye for the ladies." She raised her lips to his, put her arms around him, felt the eagerness of his response. Oh God, she thought, I'm so in love with him. She told him that.

On Friday evening, they went to Stephen's country home in Devon. On the three-hour drive down, he told her about Edge Barton Manor. "It's in Branscombe, a beautiful old village. Built during the time of the Norman Conquest."

"About nine hundred years ago," Judith interrupted.

"I really must remember that I'm dealing with an historian. The Hallett family acquired the estate when Charles the Second returned to the throne. I imagine you'll run across some references to it in your research. Quite a lovely place. I'm not very proud of my ancestor, Simon Hallett. Apparently he was quite a slippery chap. But I think and hope you will love Edge Barton as I do."

The manor was situated on a ledge near a wooded combe. Lamps glistened behind the mullioned windows, sending rays of light over the stone exterior. The slate roof had a dark sheen beneath the crescent moon. On the left a three-story gabled wing, which Stephen said was the oldest part of the building, rose majestically above the treetops. Stephen pointed out the roundheaded door with a fanlight and glazing bars, near the right wing of the mansion. "Antique dealers are always begging to buy that one. In the morning you'll be able to see the remains of the moat. It's dried up now but apparently was quite an effective defense a thousand years ago."

43]

Her research for her book had made Judith familiar with ancient houses, but as the car stopped at the main door of Edge Barton, she realized that whatever sensation she was experiencing was completely different from her reactions to other historical homes.

Stephen was studying her face. "Well, darling. You look as though you approve."

"I feel as though I'm coming home."

Arm in arm they explored the interior of the house. "For years now I've spent too little time here," Stephen said. "Jane was so ill. She preferred London, where her friends could visit easily. I came alone and stayed only long enough to attend to my constituency."

The drawing room, the dining room, the great hall, the Tudor fireplace in the bedroom above the drawing room, the Norman staircase in the old wing, the magnificent windows with concave molding, the smooth, soft Beer stone in the upper hall, which generations of children had covered with drawings of ships and people, horses and dogs, initials and names and dates. Judith stopped to examine them as a servant came up the stairs. There was a phone call for Sir Stephen. "I'll be back in a moment, darling," he murmured.

One set of initials seemed to burn from the wall. V.C., 1635. Judith ran her hands over the initials. "Vincent," she murmured, "Vincent." Dazed, she made her way down the foyer and to the staircase that led to the ballroom on the fourth floor. It was totally dark. Groping along the wall, she found the light and then watched as the room filled with people in the formal dress of the seventeenth century. The scar on her hand began to blaze. It was December 18, 1641 . . .

"Edge Barton is a magnificent home, Lady Margaret."

"I can't disagree." Margaret Carew's tone was cold as she addressed the dandified young man whose carefully curled hair, even features, and foppish dress could not conceal the impression of slyness and duplicity that emanated from Hallett, bastard son of the Duke of Rockingham.

"Your son, Vincent, is scowling at us. I don't think he favors me," he said.

"Has he a reason not to favor you?"

"Perhaps he senses that I am in love with his mother. Really, Margaret, John Carew is no man for you. You were fifteen when you married him. At thirty-two you are more beautiful than any other woman in this room. How old is John? Fifty? And virtually a cripple since his hunting accident."

"And he is the husband I love dearly." Margaret caught her son's eye and nodded to him. Quickly he crossed the room to her.

"Mother."

He was a handsome boy, tall and well developed for his sixteen years. His features made it clear he was a Carew, but as Margaret teasingly reminded him, he could thank her for his thick mane of chestnut-brown hair and his blue-green eyes. They were characteristics of the Russell family.

"Simon, you have met my son, Vincent. Vincent, you remember Simon Hallett."

45]

"I do."

"And exactly what do you remember about me, Vincent?" Hallet's smile was condescending.

"I remember you, sir, as being quite indifferent to the new taxes which threaten everyone in this room. But as my father has observed, when a man has nothing to be taxed, it is quite easy to pledge loyalty to a monarch who believes in the divine right of kings. Isn't it a fact, Mr. Hallett, that it is the hope of your breed that the estates which are confiscated for nonpayment of taxes by the crown will someday be given to the apologists of the King? To yourself? My father has noticed that your eyes are covetous when you accompany your friends to Edge Barton Manor. Is it, then, that this house holds great fascination for you, as well as your obvious interest in my mother?"

Hallett's face was flushed with anger. "You are impertinent."

Lady Margaret laughed and took her son's arm. "No, he's a very astute young man. He has given you exactly the message I asked him to deliver. You're quite right, Mr. Hallett. My husband, Sir John, is not well and that is why I do not choose to trouble him with speaking to you. Do not enter this house again under the pretext of accompanying mutual friends. You are not welcome here. And if you are indeed as close to the King as you would have us believe, tell His Majesty that the reason so many of us have fled his Court is because we cannot stomach his scorn of Parliament, his claim of divine right, his indifference to the genuine needs and rights of his people. My family has served both in the House of Lords and in the House of Commons since Parliament was created. The blood of the Tudors flows in our veins, but that does not mean we will go back to the days when the only right that the monarch acknowledged was his own will and willfulness."

Music filled the room. Margaret turned her back on Hallett, smiled at her husband, who was seated with friends, his cane beside him, and went onto the dance floor with her son. "You have your father's grace," she said. "Before his accident, I used to tell him he was the best dancer in England."

Vincent did not return her smile. "Mother, what is going to happen?"

"If His Majesty does not accept the reforms which Parliament demands, there will be civil war."

"Then I shall fight on the side of Parliament."

"Pray God, that by the time you are of age for battle, it will be settled. Even Charles must know that he cannot possibly win this battle of conscience."

Judith opened her eyes. Stephen was calling her. Shaking her head, she hurried to the staircase. "Up here, darling." When he reached her, she put her arms around his neck. "I feel as though I've always known Edge Barton." She did not realize that the scar on her hand which had flared to a deep crimson shade had once again faded to a pale, almost indistinguishable outline.

47]

*   *   *

On Monday, Judith drove to Worcester to look at the site of the last major conflict of the Civil War. It had taken place in this town in 1651. She went first to the Commandery, the timbered building that had served as headquarters for Charles II. Completely restored now, it held uniforms and helmets and muskets which visitors were encouraged to handle. When she picked up the uniform of a captain of Cromwell's army, she was aware of a sense of terrible sadness. An audiovisual presentation realistically evoked the historic engagement and the events that led to it. Eyes burning, she watched the tape, unaware that her hands were clenched into fists.

An attendant gave her a map of what the museum called the Civil War Trail, which marked the progress of the battle of Worcester. He explained: "The Royalist troops were soundly defeated at the battle of Naseby. The war was effectively over that day, won by Cromwell and his Parliamentarians. But still it dragged on. They had the final great clashing of arms here. The Royalists were led by young Charles. Only twenty-one years old, and historians say he provided 'an incomparable example of valor,' but it was no use. They'd lost five hundred officers at Naseby and never recovered from that."

Judith left the Commandery. The day was typical of January, cold, a bit raw. She was wearing a Burberry, the collar pulled up around her neck. She had twisted her hair into a chignon, and tendrils had escaped to frame her now ashen face and wide-pupiled eyes.

She followed the map as she wandered through town, pausing to consult her own notes and to jot down impressions. At the top of Worcester Cathedral she stood staring out, remembering that it was from this exact spot Charles II had watched Cromwell's preparations for the

[48

battle. And when it was obvious that the battle was lost, his Royalist troops had rushed to certain slaughter in a final attack against the Parliamentarians to cover their future monarch's escape. It was from here that Charles began his long, harrowing journey across England to sanctuary in France.

A pity he escaped, she thought bitterly as the scar on her hand began to blaze. She was no longer seeing the wintry landscape of Worcester. It was a warm July evening in 1644, and she was in a closed carriage riding to Marston Moor in the hope of finding that Vincent was still alive . . .

A drumroll accompanied a small detachment of Roundhead troops. At the sight of the approaching carriage two sentries stepped forward and with long poles barred its way.

Lady Margaret stepped from the carriage. She was wearing a dark blue simply cut daytime gown of fine linen with a white ruffled collar. A matching cape fell loosely from her shoulders. Except for her wedding ring, she wore no jewelry. Her thick chestnut hair, now shot with silver, was gathered at the nape of her neck. Her eyes, the blue-green eyes of the aristocratic Russell family, were dark with pain.

"Please," she begged. "I know that many of the wounded are lying untended. My son fought here."

"On which side?" The soldier's query was accompanied by a sneer.

"He is an officer in Cromwell's army."

49]

"From the look of you I'd have guessed him to be a Cavalier. But sorry, ma'am, there are too many women searching these fields already. Orders are to allow no more through. We'll attend to the bodies."

"Please," Margaret begged. "Please."

An officer came forward. "What is your son's name, madam?"

"Captain Vincent Carew."

The officer, a plain-faced lieutenant in his mid-thirties, looked grave. "I know Captain Carew. I have not seen him since the battle ended. He was with the charge against the Langdale regiment. That's in the wet ground to the right. Perhaps you should begin your search there."

The fields were littered with the dead and dying. Women of all ages moved among them, searching for their husbands and brothers, fathers and sons. Broken weapons and dead horses gave evidence of the fierceness of the battle. The warm, sultry evening air was filled with insects, which buzzed around the fallen bodies. Sporadic cries of agony and grief could be heard as loved ones were found.

Margaret joined the search. Many of the bodies were lying face down, but she did not have to turn them. She was looking for chestnut hair that refused to conform to the simple rounded cut adapted by so many of

[50

Cromwell's army, hair that still curled thick and loose around a boyish face.

Ahead of her a young woman of about nineteen sank to her knees and threw her arms around a dead soldier in the uniform of a Cavalier. Moaning, she rocked him in her arms. "Edward, my husband."

Margaret touched the girl's shoulder in an unspoken gesture of sympathy. And then saw what had happened. The dead soldier's sword was still grasped in his hand. Bits of cloth clung to it. A few feet away a young Parliamentarian officer was lying on the ground, his chest split open. Margaret paled as she instinctively knew that the broken threads on his tunic would match the threads on the sword. The head of chestnut hair. The handsome, patrician features so like his father's. The blue-green eyes of the Russell family, staring sightlessly up at her.

"Vincent, Vincent." She knelt beside him, cradled his head against her breast, the breast that twenty years ago his infant lips had sought. ". . . I shall fight on the side of Parliament." "Pray God that by the time you are of age for battle, it will be settled. Even Charles must know that he cannot possibly win this battle of conscience."

The young woman whose husband's sword had killed Vincent began to scream. "No . . . no . . . no. . . ."

Margaret stared at her. She is young, she thought. She'll find another husband. I will never have another son. With infinite tenderness, she kissed Vincent's lips and

51]

*forehead and laid him down on the swampy marsh.
The coachman would help her carry his body to the
carriage. For an instant she stood over the sobbing girl.
"A pity your husband's sword did not settle in the heart
of the King," she said. "If it were mine, it would have
found its mark there."*

Judith shivered. The sun had disappeared and the wind
was increasing in strength. She realized that a group of
tourists were standing near her. One of them tried to get the
attention of the guide. "What year was Charles the First
executed?"

"He was beheaded on January 30, 1649," Judith said.
"Four and a half years after the battle of Marston Moor."
Then she smiled. "Sorry. I didn't mean to interfere." She
hurried down the steps, anxious now to be away from this
place, to get home to the apartment, start a fire, have a
sherry. Funny, she thought as she drove through the ever
increasing traffic, when I began this book I had much more
sympathy for the Royalists. I believed that the Stuarts back
to Mary were either very stupid or very tricky and that
Charles I was both but should not have been executed. The
deeper I get into research, the more I believe that the M.P.s
who signed his death warrant were right, and if I'd been
there, I'd have lined up to sign it with them. . . .

The next day, her heart beating wildly, Judith walked
up the shallow step to the revolving door of the General
Register Office, St. Catherine's House, Kingsway. Let this
be the place, she begged silently, remembering the stories
her adoptive parents had told her about how the
authorities had scrutinized the parish records in Salisbury
and posted her picture in the nearby communities, hoping
to trace her family. But if she had been born in London

and stumbled onto the train ... Let it be true, she thought. Let it be true.

She had planned to be at this office yesterday, but when she looked in her book and realized she'd scheduled the visit to Worcester, she decided without hesitation to keep to her schedule. Was it because she was afraid that this would be a dead end, that the recollection of the bombing near the station, the names Sarah and Molly Marsh or Marrish, were just details that her hypnotized mind had capriciously offered?

At the inquiry desk, she waited in an unexpectedly long queue. From scraps of conversation she realized that most of the people in the line were tracing ancestors. When she finally reached the clerk she was told that the birth records were kept in the first section, recorded in large volumes marked with the various years.

"Each year is divided into four quarters and the books are marked March, June, September, December," the clerk informed her. "What date did you want? . . . May fourth or fourteenth? Then you must look in the June volume. That holds the records for April, May and June."

The room was a beehive of activity. The only place to sit was at one of the long bench-like tables. Judith slipped off the hooded hunter-green cape she had impulsively bought that morning at Harrods. "It's lovely, isn't it?" the saleswoman had said. "And so perfect with this strange weather. Not too heavy but with a sweater under it plenty warm."

She was wearing her favorite kind of outfit, a cable-knit sweater, stretch slacks and boots. Unaware of the admiring glances that followed her, she took down the ledger marked June 1942.

To her dismay she found that under the names Marrish and Marsh there was no Sarah listed, nor was there a Molly. Had everything she said under hypnosis been simply fantasy? She got back on the queue and eventually reached the clerk again.

"Isn't there a requirement that a birth be registered within a month after the child is born?"

"Quite right."

"Then I have the right book."

"Oh, not necessarily. The year 1942 was wartime. Very possibly the birth wasn't recorded until the next quarter or even later."

Judith went back to the bench and began running her finger along the pages of Marrish and Marsh, looking for the middle initial S. Or maybe Sarah was my middle name, she thought. People do call a child by her middle name if her first name is the same as her mother's. But there was no listing of a female Marsh or Marrish with that initial. Each line contained the family name and given name of the newborn, the mother's maiden name, and the district where the birth had occurred. That information was listed together with the volume and page number of the index, needed in order to obtain copies of the birth certificate. So without the right name, I'm going to hit a dead end, she thought.

She did not leave until closing time. By then her shoulders ached from the hours of poring over the ledgers. Her eyes were burning and her head throbbing. It was not going to be an easy process. If only she could enlist Stephen's aid. He could put clerical help to the task. Maybe there were ways to search records that she didn't know anything about. . . . And maybe her mind had played a trick on her, and Sarah Marrish or Marsh was a figment of her imagination.

There was a call from Stephen on her answering machine. At the sound of his voice her spirits lifted. Quickly, she dialed his private number at the office. "Burning the midnight oil?" she asked when she was put through to him.

He laughed. "I might ask the same of you. How did it go at Worcester? Impressed by our lack of brotherly love?"

She had implied that she would return to Worcester today. Certainly she would not tell him about the search for her birth family.

She hesitated, then said hurriedly, "The research was a bit slow today, but that's all part of the game. Stephen, did you enjoy the weekend as much as I did?"

"I haven't stopped thinking about it. Rather like an oasis for me at this time."

On Saturday and Sunday at Edge Barton, they had gone riding. Stephen kept six horses in his stable. His own horse, Market, a coal-black gelding, and Juniper, a mare, were his favorites. They were both jumpers. Stephen had been delighted that Judith kept pace with him as they cantered around the estate, taking the fences in stride.

"You told me you rode a little," he had accused her.

"I used to ride a lot. I've scarcely had time in the last ten years."

"It certainly doesn't show. I was shocked when I realized I hadn't warned you about that stream. Unless the rider is aware of it, the horses tend to balk."

"Somehow I expected it," she had replied.

When they returned to the stable, they had dismounted and, arm in arm, strolled toward the house. Safely out of sight of the stable hands, Stephen put his arms around her.

"Judith, it's definite. In three weeks the Prime Minister will announce her retirement and the new party leader will be chosen."

"You."

"I have her support. As I warned you, there are others clamoring for the post, but it should be all right. The next few weeks until the election are going to be pretty frantic. We'll have very little time together. Can you accept that?"

"Yes, of course. And if I can wrap up the book while you're busy campaigning, so much the better. And incidentally, Sir Stephen, I'm delighted to see you in a riding habit instead of a business suit or evening dress. Just a touch of Ronald Colman, I think. I used to love watching old movies in the middle of the night, and he was my hands-down favorite. I'm starting to feel a bit like the lovers in *Random Harvest*. Smithy and Paula found each other again at about our age."

"Judith!" Stephen's voice came from what seemed to be far away.

"Stephen, I'm sorry. I was just thinking about you and the weekend, and wondering if at this moment you look like Ronald Colman."

"Sorry to disappoint you, darling, but the comparison is unfair to the late Mr. Colman. What are you doing this evening?"

"Fixing whatever to eat and getting to the typewriter. Fieldwork is necessary but it certainly doesn't help the manuscript to expand."

"Well, do get it finished. Judith, the election will be March 13. Would a quiet April wedding suit you, preferably at Edge Barton? It's certainly the place I feel most at home in the entire world. It's meant refuge and solace and peace for me since I was born. And I sense that you have already captured something of that feeling."

"I know I have."

When Judith replaced the receiver on the cradle, she thought yearningly of preparing something simple, of going to bed and reading for a while. But she had given a precious day to the shopping at Harrods and the General Register Office.

Deciding not to pamper herself, she showered, put on warm pajamas and a robe, heated a can of soup, and went back to her desk. With satisfaction she skimmed the manuscript: the first third she devoted to the events leading up to the Civil War; the middle section to life in England during the war, the seesawing of the tides of battle, the thrown-away chances for reconciliation between the King and Parliament, and the capture, trial, and execution of Charles I. Now she was well into the return of Charles II from his exile in France, his promise of religious freedom, "liberty to tender conscience," the trial of the men who had signed the death warrant for his father.

Charles returned to England on his thirtieth birthday, May 29, 1660. Judith picked up her pen to underline her notes about the number of petitions he received from Royalists besieging him for titles and for the confiscated estates of the Cromwellians.

Her head was throbbing. The scar on her right hand began to blaze. "Oh, Vincent," she whispered. It was September 24, 1660 . . .

In the sixteen years since Vincent's death Lady Margaret and Sir John had lived quietly at Edge Barton. Only the execution of the King and the defeat of the Royalist troops had offered any consolation to Lady Margaret. At least the cause for which her son died had been victorious. But in those years she and John had grown apart. At her blazing insistence he had reluctantly signed the execution order for the King, and he had never forgiven himself.

"Exile would have been sufficient," he told her sadly

many times. "And what did we get for ourselves instead? A Lord Protector who carries himself with the attitude of royalty and whose Puritan ways have robbed England of religious freedom and of all the joys we once knew."

Loving her husband almost as much as she hated the executed King, watching John deteriorate into a forgetful old man, knowing he could not forgive her for forcing him to become a regicide, and longing daily for her lost son had changed Margaret. She knew that she had become an embittered woman. Her temper became legendary and her looking glass told her she no longer bore any resemblance to the beautiful young daughter of the Duke of Wakefield who had been the toast of the court when she married Sir John Carew. Only when she sat with John and listened as he talked more and more about the past was she able to remember how happy her life had once been.

Charles II had returned to England in May. Saying that enough blood had been shed, he offered general forgiveness except for the men who were directly involved in his father's murder. Forty-one of the fifty-nine who had signed the death warrant were still alive. Charles promised special consideration to those who turned themselves in.

Margaret did not trust the King. Clearly John had little time left. His mind was failing. Often he called for Vincent to come join him for a ride. He had begun to look into Margaret's face again with the deep love he had shown her for so many years. He spoke of going to court and planning the annual ball at Edge Barton. His shallow breathing and ashen pallor told Margaret that his heart was failing.

With the assistance of a handful of devoted servants she devised a scheme. John would set off for London to surrender to the King. The carriage would be seen leaving the estate by the tenant farmers and townspeople. And when it was dark, the coach would return. They had prepared an apartment for John in the hidden rooms that were once known as priest holes. There, in the time of Queen Elizabeth I, members of the Catholic clergy had found sanctuary as they sought to escape to France. Then the carriage would be returned to a remote spot near the road to London and made to look as though it had been attacked by highwaymen, and its occupants would be assumed to have been murdered.

The plan worked well. The coachman was handsomely paid, and on his way to the colonies in America. John's personal servant stayed with John in the hidden apartment. Margaret slipped down into the kitchen at night and with the help of Dorcas, an elderly scullery maid, prepared food for them.

When word came of the fate of the regicides who had been hanged at Charing Cross, drawn, and quartered, Margaret knew she had made the only decision possible. John would die in peace at Edge Barton.

Accompanied by a contingent of Royalist soldiers, Simon Hallett arrived at dawn on October 2. Margaret had just returned to her own room. She had spent the night with John, wrapping his frail body in her

59]

arms, feeling the chill that preceded death. She knew he had only weeks or even days to live. Hurriedly she grabbed a robe, tying it as she ran down the stairs.

It had been eighteen years since she had laid eyes on Simon Hallett. When the war ended, he'd gone to join the King in exile in France. Now his once weak features had thickened. Arrogance had replaced the sly expression that so repelled her.

"Lady Margaret, how good to see you again," he said sardonically when she opened the great wooden door. Without waiting for her permission, he stepped past her and looked around. "Edge Barton has not been tended well since last I was here."

"While you were in France languishing at the feet of your royal master, other Englishmen were home paying heavy taxes to compensate for the cost of the war." Margaret hoped that her eyes did not reveal her terror. Did Simon Hallett suspect that John's carriage had not been waylaid by highwaymen? His order to the soldiers confirmed that fear.

"Search every inch of this house. There's bound to be a priest hole. But take care. Do not cause damage. As it is, it will cost enough to properly restore the estate. Sir John is cowering here somewhere. We don't go back without him."

Lady Margaret summoned up all the contempt and scorn that was burning in her soul. "You are quite wrong," she told Simon. "My husband would meet you with a sword if he were here." And you would, John, she thought, but you are not here. You dwell in a happy past . . .

Room by room, the search continued through the great house. Cupboards were opened, walls tested for hollow sounds that would point to hidden passageways. Hours passed. Margaret sat in the great hall near the fire a servant had built wondering if she dared to hope. Simon roamed through the house, his impatience growing. Finally, he returned to the great hall. Dorcas had just brought Margaret tea and bread. Margaret knew it was all over when Simon's gaze fell reflectively on the elderly woman. In a quick bound he was across the room, had grabbed the servant by the arms and twisted them behind her. "You know where he is," he said. "Tell me now."

"Don't know what you mean, sir, please," Dorcas quavered. Her plea became a shriek as Simon twisted her arms again and the horrifying sound of cracking bone echoed through the massive room.

"I'll show you where he is," she shrieked. "No more. No more."

"Do it, then." Still twisting her arms, Simon hurried the sobbing old woman up the great staircase.

Moments later two soldiers dragged the shackled body of Sir John Carew down the stairs. Simon Hallett was replacing his sword into its sheath. "That man-servant did not live to regret his insolence," he told Margaret.

Numbly she got up and ran to her husband. "Margaret, I seem to be not well," John said, his tone bewildered. "It's very cold. Will you ask that the fire be fed. And send Vincent to me. I haven't seen the lad all morning."

Margaret put her arms around him. "I will follow you to London." As the soldiers hustled John from the house, she stared at Simon. "Even those madmen can see his condition. And if they want to put someone on trial, let them try me. It was I who demanded my husband sign the King's death warrant."

"Thank you for that information, Lady Margaret." Hallett turned to the officer in charge. "You witnessed her confession."

Margaret was barred from her husband's trial. Friends told her about it. "They said he was playing the part of the fool but had managed to concoct a clever getaway scheme. He has been given the regicide sentence, to be carried out in three days."

Hanging at Charing Cross. His body drawn and quartered. His head exhibited on a spike.

"I must see the King," Margaret said. "I must make him understand."

Her cousins had neither understood nor forgiven her for siding with the Parliamentarians. But she was of one of the great families of England. They managed to secure an audience.

The day that John was to be executed, Margaret was ushered into the presence of Charles II. She had heard that the King had told his advisers he was weary of the hangings and wanted no more of them. She would beg that Sir John be allowed to die in peace in Edge Barton, and offer herself in his place.

Simon Hallett was standing to the right of the King. He looked amused as Margaret sank into a deep curtsy. "Sire, before you hear Lady Margaret, who can be most persuasive, may I present other witnesses?"

Aghast, Margaret watched as the captain of the guard who had arrested John was admitted and told the monarch: "Lady Margaret swore that she demanded her husband sign His Majesty's death warrant."

"But that is exactly what I am here to tell you. Sir John did not want to sign it. He has never forgiven me for forcing him to it," she cried.

"Your Majesty," Simon Hallett interrupted. "Sir John Carew's entire life, his military service, his years in Parliament show him to be a man of strong convictions, not one to be swayed by a nagging wife. It is not to excuse him that I say this, but to have you understand that despite your generous and forgiving nature, you are looking into the face of a woman who is as guilty as though she herself had signed the unpardonable document. And I have one more

person I would beg you to heed—Lady Elizabeth Sethbert.''

A woman in her thirties entered. Why did she look familiar? Margaret wondered. She soon understood the reason. It was Lady Elizabeth's husband who had killed Vincent. "I shall never forget, Your Majesty," Lady Elizabeth said, staring at Margaret with stony disdain. "As I held my husband in my arms, glad he had given his life in His Majesty's service, this woman said it was too bad his sword did not settle in the heart of the King. She then said, 'If it were mine, it would have found its mark there.' When she left I inquired her name of a Parliamentary officer, since she was clearly a woman of rank. I have never forgotten the horror of that moment and have told that tale many times, which is why Simon Hallett learned of it."

The King turned his gaze on Margaret. She had heard that he fancied himself a student of physiognomy and could read people's characters by studying their faces. She said, "Sire, I am here to acknowledge my guilt. Do with me whatever you wish, but spare a sick and feebleminded old man."

"Sir John Carew is clever enough to feign madness, Sire," Hallett said. "And if with your gracious pardon he is allowed to return to Edge Barton, he will soon be miraculously restored to health. Then he and his wife will continue to put their heads together with their fellow high-placed and dangerous revolutionaries. These scoundrels plot for Your Majesty the same fate as our late King, your father, suffered."

Stunned, Margaret stared at Simon. Her cousins had told her that beneath his smiling exterior Charles II was haunted by the premonition that he was destined to experience his father's fate.

"Liar!" Margaret screamed at Simon. "Liar!" She tried to rush toward the King. "Your Majesty, my husband, spare my husband."

Simon Hallett threw himself on her, knocking her to the ground, his body covering hers. She saw the glint of a dagger in his hand. Thinking he meant to stab her, Margaret tried to wrest it from him. The dagger cut deeply into the base of her thumb; then Simon forced her fingers around it as he pulled her to her feet.

"You would murder the King!" Simon shouted. "Look, Sire, she carried a weapon into this audience."

Margaret knew it was useless to protest. Blood poured from the wound as her hands were bound and she was pulled away from the royal presence. Simon followed her out. "Let me have a word with Lady Margaret," he told the guards. "Step back please." He whispered to her, "Even now Sir John is swaying from the rope at Charing Cross and his entrails are being torn from him. The King has already created me a baronet. For my reward in saving his life from your mad attack, I shall request and be granted Edge Barton."

Over the weekend Reza Patel had tried repeatedly to ring Judith. When her answering machine went on, he did not leave a message. He wanted to sound offhand when he suggested to her that she come into his office for a blood pressure check, to be sure that the hypnotic drug had not physically affected her.

Monday she was out of her flat as well. On Tuesday evening, he and Rebecca stayed after office hours and once again studied the tape of Judith's hypnosis.

"Psychically something happened," Patel told Rebecca. "We know that. Look at her face. The anger, the hatred in it. What kind of creature did Judith bring back? And from where? If my theory is correct, the spirit, the essence, of the Grand Duchess Anastasia literally overwhelmed Anna Anderson. Will that happen to Judith Chase?"

"Judith Chase is a very strong woman," Rebecca reminded him. "That was why you needed so much of the drug to regress her to childhood. You know you can't be sure that whatever she experienced didn't end when you awakened her. She had no memory of it. Isn't it presumptuous to be so certain that you have proven the Anastasia Syndrome?"

"I wish to God I were wrong, but I'm not."

"Then can't you hypnotize Judith again, regress her to the point where she brought back whatever essence she is carrying and order her to abandon it there?"

"I don't know where I would be sending her." Patel shook his head. "Let me try to call her again."

This time the phone was picked up. He nodded to Rebecca, signaling that Judith was answering. Leaning past him, Rebecca pressed the conference call button on the answering machine.

"Yes?"

Rebecca and Patel looked at each other, puzzled. It was Judith's voice and yet not her voice. The timbre was different, the tone abrupt and haughty.

"Miss Chase? Judith Chase?"

[66

"Judith is not here."

"Her name," Rebecca whispered.

"May I ask your name, madam? You are a friend of Miss Chase?"

"Friend? Hardly." The connection broke.

Patel buried his head in his hands. "Rebecca, what have I done? Judith is two personalities. The new one is aware of Judith's existence. She is already the dominant one."

Stephen Hallett did not get home till midnight. There had been meetings all day. Rumors of the Prime Minister's decision were everywhere. He had not been wrong in believing that his election as party leader would be challenged. Hawkins, a junior minister, was especially vociferous. "While not denying Stephen Hallett's obvious merits, I must warn you, one and all, that the old scandal will be revived. The newspapers will have a field day with it. Don't forget, Stephen came within inches of being prosecuted."

"And was exonerated," Stephen shot back. He had won the skirmish. He would win the election to become party leader. But, oh God, he thought as he wearily undressed, the burden of having to live under the cloud of another man's felony. As he got into bed, he glanced at the clock. Midnight. Far too late to call Judith. He closed his eyes. Thank God that she was who and what she was. Thank God she understood why he could not allow her to begin a search for her birth family. He knew that he had asked a great deal of her by making that request. He would make it up to her for the rest of her life, he promised himself as he began to drift off to sleep.

The four-poster bed that had been in his family for nearly three hundred years creaked as he settled down. Stephen thought of the joys of sharing this bed with Judith, of the pride he would feel when she accompanied him as his wife to official functions. His last waking thought was that best of all would be their private time together in his beloved retreat, Edge Barton . . .

At ten after twelve, Judith looked up, saw the time, and was startled to realize that the soup on the tray beside her was cold, that she was chilled to the bone. Concentration is one thing but this is crazy, she thought as she made her way to bed. Tossing off her robe, she gratefully pulled the covers up, bunching them at her neck. That damn scar on her hand. It was fairly bright. As she watched, it continued to fade. It shows you're getting long in the tooth when all your old scars start surfacing, she thought, as she reached over and turned out the light.

She closed her eyes and began to think of Stephen's desire for an April wedding. That would be ten or eleven weeks from now. I'll finish this damn book and then go shopping, she promised herself. She realized she was delighted Stephen had suggested they be married at Edge Barton. In these past weeks the memory of all her childhood years with her adoptive parents, all the years she'd lived in Washington with Kenneth, had faded farther and farther away. It was as though she had begun her life the night she met Stephen, as though every fiber of her being recognized that England was her home. She was forty-six, Stephen fifty-four. His family was long-lived. We might have a crack at twenty-five good years together, she reflected. Stephen. The formal and some-times formidable manner which was a disguise for a lonely man, even, incredibly, a rather insecure man. Knowing about his father-in-law explained so much . . .

I need to know my real name, Stephen, she thought as she closed her eyes. Unless I was totally fabricating, I may be close to that knowledge now. If it is true that I was separated from my mother and sister in a doodlebug attack,

[68

I'll somehow learn the rest of the story. They were probably both killed that day. I'd like to be able to put flowers on their graves, but I solemnly promise you I won't dig up obscure cousins who may embarrass you. She fell asleep with the happy thought that she would love her life as Lady Hallett.

Judith worked at her desk all the next morning, watching with intense satisfaction the steadily growing pile of pages next to her typewriter. Her writer friends all assured her that she owed it to herself to get a computer. When I finish this one, she decided, I'll take time off. Then I can learn how to use a computer. It shouldn't be that hard to get used to one. Kenneth always called me "Mrs. Fixit"—he said that I should have been an engineer. But, she acknowledged as she stretched vigorously, traveling all over the place doing research doesn't always lend itself to finding a printer.

When she and Stephen were married, she'd get one. He'd been so afraid that she wouldn't be happy when she was busy attending official functions with him or not busy enough when left to her own devices. She was looking forward to both aspects of that life. The ten years she and Kenneth were married had been wonderful, but so hectic with both of them establishing careers. The crushing disappointment that they'd never had a child. Then these ten years of her widowhood, when work had been her goal and her salvation. Have I always been running? she wondered. Never quite at peace till now?

The sun was streaming in. *Oh, to be in England now that April's there.* Or January, or any month in England suited her totally. All morning she had been writing about the Restoration period when, as Samuel Pepys noted in his diary, there were a great many bonfires, and the Bow bells rang joyfully. Toasts were drunk to the King and maypoles were seen again in the villages. Brilliant colors replaced the drab gray of the Puritans, and the King and Queen rode in Hyde Park.

At one o'clock, Judith decided to go out, to walk in the area around Whitehall Palace and try to sense the relief of the people that the monarchy had been restored without another civil war. She especially wanted to visit the statue of King Charles I. The oldest and most beautiful equestrian statue in London, it had been given to a scrap dealer who was ordered to destroy it during the Cromwellian years. Recognizing its immense value and loyal to the dead King, the scrap dealer had not destroyed it, but kept it hidden until the return of Charles II. A magnificent base was commissioned to be made for it, and it was finally placed in Trafalgar Square looking directly down Whitehall at the site where Charles had been executed.

She had worked in her robe all morning. Now she showered quickly, applied lip gloss and mascara, and toweled dry her hair, noticing that it was getting too long. Not that it looks bad, she admitted as she examined herself critically in the mirror. But at almost forty-seven I think I'd better go for the sophisticated look. Then she raised her eyebrows. You don't look forty-seven, kiddo. The image she saw was reassuring. Dark-brown hair with hints of gold. She had been blond as a young child. The English complexion. The oval face, the wide blue eyes. I wonder if I resemble my natural mother, she reflected.

She dressed hurriedly in charcoal-gray slacks, a white high-necked sweater, and boots. My uniform, she thought. I won't be able to get away with this in town when I'm married to Stephen. She paused, deciding between the Burberry or the new cape. The cape. She collected the knapsack with her writing pads and the reference material she might need, and set out.

[70

Comely and calm, he rides
Hard by his own Whitehall:
Only the night wind glides:
No crowds, nor rebels, brawl.

Judith remembered the lines from the Lionel Johnson poem as she stood in Trafalgar Square and studied the magnificent statue of the executed King. The stately figure with shoulder-length hair, trim beard, erect head, and princely bearing did indeed have a peaceful expression. The stallion on which he sat seemed to be pawing the ground. Its right front hoof was raised as though it were eager to gallop.

And yet Charles I was so hated, Judith thought. What would the world have been like today if he had succeeded in destroying Parliament? Behind her she heard one of the inevitable tour groups approaching. The guide waited until his charges were gathered in a semicircle around him to begin his spiel. "What we now call Trafalgar Square was originally part of Charing Cross," he explained. "Fittingly enough, this statue was erected on the very spot where many of the regicides were executed, a subtle form of revenge for the dead King, wouldn't you think? The executions were not a pretty way to die. The condemned were hanged, drawn, and quartered, the entrails cut out of them while they still lived."

John dying like that . . . Sick, bewildered old man . . .

"January 30 was the day the King was beheaded. Come here next Tuesday and you'll see the wreath the Royal Stuart Society lays at the base. It's been a tradition since the statue was placed here. Sometimes tourists and schoolchildren add their own wreaths. Quite touching, it is."

71]

"The statue should be razed and the fools who lay wreaths punished."

The guide turned to Judith. "Beg your pardon, ma'am. Did you ask me something?"

Lady Margaret did not answer. She shifted the knapsack of books to her left hand and with her right hand, the crescent scar blazing, reached for dark glasses and folded the hood of the cape so it half covered her face.

For a time she walked aimlessly down the Victoria Embankment along the Thames until she reached Big Ben and the Houses of Parliament. There she waited, staring at the buildings, totally oblivious of the passersby, some of whom glanced at her curiously.

Her own words rang in her ears. "The statue should be razed and the fools who lay wreaths punished." But how, John, she wondered. How shall I go about it?

Indecisively she walked down Bridge Street, crossed Parliament Street, turned right and found herself at Downing Street. The houses at the end of the block were surrounded by policemen. One of them was 10 Downing Street. The residence of the Prime Minister. The future home of Stephen Hallett, descendant of Simon Hallett. Margaret smiled bitterly. It has taken so long, she thought. And at last I am here to do justice for John and for myself.

The statue first, she decided. On January 30, she with others would lay wreaths. But hers would have an explosive hidden within the leaves and blossoms.

She remembered the gunpowder that during the Civil War had destroyed so many homes. What explosives were used now? Three blocks away she passed a building site, stopped and watched as a sweaty, muscular young man swung a sledgehammer. A cold chill made her body shudder. The ax being lifted, smashing down. The awful moment of agony, the fight to hover in this existence, waiting, always knowing that she would somehow come back. Recognizing the moment had come when Judith Chase rushed to save her.

The muscular worker had noticed her watching him. A piercing whistle came from his lips. She smiled seductively and beckoned him to join her. When she left him, it was with the promise that she would meet him in his lodgings at six.

From there she went to the Central Reference Library off Leicester Square, where a polite assistant deposited books in front of her, whispering the titles as he laid them down: The Gunpowder Plot, Authority and Conflict in the Seventeenth Century, The History of Explosives.

That evening in the sweaty arms of the laborer, between caresses and flattery, Margaret confided that she needed to destroy a rotting coachhouse on her country property and simply hadn't the money to hire a demolition company. Rob was so clever. Could he help her get some of the stuff she'd need, show her how to use it? She'd pay him well.

Rob's mouth crushed her lips. "You're a dynamite lady. Meet me 'ere tomorrow night, love. My brother's coming up from Wales. Works in a quarry there. Easy for 'im to get what you need."

73]

There were two calls from Stephen on her answering machine when Judith reached the apartment at ten o'clock. When at nine-thirty she'd walked into a pub in Soho, she'd been shocked to see how late it was. Terrified, she realized that her last conscious memory was of standing at the statue of Charles I. That had been about two. What had she done in the intervening hours? She'd planned to search the birth records again. That's probably what I did, she thought. When I was unsuccessful again, could I have had some kind of psychological reaction? She could find no answer to that question.

With a troubled frown, she listened to Stephen's urgent request that she phone him. But first a shower, she decided. Her body ached and felt vaguely soiled. She unsnapped the cape. Whatever had made her buy it? She realized that now she felt uncomfortable in it. Jamming it in at the end of the closet, she touched the Burberry lightly. "You're more my style," she said aloud.

She let the water of the shower wash her face and hair and body. Hot water, her delicately scented soap and shampoo, tingling cold water. For some unexplainable reason, a quote from *Macbeth* ran through her mind: *Will all great Neptune's ocean wash this blood clean from my hand?* What made me think of that, Judith wondered. Of course, she thought as she toweled dry, that damn scar has been flaring again.

Her terry-cloth robe belted at her slender waist, a towel wrapped around her damp hair, her feet in comfortable slippers, Judith went to the phone to call Stephen. His voice told her instantly that he had been asleep. "Darling, I'm so sorry," she said.

He cut her off. "If I wake up during the night, I'll feel much better knowing I've spoken to you. Whatever have you been doing, darling? Fiona rang me. She expected you over this evening. Is anything wrong?"

"Good Lord, Stephen, I absolutely forgot." Judith bit her tongue nervously. "The machine was taking the calls and I just now checked for messages."

Stephen laughed. "A most single-minded lady. But better make your peace with Fiona, darling. She was already cross that she couldn't show me off as the potential party leader. Maybe we'll let her give us an engagement party after the election. We do owe her a lot."

"I owe her the rest of my life," Judith said quietly. "I'll call her first thing in the morning. Good night, Stephen. I love you."

"Good night, Lady Hallett. I love you."

I despise a liar, Judith thought as she put down the receiver, and I just lied. Tomorrow she would go to see Dr. Patel. There was no Sarah Marrish or Marsh in the records book for May 1942. Had she made up everything she had told him? And if so, was her mind now playing other tricks on her as well? Why had she lost seven hours today?

At ten o'clock the next morning, Dr. Reza Patel's receptionist violated his order to hold telephone calls and rang through to his office to announce that Miss Chase was on the phone and it was an emergency. He and Rebecca had once again been conferring on the potential danger of Judith's condition. Patel pressed the conference and record buttons on the telephone unit. Avidly he and Rebecca listened as Judith told them about the seven-hour gap in her memory.

"I think you should come in immediately," Patel told her. "If you remember, you signed an agreement that I could

75]

tape your session. I'd like you to see that tape. Perhaps it would help you. I have no reason to believe that your childhood memory was not accurate. And don't be too troubled about what you consider a memory loss. You are a woman of tremendous powers of concentration. That was obvious when I began the hypnosis. You told me yourself that hours can go by while you're working, and you're completely unaware of their passing."

"That's true," Judith said. "But it's one thing to be at my desk when that happens and quite another to be in Trafalgar Square at two o'clock and find myself in a Soho pub at nine-thirty. I'll leave for your office now."

Today she was wearing beige slacks, brown boots, a beige cashmere sweater with a brown, beige, and yellow scarf knotted on her shoulder. The Burberry felt warm and comfortably familiar as she buttoned and belted it, again regretting the three hundred pounds she'd spent for the cape.

In Patel's office, an astonished Rebecca asked, "Surely you're not planning to show her that tape?"

"Only to the point of her regression to childhood. Rebecca, she's already asking questions. She's got to concentrate on that aspect of the session and not on what may have happened to her. We still don't know how to help her. We won't know unless we can somehow learn whom she is harboring. Quickly, make a duplicate of the tape to the point where I start to instruct her to awaken."

In the taxi on the way to Patel's office, Judith realized she was deeply worried. He had used a drug on her. She remembered the time she'd done a journalistic series on LSD and its effects. She tried to remember the consequences of using LSD. Hallucinations. Memory loss. Blackouts. Oh God, she thought, what have I done to myself?

[76

But when, a short time later, she was watching the TV monitor, she found herself deeply stirred by what she was observing. Patel's skillful questioning. Her recounting of birthdays, her marriage to Kenneth, her adoptive parents. The way Patel worked backward to get her to early childhood. Her obvious reluctance to talk about the bombing. She felt tears sting her eyes as, in her hypnotized state, she wept for her mother and sister. And then realized something. The names. *Molly. Marrish.* "Stop the tape, please," she asked.

"Of course." Rebecca touched the "stop" button on the remote control she was holding.

"Can you go back? You see, I remember I had a speech impediment when I was a child. I was told I had a great deal of difficulty with the p sound. In the tape, I wasn't sure whether I heard that my sister's name was 'Molly' or 'Polly.' And turn up the volume where I say 'Marrish' or 'Marsh.' It's really not clear, is it?"

Intently they watched. "It's possible," Patel said. "You might have been trying to say something like 'Parrish.'"

Judith got up. "At least it's another avenue to search— after I finish with Marsh and Marrish, and March and Markey and Markham and Marmac and God knows how many others. Doctor, tell me frankly. Is there anything I ought to know about that treatment? Why did I lose those hours yesterday?"

She felt that Patel was weighing his words. He sat at the massive desk toying with a paper opener. In the corner she noticed the table and mirror. She'd been walking toward that table when she had the vision of a young child.

Reza Patel watched Judith glance in the direction of the table and knew exactly what she was thinking. With a flash of relief, he realized he had found a way to answer her. "You came to me last week because you were having recurring hallucinations, which I would prefer to call memory break-throughs. That process is continuing, perhaps in a slightly varied way. Yesterday you were on your way to the Register of Births. You had already suffered one intense disappoint-ment there. I would suggest that you probably returned and fruitlessly searched the records for a second time. I believe that is why your mind again did what it has taught itself to do. It blocked out. Judith, you may have caught something significant today. Perhaps the name you were trying to pronounce is Parrish, not Marrish, or a name similar to Parrish. You have been frustrated that you cannot find the information you want quickly. I beg you, give yourself more of a chance. Be aware of anything unusual, a flashback, a sense of having lost hours, a name or thought that crosses your mind that seems inappropriate to you. The mind has a strange way of trying to offer us clues when we probe the subconscious."

It made sense, but Judith repeated her question. "Then there was nothing about the treatment, about the drug you used, that might be causing some kind of reaction now?"

Rebecca studied the television remote control unit which she was still holding. Reza Patel raised his eyes and looked straight into Judith's. "Absolutely not."

When Judith left, Patel asked Rebecca despairingly, "What could I tell her?"

"The truth," Rebecca said quietly.

"What good would it do to terrify her?"

"I think what you would be doing is warning her."

Judith went directly back to the apartment. She did not want to risk going to the General Register Office again today. Instead she settled at the desk, her notebooks open around her, the aging typewriter that knew the feel of her fingers on the stand to her left. She worked steadily until early afternoon, feeling the comfort and security of knowing that the book was going well. At two o'clock, she hurriedly prepared a sandwich and a pot of tea and brought the tray back to her desk. A long afternoon of writing might complete the next chapter. She was having a late dinner with Stephen.

At four-thirty, she began to retype her notes on the trial of the regicides: *"Some would say that their trials were fair, that they were given more consideration than they had offered to their King. Standing in the crowded courtroom, over the jeers of the Royalist mob, they stoutly proclaimed their commitment to conscience, their faith that their God would judge them kindly."*

Her fingers fell from the keyboard. The scar on her hand began to throb. Judith pushed back the chair and glanced at the clock. There was an appointment she had made, wasn't there?

Lady Margaret hurried to the closet and reached for the green cape. You thought you could hide it, Judith, she jeered. She fastened it at the neck but before she pulled the hood around her face, she reached up and twisted her hair into a chignon. Hurrying back for Judith's oversized shoulder bag, she found the dark glasses and left the apartment.

Rob was waiting for her in his room. Two cans of beer were on the windowsill. "You're late," he told her.

Lady Margaret smiled coyly at him. "Not willingly. It isn't always too easy to get away."

"Where is your place, love?" he asked as he unbuttoned her cape and put his arms around her.

79]

"In Devon. Did you bring what you promised?"

"Plenty of time for that."

An hour later, lying beside him on the rumpled bed, Margaret listened with rapt attention as Rob explained: "Now you know you could get yourself blown to kingdom come with this stuff, so mind what I'm showing you. I brought you enough to pull down Buckingham Palace, but I 'ave to admit I fancy you. Same time tomorrow night?"

"Of course. And I did promise to pay you for your trouble. Will two hundred pounds do?"

At ten of nine, Judith looked up. My God, she thought. The car will be here any minute. She rushed into the bedroom to change, then decided to shower. It's just that I'm so darn stiff, she thought, sitting so long. She could not understand why again tonight she felt somehow soiled.

Monday, January 30 was cold and clear, the sun brilliantly bright, the air dry and exhilarating. Teachers kept anxious watch over streams of schoolchildren as they gathered behind the students who had been chosen to place the wreath at the statue of Charles I.

Other floral offerings were already piled there. Cameras clicked and escorted tourist groups listened attentively to the drama of the life and death of the executed King.

Lady Margaret had already placed her wreath. Now

*she listened cynically as a twelve-year-old, bespecta-
cled and shyly proud, began to recite the Lionel
Johnson poem.*

*" 'By the Statue of King Charles at Charing Cross,' "
he announced.*

*A constable was standing by, smiling at the earnest
faces of the children. The two holding the wreath were
obviously aware of their importance. Scrubbed and
shining they are, he thought. Well-trained, polite British children, honoring their badly-treated monarch.
The constable glanced at the wreaths already piled
against the base of the statue. His eyes narrowed.
Smoke. There was smoke filtering slowly through the
pile of flowers.*

*"Get back!" he shouted. "Back, all of you!" Dashing
forward, he ran in front of the children. "Turn, run, I
tell you. Get back." Frightened and bewildered, the
children turned, and the circle around the statue widened. "Back, can't you hear me?" he thundered. "Clear
a space."*

*Now the tourists, understanding danger, began to
stampede away.*

*Frozen with anger, Margaret watched as the constable
shoved aside the wreaths, picked up the brown paper
package she had placed beneath her flowers and flung
it into the clear area. Screams and frightened cries
mingled with the explosion as flying shrapnel fell on the
crowds.*

81]

As she slipped away, Margaret was aware that one tourist was recording the scene with a videocamera. Pulling her hood closer around her face, she vanished into the crowds of passersby who were rushing to assist the injured children. Big Ben was tolling noon.

She was wasting too much time walking, Judith decided as she went through the revolving door of the General Register Office at half past twelve. Granted she'd worked almost from dawn at her desk. Still, it shouldn't have taken her nearly an hour to walk here from the apartment. That hour would have been better spent examining the records.

It was becoming harder and harder to conceal what she was doing from Stephen. His interest in her research had at first delighted her. Now that she was regularly spending hours at the General Register Office and in the Library examining records of the 1942 bombings of London, she knew she sounded too vague when Stephen questioned her about her activities. And I'm getting damn careless, she thought. Somehow she had lost two hundred pounds from her wallet.

As Judith followed the familiar path to the shelves of records she thought, dear God, something else—I just never remember to ring Fiona. When I take a break, I'll do it from here.

She studiously avoided going to the P file until she satisfied herself that there was no birth entry under any possible derivation of the name Marrish that she had missed for the month of May in any 1942 volume.

An elderly woman obligingly made room for her at the crowded table.

"Absolutely frightful, isn't it?" she asked. At Judith's puzzled look she added, "Half an hour ago someone tried to blow up the statue of Charles the First. Dozens of children with cuts and bruises. They'd have been killed except for a quick-thinking constable who saw the smoke and realized something was wrong. Disgraceful, isn't it? These terrorists deserve the death penalty and let me tell you, Parliament had better face up to it."

Shocked, Judith asked for details. "I was just there the other day," she said. "The tourist guide was talking about the ceremony of laying wreaths on the statue today. People who can leave bombs around must be crazy."

Still shaking her head in disbelief, she again took down the quarterly 1942 volumes and consulted her notes. She thought of the tape Patel had given her. I said *"May"* clearly, she thought. *"Fork"* could only have been four. But did I mean four, or fourteen, or twenty-four? I was obviously trying to say "doodlebug." Her research had shown that the first doodlebug fell on London June 13, 1944. One landed near Waterloo Station on June 24. I remember getting on a train, Judith thought. I was wearing only a light sweater over the dress so it must have been fairly warm. Suppose we were going to Waterloo that day. Mother and my sister were killed. I wandered into the station and climbed on the train. I was found the next morning in Salisbury. That would explain why no one from London who might have known me saw my picture.

She had said she lived on Kent Court. A doodlebug had fallen on Kensington High Street on June 13, 1944. A few days later another had hit Kensington Church Street. *Kensington Court* was a residential street in the vicinity.

The Peter Pan statue was in Kensington Gardens, the park that adjoined the area. One of her hallucinations had been of watching a toddler touch the Peter Pan statue. Her maps and research had proved that if she had lived in the area of

Kensington it was possible that she had witnessed the first of the doodlebug attacks.

Judith felt herself begin to shiver. It was happening again. The table and the bookshelves disappeared. The room became dark. *The toddler. She could see her stumbling through the rubble, hear her sobbing. The train. The open door. The packages and sacks piled inside.*

The image vanished but this time Judith realized she had welcomed it. I *am* making breakthroughs, she thought triumphantly. It was some kind of freight car. That's why no one saw me. I laid down on something bumpy and fell asleep. The dates fit.

The next day, June 25, 1944, Amanda Chase, the Wren who was the bride of an American Naval officer, Edward Chase, came upon a two-year-old, wandering alone in Salisbury, her handmade smocked dress and wool sweater smudged and dirty. The child, silent and wide-eyed, unable to speak, suspicious at first, then reaching for friendly arms. The child without identification. The child no one claimed. Amanda and Edward Chase visited the little girl, whom they named Judith, at the orphanage, took her out on excursions. When she began to speak, she called them Mummy and Daddy. Two years later, after the efforts to find her natural family ended without success, Amanda and Edward Chase had been allowed to adopt Judith.

Judith still remembered the day she had waited for them to pick her up at the orphanage. "May I really live with you?"

Amanda, her brown eyes smiling, hugging her. "We did our best to find whoever let you go. But now you're ours."

Edward Chase, the man who became her father, tall and quiet and loving. "Judith, there's an overused line about adoption: 'We chose you.' In this case it's entirely appropriate."

[84

They were so good to me, Judith thought with renewed hope as she began another long and tedious search through the birth records. I was so happy with them.

Edward Chase, a graduate of Annapolis, had elected to make the Navy his career. After the war, he'd become Naval Military Attaché to the White House. Judith had vague memories of Easter Egg hunts on the White House lawn, of President Truman asking her what she was going to be when she grew up. Later, Edward Chase became military attaché in Japan, then ambassador to Greece and to Sweden.

Who could have asked for more loving parents? Judith wondered as she turned the book to the section with names that began with M. They had been in their thirties when they adopted her, died within a year of each other eight years ago, left their considerable assets to their "beloved daughter, Judith."

And now she was realizing their passing had freed her from a feeling of guilt or disloyalty as she tried to find the people who had begotten her. Hours passed. Marsh. March. Mars. Merrit. There was absolutely no derivation of Marrish, of *any* name beginning with M, in the records of May 1942 that had 'Sarah' as a first or middle name. It was time to look under P in hope that maybe, just maybe she *had* tried to say "Parrish."

Her fingers ran down the pages of the names beginning with P until she found the name Parrish. Parrish, Ann, District Knightsbridge; Parrish, Arnold, District Piccadilly. And then she saw it.

	Mother's Name	District	Vol.	Page
Parrish	Mary Elizabeth Travers	Kensington	6B	32

Parrish! Kensington! Oh God, she thought. Holding her index finger on that line, she raced through the rest of the page. Parrish, Norman, District Liverpool; Parrish, Peter, District Brighton; Parrish, Richard, District Chelsea; *Parrish, Sarah Courtney, Mother's Name Travers, District, Kensington, Vol. 6B, Page 32.*

Not daring to believe that she understood what she was reading, Judith rushed up to the clerk at the desk. "What does this mean?" she asked.

The clerk had a small transistor radio on her desk, the volume turned so low it was almost inaudible. Reluctantly she tore herself away from the BBC news. "Terrible, the bombing," she announced. She paused. "I'm sorry. What is your question?"

Judith pointed to the names Mary Elizabeth and Sarah Courtney Parrish. "They were born the same day. Their mother's maiden name was the same. Does that suggest they might have been twins?"

"It would certainly look so. And great care is taken about who was the older twin. Often it means who inherits the title, you see. Do you want to purchase the full birth certificates?"

"Yes, of course. And another question. Isn't Polly a nickname for Mary in England?"

"Very often. My own cousin, for example. Now to obtain the birth certificates, you'll have to fill out the proper forms and pay five pounds each. They can be mailed to you."

"How much information do they give?"

"Oh, quite a bit," the clerk replied. "Date and place of birth. Mother's maiden name. Father's name and occupation. Home address."

Judith walked back to the apartment in a daze. As she passed a newsstand she saw the glaring headlines that told of the bombing in Trafalgar Square. Pictures of bleeding children covered the front page. Sickened at the sight, Judith bought the paper and read it as soon as she was home. At least, she thought, none of the injuries were life-threatening. The paper was filled with news of the stormy session in Parliament. The Home Secretary, Sir Stephen Hallett, had made a dramatic speech: "I have long argued the need for the death penalty for terrorists. These despicable people have today planted a bomb at a place they knew would be visited by schoolchildren. If one of those children had been killed, shouldn't the terrorists be worrying now about their own necks? Does the Labour party agree or shall we continue to coddle these would-be murderers?"

Another news item said that the explosive had been gel-ignite, and a massive search had been started to trace purchases and check reports of theft of the deadly component.

Judith put down the newspaper and glanced at her watch. It was nearly six. She knew that Stephen would be calling, and that she'd better be able to say she had been in touch with Fiona.

Fiona was far too interested in the events of the day to be cross about Judith's neglect of her. "My dear, most frightful, wasn't it? Parliament in an absolute uproar. When the election is called, the death penalty will certainly be an issue. Can't help but benefit dear Stephen. People are simply outraged. Poor old King Charles. I gather they wanted to blow his statue to smithereens. Such a shame it would have been. Absolutely the most ravishing equestrian statue in the kingdom. Now there are a few statues I wouldn't mind seeing off to the scrapyard. Some of them look as though the horses should be pulling wagons, not seating kings. Oh well."

Stephen phoned fifteen minutes later. "Darling, I'll be very late tonight. I'm meeting with the Commissioner from Scotland Yard and some of his people."

"Fiona told me about the uproar in Parliament over the bombing. Have any terrorists claimed responsibility?"

"Not so far. That's why I'm meeting with Scotland Yard. As Home Secretary, acts of terrorism come under my jurisdiction. I'd hoped as a civilized nation that when we outlawed execution, it would be for all time but today certainly proves the need for the death penalty. I believe it would be a deterrent."

"I gather that many people agree with you, but I'm afraid I can't. The thought of execution makes my blood run cold."

"Ten years ago I felt exactly the same way," Stephen said quietly. "Not anymore. Not when so many innocent lives are in constant danger. Darling, I must run. I'll try not to be too late."

"Whatever time you get here, I'll be waiting."

Reza Patel and Rebecca Wadley were about to leave for dinner when the phone rang in his office. Rebecca picked it up. "Miss Chase, how good to hear your voice. How are you? The doctor's right here."

In the movement that had become automatic, Patel pressed the conference and record buttons. He and Rebecca listened as Judith told them about her discovery. "I've been longing to talk about it," she said happily, "and realized you and Rebecca are the only two people alive who know about me and can understand what's happening. Doctor, you're miraculous. Sarah Courtney Parrish. Quite a nice name, don't you think? When I receive the birth certificates, I'll have a street address. Isn't it incredible that Polly was my twin?"

"You're turning into a very good detective," Patel observed, trying to sound buoyant.

"Research," Judith laughed. "After a while you learn how to follow threads. But I have to put it off for a few days. Tomorrow I must stay at the typewriter, and there's an exhibition at the National Portrait Gallery I want to see. It has a lot of court scenes from Charles I. Should be interesting."

"What time will you be there?" Patel asked quickly. "I'm planning to visit it myself. Maybe we can have a cup of tea."

"Lovely. Would three o'clock do?"

When he replaced the receiver on the cradle, Rebecca asked Patel, "What point is there in meeting her at the gallery?"

"I have no reason to ask her to come in here again, and I'd like to see if I detect any indication of personality modification in her."

Judith changed to peach silk lounging pajamas and matching slippers, undid her hair from the chignon, brushed it loose around her shoulders, put on fresh makeup, and sprayed Joy eau de cologne on her wrists. She prepared a salad and scrambled eggs for dinner. With a pot of tea, she put the dishes on the inevitable tray and absentmindedly ate as she outlined her next chapter. At nine, she laid out a plate of cheese and crackers and the brandy snifters, then went back to her desk.

It was eleven-fifteen when Stephen arrived. His face was gray with fatigue. Silently he put his arms around her. "My God, it's good to be here."

Judith massaged his shoulders as she kissed him. Then, arms around each other, they went to sit on the overstuffed maroon damask couch that was obviously a treasured possession of Lady Beatrice Ardsley. An old comforter which covered the back and arms was tucked behind the frame and cushions, then fell protectively over the cushions to the floor. Judith poured the brandy and handed a glass to Stephen. "I really do think that in honor of the future Prime Minister I should take this exhausted comforter off and trust that you won't put your feet on Lady Ardsley's precious settee."

She was rewarded by a hint of a smile. "Be careful. If I close my eyes, I'm sure I'll end up curled on it for the night. What a hell of a day, Judith."

"How did the Scotland Yard meeting go?"

"Well enough. Fortunately, a Japanese tourist was grinding away with his videocamera and we'll have the film. There were also many people in the area snapping pictures. The media is requesting that all those pictures be turned in. There'll be a substantial reward if any of them lead to the arrest and conviction of the perpetrator. You see, one bit of luck is that the bomb must have started smoking within a minute or two after it was placed. Just possibly we'll get a picture of someone laying it at the base of the statue."

"I hope so. The pictures of those bleeding children were heartbreaking." Judith was about to say they reminded her of the hallucinations she had been having about the child caught in air raids, then closed her lips. It was hard, she thought, not to tell the man she loved so dearly that she believed she had learned her true identity.

There was a safe way to keep from revealing her secret. Slipping over on the couch, she put her arms around Stephen's neck.

Deputy Assistant Commissioner Philip Barnes was head of the Anti-Terrorist Branch at Scotland Yard. A slight, soft-spoken man in his late forties with thinning brown hair and hazel eyes, he looked more like a country preacher than a senior police official. His men had quickly learned that the soft voice could become a scathing weapon when they were on the carpet for anything from a minor offense to an incredible blunder. Still they respected Barnes to the point of awe, and some even had the courage to genuinely like him.

This morning Commissioner Barnes was both angry and pleased. Angry that the terrorists would select so meaningless a target as the equestrian statue and that they chose a day when the statue would be surrounded by children and tourists; pleased that no one had been killed or maimed. He was also frustrated. "It doesn't make sense for the Libyans or Iranians to go for the statue," he said. "If the IRA wanted to bomb a monument, they'd have gone after Cromwell. He was the one who decimated their country, not poor old Charles."

His men waited, knowing he did not expect an answer.

"How many pictures have come in?" he asked.

"Dozens," his senior aide, Commander Jack Sloane, answered. Sloane was long and lean with neutral coloring, sandy hair, light blue eyes, the rugged complexion of the year-round athlete. The brother of a baronet, he was a close friend of Stephen's. His family's country home, Bindon Manor, was six miles from Edge Barton. "Some of them still needing development, sir. It's being done now. We also have that videotape when you're ready to see it."

"How about the investigation of the explosive?"

"We may have a lead already. The foreman of a quarry in Wales has been searching the site for a quantity of missing gelignite."

"When did he realize it was missing?"

"Four days ago."

The phone rang. Commissioner Barnes's secretary had been told to hold calls except for one person's. "Sir

91]

Stephen," Barnes said even before he picked up the phone.

Swiftly he told Stephen about the missing gelignite, the tourists' pictures, the videotape. "We're just about to see it, sir. I'll report if it's promising."

Five minutes later in the darkened room, they watched as the tape was played. They had expected the usual uneven results of an amateur photographer and were pleasantly surprised to see a crisp, well-focused segment. The panorama of the area at Trafalgar Square. The close-up of the statue and its base. The floral wreaths already placed there.

"Stop," Sloane ordered.

The operator of the videocamera, familiar with this kind of order, instantly froze the film.

"Back up a frame or two."

"What do you see?" Commissioner Barnes demanded.

"That wisp of smoke. When this picture was taken, the bomb was already there."

"Damn shame the camera didn't catch the person placing it!" Barnes exploded. "All right. Keep running."

The schoolchildren. The tourists. The students holding the wreath. The self-conscious beginning of the poem. The constable rushing toward the statue, forcing the children away from it.

"That man should be put up for the George Cross," Barnes muttered.

The people scattering. The explosion. The camera panning about.

"Hold it."

Again the operator stopped the camera and retraced the previous frames.

"That woman in the cape and dark glasses. She realized she was being filmed. Look at the way she's pulling the hood around her face. Every other adult in the crowd is rushing to help the children. She's turning away." Sloane turned to one of the assistants. "I want her picture plucked out of every frame in this film. Blow it up. Let's see if we can identify her. We might be onto something."

Someone snapped on the lights. "And by the way," Sloane added. "Pay special attention to see if any of the tourists caught the woman in the cape in their snapshots."

That afternoon as Judith was dressing to go to the National Portrait Gallery, she reluctantly decided to wear a pale gray suit, heels, and her sable coat. In the few days since Stephen had been elected party leader, there had been a number of profiles of him in various newspapers, and they had all referred to him as the most eligible and attractive older single man in England. Not since Heath had there been an unmarried Prime Minister, one paper noted, and there were unconfirmed rumors that Sir Stephen had a romantic interest that would please the English people.

That quote had come from the gossip columnist, Harley Hutchinson. So I'd better not go out looking like a Greenwich Village hippie, Judith thought, sighing as she carefully brushed her hair and applied eye shadow and mascara. She then fastened a rose-shaped silver pin on the lapel of her suit and studied her reflection.

Twenty years ago, she had married Kenneth in the traditional white gown and veil. What would she wear when she married Stephen? A simple late afternoon dress, she decided. With a very small group of friends present. There had been nearly three hundred at the reception at the Chevy Chase Country Club all those years ago. To have it happen twice in a lifetime, she mused. No one deserves that much happiness.

She transferred her wallet and makeup kit to the gray

suede purse that matched her pumps, and dug out a smaller version of her oversized shoulder bag. All gussied up or not, I need my notebooks, she thought ruefully.

The National Portrait Gallery was on St. Martin's Place and Orange Street. The special exhibition was of court scenes from the Tudors through the Stuarts. The paintings had been borrowed from private collections all over Britain and the Commonwealth, and the lesser figures in the paintings who could be identified were listed in framed plaques. When Judith arrived, the gallery was still quite crowded, and with some amusement she watched as people peered down the printed lists within the plaques, obviously hoping to locate some long-forgotten ancestor.

She was particularly interested in seeing the court scenes in which Charles I, Oliver Cromwell, and Charles II were depicted. Working her way backward, she compared the festive dress of the returned "Merry Monarch," Charles II, to the sternly plain Puritan-type garb of Cromwell's intimates. The court scenes of Charles I and his consort, Henrietta Maria, were especially intriguing. She knew that, ignoring the stony disapproval of the Puritans, Queen Henrietta had delighted in pageants. One painting in particular caught her eye: The setting was Whitehall Palace. The King and Queen were the central figures. The members of the court were obviously dressed for a pageant. Shepherds' crooks, angel wings, halos, and gladiators' swords abounded.

"Miss Chase, how are you?"

Judith had been drinking in the painting.

Startled, she turned around and saw Dr. Patel. His even-featured face was smiling but she noticed that the expression in his eyes was serious. Lightly she touched his arm. "Doctor, you seem very somber."

He bowed slightly. "And I was thinking that you look

very beautiful." He lowered his voice. "I will say it again. Sir Stephen is indeed a fortunate man."

Judith shook her head. "Not here, please. From what I can see, this place is alive with press." She turned to the painting. "Isn't this fascinating?" she asked. When you think this was painted in 1640, just before His Majesty dissolved the Short Parliament."

Reza Patel stared at the picture. Beneath it the plaque read: *"Unknown Artist. Believed to have been painted between 1635 and 1640."*

Judith pointed to a handsome couple standing near the seated King. "Sir John and Lady Margaret Carew," she told Patel. "They were both upset that day. They knew what would happen if the King dissolved Parliament. Lady Margaret's ancestors had been M.P.s since the inception of Parliament. Her family was terribly split over allegiance at that time."

Patel read the information on the plaque. Other than the King and Queen, their eldest son, Charles, Duke of York, and a half dozen royal relatives, the other figures in the painting were unidentified. "Your research must be superb," he said. "You should have offered it to the historians here."

Lady Margaret realized she should not have told Reza Patel about John and herself. Turning abruptly from him, she hurried from the gallery.

At the door he caught up with her and stopped her. "Miss Chase, Judith. What is wrong?"

She stared him down. Her tone haughty, she said, "Judith is not here now."

"Who are you?" he asked urgently. Startled, he observed the angry red scar on her right hand.

She pointed to the painting. "I've already told you. I am Lady Margaret Carew."

Breaking away from him, she hurried outside.

Stunned, Patel went back to the painting and studied the figure whom Judith had indicated was Lady Margaret Carew. He realized there was a striking resemblance between her and Judith.

Sick with apprehension, he left the gallery, unaware of the pleasant buzz of conversation of the people who tried to greet him. At least, he told himself, I know who is present in Judith's body. Now he would have to learn what had happened to Margaret Carew and try to anticipate her next move.

The wind had become sharp. He turned to walk down St. Martin's Place and felt his arm taken. "Dr. Patel," Judith laughed. "I'm so terribly sorry. I was so engrossed in looking at the paintings that I started home before I remembered that we planned to have tea. Forgive me."

Her right hand. As Reza Patel watched, the scar faded into a barely discernible outline.

The next day, February 1st, brought teeming, chilling rain. Judith decided to stay in the apartment and work at her desk. Stephen phoned to say he was going to Scotland Yard and then to the country. *"Vote Conservative, Vote Hallett,"* he joked. "A pity, you Yankee, I can't count on your vote."

"You'd have it," Judith told him. "And maybe you can use this. My father used to tell me that in Chicago half the poor souls in the cemeteries were still on the voters' list."

"You must teach me how it's done." Stephen laughed. His tone changed. "Judith, I'll be going to Edge Barton for a few days. The trouble is, I'll hardly be home, but would you like to come down? Knowing you were there at the end of the day would mean so much to me."

Judith hesitated. On the one hand, she wanted desperately to go back to Edge Barton. On the other, Stephen's total preoccupation with the upcoming campaign freed her to quietly try to discover her past. Finally she said, "I want to be there. I want to be with you. But I don't work as well away from my desk. We'll scarcely see each other, so I think it's better if I stay put here. By the time the election comes, I intend to be mailing a completed manuscript to my editor. If I can achieve that, I assure you, I'll feel like a new woman."

"Once the election is over, I won't be patient, darling."

"I hope not. God bless, Stephen. I love you."

In Scotland Yard a room had been set aside to display the enlarged snapshots that had been turned in. Several of them included glimpses of the woman in the dark glasses and cape. None of the pictures offered much more than a profile. The hood of the cape almost covered the woman's face, even before she pulled it closer when she noticed the video-camera. All the pictures that included her had been blown up and her image taken from them. "About five eight or so," Commander Sloane observed. "Quite slender, don't you think? Not more than eight or nine stone. Dark hair and an angry mouth. Doesn't help much, does it?"

Inspector David Lynch came into the room, his footsteps brisk. "Think we have something, sir. Another set of pictures just arrived. Look at this, won't you?"

The new pictures showed the woman in the cape placing a wreath at the base of the statue of Charles I. The camera

97]

had caught the corner of the brown paper parcel beneath the wreath.

"Well done," Sloane said.

"That isn't the half of it," Lynch told him. "We've been asking questions at all the local construction sites. A foreman tipped us off that a very attractive woman in a dark cape was flirting with one of his crew, Rob Watkins, and that Watkins bragged she was coming to his lodgings." Lynch waited, obviously enjoying what he was about to say. "We just talked to Watkins's landlady. Not ten days ago, he had a visitor. She came two evenings about six o'clock, stayed a couple of hours in his room. The lady had dark hair, dark glasses, looked to be in her late thirties or early forties, and she wore a dark green cape with a hood, a very expensive one, the landlady reports. Also wore very expensive leather boots, carried an oversized shoulder bag, and as the landlady reported, 'thought she was the Queen herself, the manner of her. Very haughty.' "

"I think we'd better have a chat with Mr. Rob Watkins immediately," Sloane said. He turned to an assistant. "Take down all the enlarged pictures of the lady in the cape. Let's see if we can get this fellow to pick her out of the crowd without giving him any help."

"Another interesting thing," Lynch went on. "The landlady says the woman was undoubtedly English, but that she had a strange accent, or manner or speaking."

"What's that supposed to mean?" Sloane snapped.

"From what I gather it was the *cadence* of her speech that seemed odd. The landlady says it was like listening to one of those old films in which people use words like 'forsooth.' "

He shook his head at the expression on Commander Sloane's face. "Sorry, sir. I don't understand it either."

*   *   *

[98

On February 10 the Prime Minister made her long-expected announcement. She would go to the Queen and ask Her Majesty to dissolve Parliament. She would not be seeking reelection.

On February 12 Stephen was elected Conservative Party Leader. On February 16 the Queen dissolved Parliament and the campaign began.

Judith joked to Stephen that if she wanted to see him she turned on her television set. When they did manage to meet it was usually at his home. His car would pick her up and Rory would drive around the house to the back entrance. That way it was possible to avoid the attention of the ever-present media.

Nevertheless, Judith realized that it was a blessed coincidence that Stephen was away campaigning at the same time that she was completing her book. Eagerly she awaited the moment the birth certificates would arrive. Her moods ranged from anticipation to fear. Suppose Sarah Parrish was only someone she had *known* as a small child? What then?

She knew that when she was married to the Prime Minister of England, she would always be recognizable. There would be no private mission like this possible for her then.

Stephen called her early every morning and again late in the evening. His voice was often hoarse from the speech-making. She could sense his fatigue as they talked. "It's going to be much closer than we anticipated, darling," he told her. "Labour is fighting hard, and after over a decade of a Conservative government, there are many who will vote for change for the sake of change." The worry in his voice was enough for Judith to completely absolve him of selfishness in not helping her search for her identity. She could only compare his disappointment if he failed to become Prime Minister to what her own anguish would be if she suddenly sat in front of her typewriter and realized that she could no longer write, that the gift was gone . . .

To accommodate her need to finish the book and to continue her search, Judith set her alarm earlier and earlier. Now she arose at four in the morning, worked until noon, prepared a sandwich and a pot of tea, and worked until eleven.

Every few days she walked in the Kensington area, thinking that given enough concentration, one of the old apartment buildings that lined the lovely streets might suddenly look familiar. Now she wished she could see the phantom toddler running ahead of her, running into the entrance of the dwelling that might have been their home. In the hallucinations she had experienced, had she seen herself or Polly? she wondered, and was rewarded by the immediate thought, *I always followed Polly. She could run faster . . .* The window to the past was opening a little more . . . Why was it taking so long for the birth certificates to come?

It was not the social season in London. Fiona was in a hard fight for her own seat in Parliament. The parties and dinners to which Judith received invitations were easy to refuse. She kept track of time carefully and was certain she had no more memory lapses. Dr. Patel phoned her regularly, and it amused her that his tone at the beginning of the conversation was always apprehensive, as if he expected her to report some sinister aberration.

On February 28, she completed the first draft of her book, read it through, and realized there would be very little rewriting needed before sending it to her publisher. That night Stephen arrived from Scotland, where he'd been campaigning for the Conservative candidates.

They had not seen each other for nearly ten days. When she opened the door for him, they stood for a long moment looking at each other. Stephen sighed as he held her close before he kissed her. Judith felt the warmth and strength of his arms, the beating of his heart, as he drew her to him. Their lips met and her arms tightened around his neck. Again she was aware that as dearly as she had loved Kenneth, in Stephen's arms she felt the completion of all that was possible between a man and woman.

Over drinks they compared notes, each agreeing that the other looked exhausted. "Darling, you're much too thin," Stephen told her. "How much weight have you lost?"

"I'm not keeping track. Don't worry. I'll put it all back when the book goes in. And incidentally, Sir Stephen, you've shed a few pounds yourself."

"The Americans think they have a market on rubber chicken. They're quite wrong. By the way, I'd better phone the house and tell them to expect us for dinner."

"No need. I sent out for all the makings. Very simple. Chops and salad and a wonderfully large baked potato for carbohydrate energy. Will that do?"

"And not a single constituent to wish me luck or badger me about taxes."

They worked together in the tiny kitchen, Judith preparing the salad, Stephen proclaiming himself a master at grilling chops to the point of perfection. Stephen, his sleeves rolled up, a chef's apron enveloping him, seemed to Judith to visibly shed the lines of fatigue from around his eyes. "When I was a boy," he said, "my mother gave all the servants Sundays off unless we were having weekend guests. She loved to go down into the kitchen and cook for my father and me. I've always missed those wonderful days when we were completely alone. I suggested we carry on the tradition when Jane and I were married."

"What did Jane say?" Judith asked, suspecting the answer.

101]

Stephen chuckled. "She was appalled." He gave another glance at the chops. "About three minutes more, I think."

"Salad ready to go on the table. Potatoes and rolls already there." Judith rinsed her hands, dried them, and cupped Stephen's face in her palms. "Would you like to reinstate the old tradition? When I'm not a slave to the typewriter, I'm a darn good cook."

Four minutes later, as they were still wrapped in each other's arms, Stephen sniffed, then said in an alarmed voice, "Good God, the chops!"

The search for the woman who had set the bomb at the base of King Charles's statue had come to a dead end. The young construction worker, Rob Watkins, had been interrogated relentlessly but to no avail. He quickly identified the woman in the dark cape in the photos taken at King Charles's statue as the woman to whom he had given the gelignite, but adamantly stuck to his story that Margaret Carew had told him she planned to use it to demolish an old house on her property in Devonshire. Watkins's background was exhaustively researched. Scotland Yard concluded that he was exactly what he seemed to be: a laborer who fancied himself a womanizer, totally uninterested in politics, and the sort whose brother would help himself to anything he wanted from a quarry. The mantel of the fireplace in his parents' cottage in Wales was newly constructed of valuable slabs of marble that exactly matched the marble used in the brother's last job.

Reluctantly Deputy Assistant Commissioner Philip Barnes agreed with his senior aide, Commander Jack Sloane, that Watkins had been used for a fool by the dark-haired woman in the cape. Watkins's insistence that the woman who called herself Margaret Carew had a vivid scar at the base of her right thumb was the one clue on which they could pin some hope.

Watkins's information was kept from the media. He was charged with receiving stolen property and remanded on bail, which he was unable to raise. The charge of aiding a terrorist was held over his head pending his future cooperation. Every constable in England was given an enlarged picture of the woman in the cape and dark glasses, with instructions to be on the lookout for her. They were particularly warned to watch for a dark-haired woman around forty years old with a scar on her hand.

As the election loomed closer, the story about the bombing of the statue receded from public interest. No one had been seriously injured, after all. No group had claimed responsibility. Black humor began to emerge on the television programs. "Poor old Charles. Not satisfied with chopping off his head, three hundred years later they're trying to blow him up. Give him a break."

Then on March 5, there was an explosion in the Tower of London in the room where the Crown jewels were on display. Forty-three people were injured, six seriously, and a guard and an elderly American tourist were killed.

On the morning of March 5, Judith realized that she was not satisfied with her description of the Tower of London. She felt that she had not managed to convey the awesome fear that must have been experienced by the regicides and their accomplices who had been lodged there. She knew that a visit to the site she was describing could often help her to find the mood she was seeking to portray.

The day was crisp and windy. She buttoned her Burberry, tied on a silk kerchief, dug gloves out of her pockets, and decided against carrying her shoulder bag. The long hours were getting to her, she admitted to herself, and the weight of the bag was causing her shoulder to ache. Instead, she put money and a handkerchief in her pocket. She did not intend to take notes. She simply wanted to wander around the Tower.

As usual the inevitable tourists filled the courtyards and rooms. Guides speaking in a dozen languages explained the history of the massive palace. "In 1066 when the Duke of Normandy was crowned King of England, he immediately began to fortify London against possible attack. Originally the Tower was conceived and built as a fort, but some ten years later a massive stone tower was built and became known as the Tower of London."

It was a history she knew well, but Judith found herself following at the edge of the group as it was led through the towers and apartments selected for the tour. The apartment in the Bloody Tower where Sir Walter Raleigh was imprisoned for thirteen years fascinated tourists. "It's bigger than my own studio," a young woman commented.

It's much better lodging than most of the poor wretches had, Judith thought, and realized she was chilled and shivering. A sense of panic and fear raced through her and she leaned against the wall. Get out of here, she told herself, then thought, Don't be ridiculous, this is the sensation I want to get across in the book.

Her hands clenched in her pockets, she continued with the tour to the Jewel House in the old Waterloo Barracks where the Crown Jewels were housed. "From the time of the Tudors this tower accommodated prisoners of rank," the guide explained. "During the Cromwell years Parliament had the coronation ornaments melted down and the gems sold. Desperate pity. But when Charles the Second was reinstated, as much of the old regalia as could be found was brought together, and new ornaments were made for his coronation in 1661."

[104

Judith walked through the lower chamber of the Jewel House slowly, stopping to stare at the Anointing Spoon; the Sword of State; St. Edward's Crown; the Eagle Ampulla, which held the holy oils for anointing the monarch; the Scepter, which contained the Star of Africa diamond . . .

The Scepter and the Ampulla were made for his coronation, Margaret thought. John and I heard about the grandeur of it all. Oils to anoint a liar's breast, a scepter to be held by a vengeful hand, a crown to be placed on the head of another despot.

Abruptly Margaret hurried past the Yeoman Warder. The room where they kept me is in the Wakefield Towers she thought. They told me I was fortunate not to be lodged in the dungeon while I awaited my execution. They said that the King was merciful to that extent only because I was the daughter of a duke who had been his father's friend. But they found ways to torture me. Oh God, it was so cold and they delighted in describing John's death. He died calling for me and Vincent, and they put his head on a stake where I would see it on the way to my execution. Hallett planned all that. Hallett visited me and mocked me with his tales of life at Edge Barton.

"Miss Chase, are you all right?"

The solicitous voice of the guard followed Margaret as she rushed blindly up the winding stairs, brushing aside the clusters of slowly moving tourists. In the courtyard she rubbed her hand over her forehead, noticing that the scar was as vivid as it had been when she was imprisoned here. Hallett took my hand and examined

105]

the scar, she remembered. He told me it was a shame
that so beautiful a hand should be so marred. Turning,
she stared at the old Waterloo Barracks. The crown
and jeweled trappings created for Charles II will never
be placed on the head and in the hands of Charles III,
she vowed.

"The lady in the dark green cloak again." Deputy Commissioner Barnes spat out the words. "Every constable in London was told to be on the lookout for her, and she managed to set a bomb in the Tower of London, of all places! What is the matter with our people?"

"There were a lot of tourists, sir," Sloane said quietly. "A woman clustered in a group doesn't stand out, and this year capes are very popular. I imagine the constables were alert for the first few weeks, then since there were no other incidents, rather put the woman to the back of their minds . . ."

There was a tap on the door and Inspector Lynch hurried in. It was clear to his two superiors that he was shaken. "I've just come from the hospital," he announced. "The second guard in the Jewel House won't survive, but he's conscious enough to talk. He keeps repeating a name—Judith Chase."

"Judith Chase!" Philip Barnes and Jack Sloane spoke simultaneously and with equal astonishment.

"Good God, man," Barnes said. "Don't you know who she is? The author. Absolutely marvelous." He frowned. "Wait a minute. Didn't I read she's doing a book on the Civil War, on the period between Charles the First and Charles the Second: Maybe we're onto something. Her picture is on the back of her last book—we have it at home. Get someone to go out and buy it. We can compare the lady's picture with the ones we have and show it to Watkins. *Judith Chase!* What kind of world do we live in?"

[106

Jack Sloane hesitated, then said, "Sir, it's very important that no one know that we are investigating Judith Chase. I'll get the book. I don't want even your secretary to know of our interest in the lady."

Barnes frowned. "What is your point?"

"As you know, sir, my family home is in Devonshire, about five miles from Edge Barton, Sir Stephen Hallett's country place."

"What of it?"

"Miss Chase was a guest of Sir Stephen's at Edge Barton last month. The rumor is that as soon as the election is over, they will marry."

Philip Barnes walked to the window and stared out. It was a gesture his men recognized. He was weighing and analyzing the potential disaster. Sir Stephen as Home Secretary was the cabinet minister concerned with the administration of justice. Sir Stephen if elected Prime Minister would be one of the most powerful men in the world. A hint of scandal about him now could easily change the course of the election.

"What exactly did the guard say?" he asked Lynch.

Lynch pulled out his notepad. "I copied it, sir. 'Judith Chase. Back again. Scar' "

Judith's picture, cut from the book jacket, was shown to Rob Watkins. "That's her!" he exclaimed, then as his shocked listeners waited, his expression became uncertain. "No. Look at 'er 'ands. No scar. And the mouth, and the eyes. Sort of *different*. Oh, they look alike. Enough to be sisters." He tossed aside the picture and shrugged. "Wouldn't mind taking this one out. See if you can set it up."

Aghast, Judith heard about the bombing at the Tower of London when she turned on the television for the eleven o'clock news. "I was there this very morning," she told Stephen when he phoned a few minutes later. "I just wanted to sense the atmosphere. Stephen, those poor people. How can anyone be that cruel?"

"I don't know, darling. I just thank God you weren't in that room when the bomb went off. I do know one certain fact. If my party wins and I become Prime Minister, I'm going to force through the death penalty for terrorists, at least for the ones who cause fatalities."

"After today, more people will agree with you, even though I still can't. When will you get back to London, darling? I miss you."

"Not for another week or so, but Judith, at least we're on countdown. Ten more days until the election and then, win or lose, we'll begin our time."

"You'll win and I'm down to the fine editing. I'm awfully pleased with what I wrote this afternoon about the Tower. I really think I managed to convey how it must have been to be a prisoner there. I love it when the work is really going well. I absolutely lose any sense of time, and it's glorious immersion."

After Judith said good-bye to Stephen, she went into the bedroom and was surprised to notice that the doors of the second section of the wardrobe, the area Lady Ardsley had reserved for her own clothing, were slightly ajar. Probably they weren't completely closed from the beginning, Judith thought, as she pushed them firmly together until she heard the click of the lock. She did not notice the cheap knapsack that was half hidden behind the row of prim dresses and tailored suits which constituted Lady Ardsley's London wardrobe.

At ten the next morning, Judith was startled to hear the intercom buzzer sound in the foyer. One of the joys of

[108

London is that nobody ever drops in without phoning first, she thought. Reluctantly she left her desk and went to the intercom. It was Jack Sloane, Stephen's friend from Devonshire, asking for a few minutes of her time.

He was an attractive man, she thought as she watched him sip the coffee he had quickly accepted. Forty-five or so. Very British with his fair hair and blue eyes. Diffident, with that touch of shyness that characterized so many well-bred Englishmen. She had met him at several of Fiona's parties and knew he was with Scotland Yard. Was it possible that rumors about her and Stephen had caused him to begin checking on her in an official capacity? She waited, letting him lead the conversation.

"Terrible thing about the bombing at the Tower yesterday," he said.

"Appalling," Judith agreed. "Actually I was there in the morning, just a few hours before it happened."

Jack Sloane leaned forward. "Miss Chase, Judith, if I may, that's why I'm here. Apparently one of the guards in the Crown Jewel area recognized you. Did he speak to you at all?"

Judith sighed. "I'm going to sound like an idiot. I'd gone to the Tower for atmosphere for one of the chapters in my new book which didn't seem quite right. I'm afraid when I'm concentrating, I turn pretty inward. If he spoke to me, I didn't hear him."

"What time was that?"

"About ten-thirty, I think."

"Miss Chase, try to help. I'm sure you're a keen observer, even though, as you say, you were intent on your own research. Someone managed to smuggle in a bomb in the afternoon. It was one of those plastic devices, but rather crudely made from what we can see. It couldn't have been there more than a few minutes before it exploded. The

109]

moment the guard noticed the bag and picked it up, it was detonated. When you went through security to get into the Jewel House, did you feel that the guards were attentive when they passed your handbag through the detection equipment?"

"I didn't carry a bag yesterday. I just put money in the pocket of my raincoat." Judith smiled. "For the last three months I've been doing research all over England, and my shoulder is worn down from lugging books and cameras. Yesterday I realized I didn't need anything but my cabfare and cash for an admittance ticket so I'm afraid I can't help you."

Sloane stood up. "Would you mind taking my card?" he asked. "Sometimes we see something and tuck it away subconsciously. If we send our minds on a search-and-retrieve pattern, not unlike the way we use computers, it's amazing how often helpful information may emerge. I'm very glad that you were so fortunate as not to be in the Tower at the time of the bombing."

"I was back at my desk all afternoon," Judith told him, gesturing toward the study.

Sloane could see the pile of manuscript pages by the side of the typewriter. "Looks quite impressive. I envy you your talent."

His eyes darted about absorbing the layout of the flat as they walked to the door. "After the election and when things are quieted down, I know my family is anxious to meet you."

He knows about Stephen and me, Judith thought. Smiling, she held out her hand. "That would be lovely."

Jack Sloane glanced down swiftly. There was the faintest outline of an old scar or even a birthmark on her right hand, but nothing like the angry reddish-purple crescent Watkins had described. A very nice woman, he thought as he went

[110

down the stairs. On the main floor he opened the outside door just as an elderly woman came up the steps carrying a large bundle of groceries. She was breathing rapidly. Sloane knew the lift was out of order.

"May I carry these for you?" he asked.

"Oh thank you," the woman panted. "I was wondering if I'd make it up the three flights, and I know perfectly well the handyman will be among the missing as usual." Then she looked at him sharply, as though wondering if he was simply trying to gain admittance to her apartment.

Jack Sloane knew what she was thinking. "I'm a friend of Miss Chase on the third floor," he said. "I just left her."

The woman's face brightened. "I'm right across the hall from her. What a lovely person she is. And so pretty. Wonderful writer. Did you know that Sir Stephen Hallett calls on her? Oh, I shouldn't talk about that. Quite rude of me."

They were going up the stairs slowly, Jack carrying the bags. They exchanged names. Martha Hayward, she told him. Mrs. Alfred Hayward. From the tinge of sadness as her voice lingered over the name, Jack was sure that her husband was no longer living.

He deposited the groceries on Mrs. Hayward's kitchen table and, his good deed accomplished, turned to go. As he said good-bye, he asked a question he had not expected to hear emerge from his lips: "Does Miss Chase ever wear a cape?"

"Oh yes," Mrs. Hayward said warmly. "I've not seen her in it much, but quite lovely it is. Dark green. When I admired it last month she said she had just bought it in Harrods.

Reza Patel read the morning newspapers in his office. His hand trembling as he held the coffee cup, he studied the pictures of the dead and wounded victims of the bombing in the Tower of London. Fortunately, or unfortunately, the bomb had fallen short of its mark. It had been left where it would do maximum damage to the royal crowns and coronation fittings, but when the guard picked it up, he had caused the force of the explosion to occur away from the heavy metal glass enclosures over the priceless treasures. The glass cases had been shattered but their precious contents were unharmed. Touching the package had cost the guard his own life and the life of the tourist nearest him.

A separate article gave a history of the royal trappings, how they had been broken and dismantled after the execution of Charles I and restored for the coronation of Charles II. "Charles the First and Charles the Second again," Patel said, his voice anguished. "It's Judith. I know it."

"Not Judith—Lady Margaret Carew," Rebecca corrected him. "Reza, don't you have an obligation to go to Scotland Yard?"

He slammed his fist down. "No, Rebecca, no. I have an obligation to Judith to try to rid her of this malignant presence. But I don't know if I can do it. She is the most innocent victim of all, don't you see that? Our only hope is that she is a strong personality. Anna Anderson willingly enslaved herself to the essence of the Grand Duchess Anastasia. Judith subconsciously will fight for her own identity. We have to give her time."

Repeatedly throughout the day, Patel tried to phone Judith but reached only her answering machine. Just before he left the office he tried once more. Judith answered, a Judith whose voice was brimming with joy. "Dr. Patel, I received the birth certificates. Can you believe they were misaddressed? That's why they've taken so long to get here. We lived in Kent House at Kensington Court. Remember? I tried to tell you I lived on Kent Court. That's pretty close,

[112

isn't it? If I'm right about all this, my mother's name was Elaine. My father was an RAF officer, Flight Lieutenant Jonathan Parrish."

"Judith, what good news! What is your next step?"

"Tomorrow I'm going to Kent House. Maybe somebody will remember something about the family, someone who was young then and is still living in the building. If that doesn't work, I'll find out how to trace RAF records. My only worry about *that* is that Stephen might hear about it somehow, if I start poking into government records, and you know his feelings."

"I know. And how is the book coming?"

"About a week more and I'll be totally finished editing it. Are you aware that the polls show the Conservatives are pulling ahead? Wouldn't it be wonderful if just as I finish the book, he wins the election, and as a bonus I trace the family I came from?"

"Wonderful indeed. But don't work too hard. Have you had any problems with time lapses?"

"Not a one. I just sit at this typewriter and day fades into night."

When Patel hung up, he looked over at Rebecca who had been on the extension. "What are you thinking?" she asked him.

"There is hope. When Judith finishes this book, she will no longer be concentrating on the Civil War. Finding her roots will satisfy a deep hunger in her. Marriage to Sir Stephen will be a full-time commitment. Lady Margaret's grasp on her will fade. Watch and see."

Commander Sloane reported back to Deputy Assistant Commissioner Barnes at Scotland Yard. Only Inspector Lynch was allowed in the room with them. "You've spoken to Miss Chase?" Barnes asked.

Sloane noticed that in the weeks since the first bombing, Barnes's thin face had settled into rows of lines that ran down his cheeks and across his forehead. As head of the Anti-Terrorist Branch, Barnes usually reported to the Assistant Commissioner for Crime, who was the highest-ranking officer in Scotland Yard after the Commissioner. He knew that Barnes had assumed the awesome responsibility of not telling his superiors of the possible connection of Judith Chase to the bombings. Either of them would have gone to Stephen Hallett unhesitatingly. The Commissioner did not like Stephen, and would welcome an opportunity to embarrass him. Sloane admired Barnes's decision to withhold Judith's name; at the same time he did not envy Barnes the consequences if it proved to be a mistake.

The office was warm enough, but the bleak overcast day made Sloane long for a cup of coffee. He hated the report he knew he had to give.

Barnes switched on the intercom and told his secretary to hold all calls, hesitated, then barked, "Except for the obvious ones." Leaning back in his chair, he held his hands together, the fingers pointing up, always a sign to his staff that there had better be answers to his questions.

"You spoke to her, Jack," Barnes snapped. "What about it?"

"She has absolutely no scar. She does have the faintest of marks on her right hand, but you'd have to be within an inch of her hand to see it. She was in the Tower yesterday *morning*, not in the afternoon. She didn't speak to the guard and if he spoke to her, she didn't hear him."

"Then her story dovetails with the guard's account. But what did he mean when he said 'back again'?"

"Sir," Lynch volunteered. "Doesn't it seem to be the same situation as Watkins claims—not the same woman, but one with a strong resemblance?"

[114

"It would seem so. I suppose we should thank God that we don't have to worry about arresting the intended wife of the next Prime Minister, if that's what she is," Barnes said. "Gentlemen, obviously the fact that the guard saw Miss Chase and that she verified she had been in the Tower in the morning must be part of the official report. But no emphasis—and I repeat no emphasis whatsoever—on 'back again.' It's clear that someone who resembles Miss Chase, the one who told Watkins her name was Margaret Carew, is the woman we're looking for, but in fairness to both Miss Chase and Sir Stephen, her name must *not* be dragged into this."

Commander Sloane thought of his long friendship with Stephen, of how concerned Judith Chase had been when she discussed the bombing with him. Frowning, his voice subdued, he said: "There's one other fact you must know. Judith Chase has an expensive dark green cape, which she bought in Harrods about a month ago."

Judith stood in front of Kent House, 34 Kensington Court, and looked up at the crenellated parapets and ornate tower of an apartment building that had been designed in the Tudor style. Mary Elizabeth Parrish and Sarah Courtney Parrish had been brought to this house after their birth at Queen Mary Hospital. She rang the bell for the porter and wondered, as she stared at the faded marble on the foyer floor, if her mind was playing tricks. Did she remember running across that marble to that staircase so long ago?

The porter's wife was a woman in her late fifties. Wearing a long sweater over a shapeless woolen skirt, her feet encased in blue and white imitation-leather shoes, her pleasant face devoid of makeup but framed by wavy white hair, she held the door partially open. "I'm afraid we don't have a single flat to let," she said.

"That's not why I'm here." Judith gave the woman her

115]

card. She had already decided on what she would say. "My aunt had a dear friend who lived in this building during the war. Her name was Elaine Parrish. She had two little girls. It's so long ago, but my aunt was hoping to trace them."

"Oh love, I don't think there'd even be records. The place has been sold time and again, and what would be the point of keeping files on people who moved out, how many years would that be? Forty-five or fifty! Oh, that's hopeless." The porter's wife began to close the door.

"Wait, please," Judith begged. "I know how busy you are, but if I could pay you for your time?"

The woman smiled. "I'm Myrna Brown. Come in, won't you, love? There *are* some old records in the storeroom."

Two hours later, her nails chipped, feeling dusty and soiled from the grimy files, Judith left the office and sought out Myrna Brown. "I'm afraid you're right. It's pretty hopeless. There's been quite a turnover in the twenty years of records that you have here. There's just one thing. Apartment four B. From what I can tell, there was no record of it changing tenants until four years ago."

Myrna Brown threw up her hands. "I must be daft. Of course. We've just been here three years, but the porter who retired told us all about Mrs. Bloxham. Ninety years old when she finally gave up her flat to go to a retirement home. Bright as a button, they say, and left under protest, but her son wouldn't have her alone any longer."

"How long was she here?" Judith felt her mouth go dry.

"Oh, forever, dear. She came as a twenty-year-old bride, I gather."

"Is she still alive?"

"I haven't the faintest. Not likely, I'd say. But then you never can tell, can you?"

[116

Judith swallowed. So near. So near. To gain her composure she glanced around the small living room with its brilliantly flowered wallpaper, stiff horse-hair couch and matching chair, electric heating units set under long narrow windows.

The heating unit. She and Polly had been having a race. She'd tripped and fallen against the heater. She could remember the frightful smell of burning scalp, the feeling of her hair sticking to the metal surface. And then arms holding her, soothing her, carrying her down the stairs, calling for help. The young, frightened voice of her mother.

"Surely Mrs. Bloxham's mail had to be forwarded to her."

"The post office isn't allowed to release addresses, but why don't we call the building management office? They just might have it."

Late that afternoon, in a rented car, Judith drove through the gates of the Preakness Retirement Home in Bath. She had phoned ahead. Muriel Bloxham was still a resident, she was told, but quite forgetful.

Matron led her to the "social" room. It was a large-windowed, sunny area with bright curtains and carpeting. Four or five old people in wheelchairs were clustered around a television set. Three women who appeared to be in their late seventies were talking and knitting. One gaunt-faced, white-haired man was staring straight ahead, his hand making conducting motions. As she passed him, Judith realized he was humming to himself in remarkably accurate pitch. Dear God, she thought, these poor people . . .

Matron must have seen the expression on her face. "There's no question that some of us live beyond our time but I can promise you that all our guests are quite comfortable."

117]

Judith felt reproved. "I can see they are," she said quietly. I am so weary, she thought. The end of the book, the end of the campaign, perhaps the end of the trail. She knew Matron probably thought she was a relative of old Mrs. Bloxham's—perhaps a relative with a guilt complex who was paying a hurried duty visit.

They were at the window, which looked over the parklike grounds. "Well now, Mrs. Bloxham," Matron said in a hearty voice. "We've got company today. Isn't that nice?"

The woman, slight but still erect in her wheelchair, said, "My son is in the United States. I don't expect anyone else." Her voice was firm and sensible.

"Now is that any way to treat a guest?" Matron boomed.

Judith touched Matron's arm. "Please. We'll be fine." There was a chair at a small table. She pulled it over and sat by the old woman. What a wonderful face, she thought, and the eyes still so intelligent. Muriel Bloxham's right arm was lying on the blanket that covered her up. It looked thin and shriveled.

"Well now, who are you?" Bloxham asked. "I know I'm getting old, but I don't recognize you." Her voice was weak but quite clear. She smiled. "Whether I know you or not, I welcome company." Then a troubled look came over her face. "Should I know you? They tell me I'm getting forgetful."

Judith realized immediately that talking was an effort for the old woman. She would have to get to her questions immediately. "I'm Judith Chase. I think you might have known my relatives a long time ago, and I want to ask you about them.'

Bloxham's left hand reached up and patted Judith's face. "You're so pretty. You're American, aren't you? My brother married an American, but that was a long time ago."

[118

Judith closed her fingers around the chilly blue-veined hand of the older woman. "I'm talking about a long time ago," she said. "It was during the war."

"My son was in the war," Mrs. Bloxham said. "He was a prisoner, but at least he came back. Not like some of the others." Her head went down on her chest and her eyes closed.

It's no use, Judith thought. She's not going to remember. She watched as Muriel Bloxham's breathing became even. Judith realized she had fallen asleep. As Mrs. Bloxham napped, Judith studied every feature of the old woman. *Blammy minded Polly and me. She made little cakes and read us stories.*

It was nearly half an hour before Muriel Bloxham opened her eyes. "I'm sorry. That's what comes of being so old," she said. Again her eyes were alert.

Judith knew she could not waste time. "Mrs. Bloxham, try to think. Do you remember a family named Parrish who lived in Kent House during the war?"

Bloxham shook her head. "No, I never heard that name."

"Blammy, try," Judith begged. "Try."

"Blammy." Muriel Bloxham's face brightened. "No one's called me that since the twins."

Judith tried not to raise her voice. "The twins."

"Yes. Polly and Sarah. Such beautiful little girls. Elaine and Jonathan moved in when they were married. Her, so fair. Him, dark hair, tall and good-looking. So much in love they were. He was shot down the week after the twins were born. I used to go in and help Elaine. She was heartbroken. Then after those doodlebugs fell nearby, she decided to take the girls to the country. Neither one of the two had family, you see. I arranged for her to stay with friends of mine in Windsor. The day they left, a bomb hit near the station."

Mrs. Bloxham's voice quavered. "Terrible. Terrible.

119]

Elaine dead. Little Sarah blown to bits like some of the others. They couldn't even find her body. Polly injured so badly."

"Polly didn't die!"

Mrs. Bloxham's face receded into blankness. "Polly?"

"Polly Parrish, Blammy. What happened to her?" Judith felt tears welling in her eyes. "You can remember."

Blammy began to smile. "Don't cry, love. Polly's doing fine. She writes to me sometimes. She's got a bookshop in Beverley, in Yorkshire. Parrish Pages, it's called."

"I'm sorry, miss, but you'll have to leave. I've let you stay beyond visiting hours." Matron looked disapproving.

Judith got up, leaned over and kissed the top of the old woman's head. "Good-bye, Blammy, God bless. I'll be back to see you."

As she walked away, she heard Muriel Bloxham telling Matron about the twins who used to call her Blammy.

The vast intelligence-gathering mechanism of Scotland Yard quietly began the search into the life of Judith Chase. Within a few days the results were piled on the desk of Commander Sloane. Records that dated back to childhood, psychological reports, articles she had written for the *Washington Post,* social mentions, school marks, activities, clubs, discreet interviews with co-workers in Washington, her publisher, her accountant.

"It all amounts to a paean of praise," Sloane commented to Philip Barnes. "There isn't a single hint of antigovernment protest or radical affiliations from the time she was born. Three times the president of her class in boarding school, president of the student council at Wellesley, literacy volunteer, generous with charities. It's a damn good thing we didn't make fools of ourselves, sir, by tipping our hand that we're looking into her."

[120

"There's only one item that jumps at me." Barnes had the boarding-school yearbook open. Under her class picture, with the usual brief biography, there was one sentence that he underlined. *"Miss Fixit. Says she'll be a writer but watch and see if she isn't building bridges."*

"Those bombs were crude but quite effective. If Watkins only supplied the gelignite, it took a fairly decent mechanical ability to set them up so that they escaped detection."

"I can't find that significant, sir," Sloane protested. "My two sisters have natural mechanical ability, but I doubt that they would use it for terrorist purposes."

"Nevertheless, I want day and night surveillance on Miss Chase continued. Have Lynch or Collins anything to report?"

"Not really, sir. She's spending most of her time in her apartment, but yesterday she did go to Kent House on Kensington Court. She was inquiring about a family who lived there many years ago—people her aunt knew."

"Her aunt?" Barnes looked up sharply. "She doesn't have any relatives."

Sloane frowned. That was what had been bothering him. "I should have caught that, but she went from Kent House to a retirement home in Bath and spoke to a very old woman, so it seemed innocent enough."

"Who was she inquiring about?"

"We can't be sure, sir. When Lynch tried to talk to the old woman, she was pretty well out of it. Seems her mind drifts back and forth."

"Then I suggest you go visit that old woman and see if *you* can talk to her. Don't forget, Judith Chase was a British war orphan. For all we know, she's located people from the past who might be influencing her."

Barnes got up. "Only six days to the election. It's still

close but I think the Conservatives have it. That's why we need to clear Judith Chase absolutely before we're in the embarrassing predicament of bringing the new government down before it's even in office!"

When Judith returned home from Bath, she felt as if she had pushed herself emotionally and physically to a point beyond exhaustion. She drew a hot bath, lingered in it for twenty minutes, then put on a nightgown and robe. Staring into the mirror, she realized that she was deadly pale, her hair really needed trimming now, and her face was so thin it was no longer becoming. I'll *have* to give myself a day off, she thought—tomorrow I'll go for a facial, and manicure, and have my hair done . . . She'd leave the book alone for a day or two, then go over the pages she'd flagged for editing. And tomorrow she'd call Parrish Pages in Beverley and find out if Blammy had been right about Polly Parrish . . .

Polly, *alive!* My *sister,* Judith thought. *My twin sister!* The realization that she might actually have a close relative was both thrilling and frightening. I'll go up and visit the bookshop, she thought. I'll just browse through it for now. She knew she could not identify herself to Polly until she knew more about her. But later, after the campaign, Stephen could have her checked out. He wouldn't object to that as long as no one knew the reason for the investigation. But she'll be fine, Judith promised herself, as she got into bed, too weary even to heat a cup of soup. Funny, she's in the book world too . . . I wonder if she's ever tried to write . . .

She slept so soundly that the phone rang a dozen times before she heard it. Stephen's concerned voice pulled her awake. "Judith, I was just getting worried. Are you that tired?"

[122

"That *happy*," she said. "I'm taking a couple of days off to clear my head, then wrapping up the book and turning it in."

"Darling, I won't get to London until the election after all. Do you mind?"

Judith smiled. "I'm almost glad. I look like something the cat dragged in. Another few days will give me a chance to make myself presentable."

She fell back asleep thinking, *Stephen, I love you . . . Polly, it's me . . . It's Sarah . . .*

Margaret felt her hold on Judith weakening. With the book completed, she knew that Judith would turn her attention away from the Civil War. Margaret had used her energy preparing for the time she could conquer Judith. Now she knew she could copy Judith's speech without the cadence that Rob Watkins had found so amusing. She felt familiar in Judith's world. She had realized today what Judith missed. They were being followed.

There was so much to be done. She had chosen where the next bomb would be placed. Did she have the strength to overcome Judith again?

Inspector Lynch spent a good part of the next day outside the beauty salon in Harrods. When Judith emerged at five o'clock, her hair was shining, her face was glowing, her nails were elegant ovals. She looked rested and happy.

Damned waste of time, Lynch thought as he followed her to a restaurant where she ate a bowl of steaming pasta and sipped Chianti, then went directly home. As much a terrorist as my grandmother, he mumbled to himself as he took up his post in a car across the street from the door of her apartment building. His relief, Sam Collins, would be here soon. Collins, a thoroughly trustworthy officer, had been told that they'd received an anonymous note implicating Miss Chase in the bombings, and though they thought it was ridiculous, they had to follow up on it. He had been warned it was "top secret."

Tonight Lynch noticed that the light went on in Judith's front window. That would be the study, as Commander Sloane had described the apartment, so she was working again. A few minutes later, Collins arrived. "You'll have a quiet night, I can promise you," Lynch told him. "She's no gadabout."

Collins nodded. He was a heavy-featured man who looked as if he should have a lunch pail in his hand. Lynch knew he was also amazingly agile.

Judith had not planned to work, but after the massage and facial and pedicure and manicure and hairdo, she felt so pleasantly revived that she thought she might be able to revise the pages she had flagged for editing. The exhilaration of the morning phone call she'd made to Beverley had kept her glowing all day. Information readily gave her the number of Parrish Pages. She'd phoned and inquired about the hours the bookstore was open. Then casually she asked, "Is Polly Parrish still the proprietor?"

The reply was "Oh yes. She'll be in shortly. May I have her call you?"

"That's quite all right. Thank you."

All day Judith had thought, Tomorrow. I'll see her tomorrow. And in a few more days the election will be over. In the past weeks, she'd pushed aside the thought of the years ahead with Stephen. Now she wanted to go to Edge Barton and spend uninterrupted days and weeks with him. Uninterrupted days and weeks when Stephen was Prime

Minister? Judith smiled ruefully—they'd be lucky to have uninterrupted *hours*!

Leaning her hand on her chin, she looked affectionately around Lady Ardsley's tiny library, the room she was using as a study. Old volumes intermingled with Renaissance romances, Victorian gewgaws brushing fine old porcelain, a starched doily atop a truly beautiful Jacobean table.

Edge Barton, with its great high ceilings and wonderfully large rooms, its graceful windows and ancient doors . . . The interior needed some tender, loving care, a woman's touch. Some of the furniture should be reupholstered. The draperies wanted replacing. Judith thought how good it would be to put her own touch on Edge Barton . . .

Get back to work. The Royal Hospital.

It was almost as though a command rang through her mind. Startled, she brushed her hair back from her forehead and noticed that the scar on her hand was faintly pink. I'm going to see a plastic surgeon about that damn scar, she vowed. It's crazy the way it comes and goes.

She flipped her manuscript to the last chapter where she had flagged the section on the Chelsea Royal Hospital. A lovely and wonderfully preserved building, it had been built by Charles II as a residence for veterans and invalid soldiers.

Charles II's veterans. The Simon Halletts of the world clinging to the coattails of the Merry Monarch! That's what they called him, the Merry Monarch. Vincent fallen in battle, John executed, myself tricked and murdered—and the Merry Monarch built a residence for his soldiers where they could live "as in a college or monastery."

Margaret pushed the manuscript aside, deliberately shoving whole sections of it onto the floor around the

125]

desk. She got up swiftly, went into the bedroom, and took from the wardrobe the bag Rob Watkins had given her. The light was brighter in the kitchen. She brought the bag there and laid out its contents on the table.

Outside, Sam Collins observed with growing interest the succession of lights that went on in the Ardsley apartment. Judith Chase must have left the study without extinguishing the light, so she probably planned to go back there. It was only a quarter to eight. Did the bedroom light signify she was planning to retire, or perhaps change into more comfortable clothing? He watched as the kitchen light went on, then consulted the diagram of the flat that Sloane had given him. The windows of the study, kitchen, living room, and bedroom all faced the street; the entry door and the foyer connecting the rooms were to the rear.

Sam realized that the weather was changing rapidly. The evening had started bright with stars and a crescent moon. Now thick clouds had settled in and the damp air was filled with the threat of rain. The few passersby were scurrying along, obviously anxious to get to their destinations quickly.

From the privacy of his nondescript car Sam continued to survey the Ardsley flat. As he watched, the kitchen light and then the bedroom light went out. Probably just changed her clothes and made a pot of tea, he thought, and started to lean his head on the backrest. Then he froze. The shade on the study window had moved. For an instant he had a clear glimpse of Judith Chase. She was looking down directly at his car. She was wearing some kind of outer garment.

Sam pulled back into the shadowed interior of the car. She knows I'm here, he decided. She's planning to go out. He had inspected the premises his first night on the job, and

[126

knew there was a service door in the rear of the building and a narrow courtyard which could be used to exit between buildings to the next street.

He waited a moment, then decided that Judith was going to leave the study light on. He slipped from the car and darted along the concrete walk that separated the houses. The back door opened and Judith came out. Sam stepped back and peered around the side of the building. There was just enough light for him to see that she was wearing a dark cape. That tip might be on target, he thought. She may *have* some connection to the bombings! What's she up to now? A secret meeting with terrorists? Pleasurably he anticipated being the one who broke the case of the London bomber. Won't hurt the old career, he thought . . .

Margaret moved swiftly through the lightly traveled streets. The Scotland Yard man was undoubtedly dozing off in his car by now. Beneath her cape she was carrying the package she had prepared. It was innocently encased in a small shopping bag from the nearby market, grapes and apples plainly visible at the opening between the handles—the obvious kind of bag with which to enter a veterans home. The visiting hours would be over soon. She had barely enough time.

Silently Sam Collins followed the slender figure as she walked swiftly across town and headed toward the Thames. Nearly half an hour later when she turned onto Royal Hospital Road, his eyes widened in surprise. What was she up to? Was she simply planning to visit a pensioner? Had she noticed that she was being followed and chosen to use the back door only to escape the annoyance of a pursuer? She was wearing a dark green cape, but Sam's own wife had commented on how fashionable capes were this season and bought one for their daughter's birthday.

The domed vestibule of the magnificent building had a stream of briskly moving people. The clock on the reception desk showed the time to be eight-twenty. Sam watched as Judith went directly to that desk and laid a small bag of fruit on it.

After she got her visitor's pass, he'd ask the receptionist the name of the pensioner she was seeing, he decided. Then that unfailing instinct made him walk to the desk and stand behind her as if he too were requesting a pass.

"I should like to visit Sir John Carew," Margaret said in a low, hurried voice.

Carew! Collins moved forward. "May I have a word with you, ma'am?"

Margaret spun around, fury blazing in her eyes. She watched as the heavyset man, the man who must have been following her, stared at her hand. The scar was blazing now, a vivid reddish purple.

She grabbed the bag from the reception desk and flung it across the vestibule at a trio of porters who had just come down the hall.

Instinctively Sam knew the package contained a bomb. In seconds he was across the room and diving for it . . .

Margaret was in the courtyard when the detonated bomb exploded, reducing the vestibule to flying debris, collapsing walls, and screaming victims. Window glass shattered. A jagged piece grazed her cheek as she

[128

slipped into the dark protection of the lightly falling rain.

Reza Patel and Rebecca were watching television in their apartment when the news flash came about the tragedy at the Royal Hospital. Five dead, twelve severely injured. Patel, his face ashen, phoned Judith. She answered immediately. "I'm right at my desk, doctor. Working as usual." To Patel, her voice sounded cheerful and normal. Then Judith laughed. "I only hope my readers don't have the same reaction to my book as I had tonight. I literally fell asleep reading it."

I must have been practically unconscious, Judith thought, as she spotted a page she had missed when she picked up the manuscript from the floor. She turned off the study light, went into the bedroom, and undressed quickly. Stephen had told her he had a very late meeting and wouldn't try to call her tonight.

She realized that her legs were aching. You'd think I'd been running in a marathon, she thought. She decided that an aspirin might help her relax. For an instant she studied herself in the cabinet mirror as she reached for the packet of aspirins. Her new hairdo was disheveled. The tendrils around her face were now ringlets and as she pushed them back, she realized they were slightly damp. The heat in the study must have been too high, she decided. But I never perspire . . .

She creamed her face and was startled to see a drop of blood on her cheek. There was a small scratch there. She didn't remember any twinge of pain during the facial, but the facialist did have long nails . . .

As she made her way back to the bed, she noticed with irritation that the doors to Lady Ardsley's wardrobe were slightly ajar again. I'll tie them together, she thought.

129]

Wouldn't it be terrible if she ever happened to stop by and thought I was going through her things?

In bed, the lights out, she tried to relax but her legs were aching, her head was throbbing, and an overwhelming sense of depression settled over her. It's just all the work, she thought, and not talking to Stephen tonight. She whispered, "Stephen and Polly," but the names brought no comfort. Heartsick, she felt as if both of them were slipping away from her.

Deep lines of sorrow and anger were etched on the face of Deputy Assistant Commissioner Barnes. Commander Sloane and Inspector Lynch, their eyes red-rimmed with fatigue, managed to sit erectly in the chairs at Barnes's desk. They knew that no matter how grave the problem, Barnes did not appreciate evidence of weariness. They had both been at the scene of the bombing all night, but with no results. A doctor coming down the hallway had noticed a package fly across the vestibule, and a burly man rushing toward it. Some instinct made him jump back into the hallway—a reaction that had undoubtedly saved the doctor's life. The other injured victims had noticed no one carrying a package. The three porters at whose feet the bomb had fallen, the receptionist, and Inspector Collins were dead.

"The question," Barnes said sharply, "is whether Collins was following Judith Chase. Every evidence points to that fact. The only other possibility is that someone emerged from her flat or another flat in her building who caused Collins to become suspicious. You called Miss Chase, Jack?"

"Yes sir, about an hour ago. I used the fairly lame excuse that we're desperate to uncover any lead, however small, and asked her if she had recalled anything at all unusual when she was in the area of the Crown Jewels."

[130

"And her answer?"

"Straightforward. Absolutely nothing. Repeated how concentrated her mind is when she's doing research. That she pretty much blots out all the extraneous."

"Did you detect any nervousness in her tone?"

Lynch frowned. "Not nervousness, sir. Subdued, I'd think. She did say she was finished with her book and it had taken a lot out of her. Was planning to stay in bed all day and read it, then send it off to her agent."

Barnes slammed his fist on the desk, a gesture that warned his subordinates they would be on the carpet. "Why in hell didn't Collins notify us he was leaving the car? It wouldn't have taken thirty seconds to use the car phone."

"Maybe he didn't have those thirty seconds, sir."

"Or maybe he didn't bother. God damn it, Sam was one of our best men. He saved a dozen lives when he threw himself on that bomb. Jack, that old woman Judith Chase visited. What exactly did she tell you?"

"Absolutely nothing, sir. Not a single connected thought. Matron tells me that she can be absolutely lucid. Then she drifts off for days at a time. The only information I got was that right after Miss Chase left, Mrs. Bloxham told Matron about two-year-old twin sisters, Sarah and Polly, who used to call her Blammy."

"Twins!" Inspector Lynch jumped up, his fatigue forgotten. "Sir, as you know, Judith Chase was found wandering in Salisbury when she was two years old. No one ever claimed her, even though she was a very well-dressed child. Is it possible she's been trying to find, or may have found, her birth family? And located a twin sister?"

Barnes bit his underlip and impatiently pushed back the strands of hair that had fallen over his forehead. "A twin sister who may closely resemble her and who may have some nasty political affiliations? It would make sense.

131]

God, the election is day after tomorrow. We've got to crack this. Judith Chase was asking questions of that old woman only two days ago. That doesn't sound as though she had found everything she's looking for. So we can't assume she's in touch yet with people from her past. If she isn't—and if we can find out who they are, and if necessary *warn* her away from contacting them—we may be able to keep her and Sir Stephen out of this. Or if she's found them and has somehow fallen in with a bad crowd, I want to know before Sir Stephen becomes Prime Minister. Jack!"

Sloane stood up. "Sir."

"Get back to that nursing home! Get a psychiatrist. Tell him what you're trying to learn. Maybe he'll have a way of questioning Mrs. Bloxham, if that's her name. Chase was asking questions of the porter's wife at Kent House the other day, wasn't she?"

"Yes."

"Go over and see the porter's wife again. Also, I want a check of all the pensioners in the Royal Hospital last night. Find out which ones had visitors who might have left around eight-thirty. Speak to those visitors. Someone may have seen Collins and whoever he was following coming in. And for God's sake, make *sure* Judith Chase doesn't take a step without someone right behind her."

The phone on Barnes's desk rang insistently. His secretary's voice was breathless. "I'm sorry to interrupt. The Commissioner wishes you to know that Sir Stephen has called an emergency meeting to learn the progress of the investigation."

Stephen phoned Judith at nine o'clock the next morning, waking her from the deep, exhausted sleep into which she

[132

had fallen. Her hand gripped the phone when she heard his voice. She felt as if she had been swimming in warm, dark water, trying to make her way to land. Forcing herself awake, she murmured his name, then pulled herself up on one elbow as he said, "I'm in the car, darling, just ten minutes away. I'm heading for an emergency meeting with Scotland Yard. I must go directly back to the country, but how about a cup of coffee for a man who's frantic to see you?"

"Stephen, how wonderful! Of course."

Judith dropped the phone and rushed from bed. In the bathroom mirror, she saw that her eyes were swollen with sleep. A drop of dried blood outlined the slight cut on her face. I look a mess, she thought. Yanking on the spigots for the shower, she pulled off her nightgown, grabbed a shower cap, and deliberately let the water run first hot, then cold to shake her from the lethargy.

A light makeup base covered the scratch. A touch of blush helped hide the paleness of her face, a quick brushing smoothed down the lost hairdo. A soft wool caftan with a vivid design of orange, blue, lilac, and fuchsia swirls over a black background enveloped her in color. She hurried into the kitchen, got the coffee brewing, and began to set the small table at the window. She noticed something on the floor and bent to pick it up. It was a twisted piece of wire. Where did that come from? she wondered as she tossed it into the wastebasket. The intercom buzzed. She picked up the speaker and said, "Coffee's ready, sir. Come right up."

When she opened the door for Stephen, they flew into each other's arms.

Over sips of coffee and bites of toast and marmalade, Stephen told her the shocking news about the bombing at the Royal Hospital.

133]

"I worked late and never turned on the television," Judith said. "Stephen, what kind of depraved mind sets a bomb in a veterans home?"

"We don't know. Usually some group claims responsibility. When that doesn't happen, it's often sheer luck to find the perpetrator. The public outcry this morning is enormous. Even Buckingham Palace has officially expressed deep concern, as well as sending condolences to the families of the victims."

"What will this do to the election?"

Stephen shook his head. "Darling, I'd hate to spend the rest of my life thinking that I got into office because someone was blowing up London, but my adamant stand on the death penalty for terrorists is certainly making a difference in the polls. Labour still won't change its mind now about the death penalty, and their cry for life without parole sounds pretty weak to a nation that has to wonder if the next time its children go on a school outing to a monument, or to the hospital for a tonsillectomy, they may be blown up."

The five minutes Stephen had said he could stay became thirty. When he left, he said, "Judith, I honestly think I'm going to *win* the election. If and when that happens, I'll be summoned to Buckingham Palace and asked by Her Majesty to form a new government. It would not be appropriate for you to come to that meeting, but would you ride in the car with me?"

"There's nothing I want more."

"There's a *lot* I want more, but that will be a good start for the rest of our lives." Stephen kissed her again and reached for the doorknob. In an involuntary motion, Judith touched his arm and turned him again to her. "Did you ever hear that old song 'Let me stay, let me stay in your arms'?" she asked almost sadly.

[134

For a long minute he held her close to him, and Judith heard herself praying, Please, don't let anything spoil this. Please.

When Stephen left, she poured another cup of coffee and went back to bed. I probably have some kind of virus, she insisted to herself. That's why I feel so punk. She knew she could not make the trip to Yorkshire today. I'll give myself the day off and do the final editing on the manuscript. I don't want to feel like this when I see Polly.

At noon the phone rang. Dr. Patel was anxious to know when she was planning to go to Beverley.

"Not till tomorrow," Judith said. "I decided to put off going today. I think I've got a bit of a bug. I feel pretty achy. But you can be sure I'll call you the minute I've seen her."

Reza Patel tried to make his voice sound casual. "Judith, you're an expert on the seventeenth century. During your research, did you ever come across the name Lady Margaret Carew?"

"Of course I did. Fascinating gal. Apparently talked her husband into signing the death warrant of Charles the First, lost her only son in one of the great battles of the Civil War, then tried to assassinate Charles the Second when he got back on the throne. He was so darn mad he went out of his way to attend her execution."

"Do you know the date of the execution?"

"I have it somewhere in my notes. Why do you ask?"

Patel had been anticipating the question. "Remember when I met you at the Portrait Gallery? Another friend was there and thought he recognized Lady Margaret in a group portrait. At least, she very much resembles the woman whom his branch of the family disowned. He's just curious."

135]

"I'll go through my notes. But maybe he should forget about her. Lady Margaret was big trouble."

When they broke the connection, Patel turned to Rebecca. "I know it was risky, but the only hope for Judith is to send her back to the moment of Lady Margaret's death. If I'm going to do that, I must know exactly when she died. Judith didn't suspect anything."

Rebecca Wadley felt as if she was constantly being cast in the role of Cassandra. "By this time tomorrow, whether or not she reveals herself, Judith may be positive she has found not only a living relative but a twin sister. Why would she put herself under hypnosis again? Are you planning to tell her the truth?"

"No!" Patel shouted. "Of course not. Don't you see what that would do to Judith Chase? She would feel morally responsible no matter what I told her. I've got to find a way to send her back without her knowing the reason."

Rebecca had the morning papers open on her desk. They were filled with pictures of the carnage at the Royal Hospital. "You'd better do it fast," she told Patel. "Like it or not, you're now in the position of protecting a murderer."

The day in bed did not help Judith. An exhaustive reading of her manuscript enabled her to pick up minor typos and repetitive phrases—and made her realize that on the one hand it was her best book to date, and on the other it was far more biased against Charles I and Charles II than she had ever intended when she set out to write it. I made a strong case for Parliamentary law, she thought, and I'd have to rewrite the whole book to change it now. Somehow she could not feel the surge of relief and well-being that usually accompanied the completion of a book.

Her sleep that night was again troubled and at five in the morning, she gave up and lay awake in Lady Ardsley's overfurnished bedroom. What is the *matter* with me? she asked herself. Six months ago when I came to England I didn't have a single human being to call family. Now I'm going to marry the man I love and today I'll see my twin sister. Why am I crying? Impatiently she brushed the tears from her eyes.

At 6:30 she got up to prepare for the trip to Beverley. She was taking an eight o'clock train. It's nothing but nerves, she told herself as she showered and dressed. I want to see Polly and I'm afraid to see her.

She had a fleeting thought that it might be wise to wear her new cape, because the hood concealed much of her face, but for some reason the thought was distasteful. Instead, she reached for her old Burberry and fished in the drawer for a soft, wide kerchief which she tied around her head. The outsized dark glasses and the scarf would be enough to conceal her appearance, she decided, in case she and Polly resembled each other closely.

On the way to the station she stopped to have a copy made of her manuscript and mailed the original to her agent in New York with a brief note. Then she went to Kings Cross to catch her train.

Did she only imagine, she wondered, that now she was remembering clearly the moment when the bombs fell? Her hand groping for her mother's, Polly screaming, the darkness, the sound of running feet, and herself after them sobbing, thinking her mother was leaving her. As she stepped up onto the train, she could feel how high the steps had been to a two-year-old. As she settled in a window seat, she remembered—or thought she remembered—the lurch as the train pulled out of the Waterloo station. She could feel the sack she had laid on, stiff and unyielding. Mailbags, she thought, crammed to the top, tied with a drawstring. So absorbed was she in the memory that she did not notice the thin-faced, fortyish man who was sitting one seat behind her across the aisle, nor did she suspect that despite the pretense of burying his face in the morning newspaper, Inspector David Lynch never took his eyes off her.

In Scotland Yard there had also been a breakthrough. Commander Sloane had visited the nursing home and found Mrs. Bloxham absolutely clear in her memory. Her voice quivering with emotion, she told him about the beautiful twin girls who had lived with their widowed mother in the flat next to her, how the mother, Elaine Parrish, had been killed in a doodlebug raid just as she was taking the girls to the country, how little Sarah's body had never been found, how Polly owned her own bookstore in Beverley in Yorkshire. On his return to the office his delight at being able to report the information was tempered by the news that Judith was on her way to Yorkshire and was being followed by Inspector Lynch. "I wish we'd had a chance to investigate Polly Parrish before Miss Chase reveals herself to her, if that's her purpose," he told Commissioner Barnes.

There was another break, if you could call it that, Sloane was told. The questioning of visitors to the hospital the night of the bombing had had results. A man who'd left at 8:20 had held the door open for a woman in a dark green cape who swept past him without even a nod. He remembered noticing a vivid scar on her hand. A few steps behind her a burly man caught the door before it closed. "So we have the lady with the scar and the cape again," Barnes said. "Tomorrow we bring Judith Chase in for questioning."

"On what grounds?" Sloane asked.

"On the grounds that we tell her we believe the person we're looking for strongly resembles her and we want to ask if she's located any of her birth family. We'll also ask her if she knows a woman named Margaret Carew."

[138

"And if she does?" Sloane asked.

"Tomorrow is the election. We warn Sir Stephen away from her. Of course, if any of the newspapers are onto their involvement, he may still have to resign his post as party leader, and that means someone else will become Prime Minister."

"A damn shame for him and for the country!" Sloane exploded.

"A worse shame if the lady in the cape, whoever she is, keeps on with her dirty work and is linked to him."

The trip took three hours. Judith changed trains in Hull. From there it was a short ride to Beverley. As she walked through the marketplace she was only vaguely aware of the exquisite ecclesiastical architecture that characterized the beautiful town. A constable directed her to Queen Mary Lane, the narrow sidestreet where the Parrish bookshop was located. The wind was light but sharp. She drew the kerchief forward, and turned up her coat collar. She was already wearing the oversized dark glasses. She passed a chemist, a greengrocer, a florist. Then she saw the sign. Parrish Pages. She was at the bookstore.

Judith opened the door of the shop and heard the faint ringing of a bell announce her arrival. A pleasant-faced young woman with large round glasses was at the cashier's desk. She looked up and smiled, then continued to wait on a customer.

Judith was grateful to see that there were at least half a dozen people browsing along the shelves. It gave her time to observe the interior of the shop. It was a long and rather narrow area in which every inch of space had been used to advantage without sacrificing the comfortable atmosphere of a home library. The back area was arranged like a living room with an old leather couch, an oversized velour chair, and end tables with reading lamps. A woman was sitting, working at a heavy oak desk—a woman whose profile made Judith think she was looking in the mirror. Her heart began to race and she felt her hands go clammy. Polly! It had to be Polly.

"Are you looking for any book in particular?" It was the young woman from the cashier's desk.

Judith swallowed over the lump that had formed in her throat. "I'm just browsing but I'm sure I'll find something I'll want. This is a lovely shop."

"Your first time then?" The clerk smiled. "Oh, Parrish Pages is famous. People come from miles around. And have you heard about Miss Parrish?"

Judith shook her head.

"She's a very well known storyteller. Invited all over to perform, but prefers to have her own program on the radio station up here on Sundays and during the week has two classes of storytelling for children. Much easier doing it that way than traveling. She's right at her desk. Would you care to meet her?"

"Oh, I don't think so. I don't want to bother her."

"No bother. Miss Parrish enjoys meeting new visitors."

Judith felt herself being propelled to the back of the store. She was standing in front of the desk. Polly looked up and Judith felt her heart pound in her throat.

Polly was a few pounds heavier than she. Her dark brown hair was generously shot with silver. Her face was devoid of makeup but naturally very pretty, with an expression of both strength and warmth.

"Miss Parrish, we have someone here for the first time," the clerk said.

Polly Parrish smiled and extended her hand. "How nice of you to stop in."

Judith held out her own hand and realized that she was

[140

making physical contact with her twin. "I'm ... I'm Judith Kurner," she said, instinctively using her married name. Polly, she thought, Polly. For a moment it was on the tip of her tongue to say, *"It's me, it's Sarah,"* but she knew she would have to wait. Polly was a well-known storyteller. She had her own program and this charming bookshop. Oh, Stephen, she thought, we won't have to hide *this* relative!

Inspector Lynch was watching from a corner aisle. His mouth narrowed into a whistle. Except for the hair the woman looked exactly like Judith Chase. Cover the gray or put a dark wig on Polly Parrish and you'd have a mirror image of Judith Chase. Wouldn't it be a blessing if when they ran a check on Parrish, they could link her to a terrorist group? He realized instantly that Judith was not going to identify herself to Parrish. She's here looking her over, he thought. That's the reason for that kerchief and the dark glasses. Good thing she has that much sense!

Lynch knew he wanted to clear Judith Chase of any suspicion of being the woman in the cape. Reading her books and the dossier Scotland Yard had compiled on her had made him like and admire her. He had to remind himself to stay totally objective. Then he frowned.

At exactly the same moment as Judith saw it, he realized that Polly Parrish was sitting in a wheelchair.

It was nearly six o'clock when Judith returned to the apartment. After she left Polly, she had had tea in a small restaurant around the corner from the bookshop. The Irish waitress had responded loquaciously to her skilled but seemingly casual questions. Polly Parrish had been raised right here in Beverley. Lovely family took her in when she was finally discharged from hospital. Shattered her spine in a doodlebug raid that killed her mother and sister. Lived alone, in the dearest little cottage, just a few miles away. She'd been written up in several magazines and newspapers. And oh, when she told a story, people of every age, from little ones to oldsters, just sat in awe and drank in her every word. "Miss, I tell you, it's as though she's spinning magic."

"Does she tell the old legends or make up her own stories?" Judith had managed to ask over the tightness in her throat.

"Both." Then the waitress had paused in her narration and said, "You know, I can't help but think she's lonely, don't you see? Plenty of friends, but no one really her own."

But she *has* someone of her own now, Judith thought again as she hung up her coat. She has *me*!

On the trip back to London, other memories had tumbled into her consciousness. Polly and she playing in the Kent House flat. We had matching white wicker doll carriages, Judith remembered. The hood of mine was yellow, the hood on Polly's pink.

Tomorrow was election day. At the station she had bought the leading newspapers. All of them predicted a Conservative sweep. Far from embracing the cry of Labour for change, all surveys showed that the average voter was most deeply concerned about terrorism and that Sir Stephen Hallett's demand for the return of the death penalty would cause many died-in-the-wool Labourites to cross traditional party lines to ensure that he became Prime Minister.

The book was completed. She had found Polly. Tomorrow the Conservatives would win the election, and the next day Stephen would become Prime Minister. How was it possible, Judith wondered, that she was not brimming over with joy? Why did she feel so overwhelmingly sad, so without hope?

Battle fatigue, she decided, as she prepared a salad and

[142

omelet. She sat at the kitchen table, reading the newspapers as she ate, and remembering that yesterday morning Stephen and she had sat side by side on the narrow banquette. She could feel the warmth of his shoulder brushing against hers, his hand over hers, as they sipped their coffee. In a few days she would be openly at his side. With the election behind him, the need for privacy would be over. She smiled as she poured tea from the plump china teapot—that annoying columnist Harley Hutchinson would probably try to claim that he'd known about them right along!

It was only after she'd washed and dried the few dishes and put them away that she went into her study and noticed that there was a message on the answering machine. Commander Jack Sloane of Scotland Yard would very much appreciate it if she would plan to come to the Yard in the morning. Would she phone him to set up a convenient time?

At eleven o'clock on election day, Sloane was in the office of Deputy Assistant Commissioner Barnes. The demeanor of both men was sober.

"It's a tricky business," Barnes acknowledged. "I'm not prepared to tell Miss Chase she's under investigation yet. Lynch said that Polly Parrish, the sister, without the streaks of gray in her hair could be a clone of Chase. You've had the birth records traced and read the father's RAF file?"

Sloane nodded. "There were no other siblings."

"That doesn't mean there might not be a cousin, or a perfect stranger who closely resembles Miss Chase. The only direct link we have is that Collins was surveilling Judith Chase, and he was at the hospital when the bomb went off. Do you know what counsel could do with that kind of testimony? He'd round up half a dozen Chase look-alikes, and the case would fall apart."

"And in the meantime we'd have destroyed the reputation of Judith Chase."

"Exactly."

"That scar that Watkins and the witness from the hospital spoke of—is there any chance that it's a fake, that she paints it on her hand as some kind of weird symbol?"

"Watkins has been grilled about that. He claims he examined it closely, felt the texture. He said that obviously no one had bothered to sew it up, and the skin is all raised and puckered. To prove his point he mentioned that when he was in bed with her, he asked her to rub it across his back, that it gave him quite a sensation."

Jack Sloane's expression showed his disgust. "Judith Chase is not the kind of woman to go to bed with that bloody lout."

"We don't know who Judith Chase is," Barnes said sharply. "And it's time we found out. You told her eleven o'clock, here, didn't you?"

"Yes sir. It's just on eleven now." Sloane hoped that Judith would not keep the deputy assistant commissioner waiting: Barnes had a passion for promptness. He did not have to worry. At that moment the secretary announced Judith's arrival.

The vague unease she had been feeling for the last two days had caused Judith to dress carefully. The day held a hint of spring, and she'd worn a fuchsia walking suit, exquisitely cut, with a slender skirt and semifitted fingertip jacket. A black and fuchsia scarf was tied at her neck. A gold pin shaped like a unicorn was fastened to her jacket. Her narrow black calf Gucci shoulder bag matched her slender low-heeled shoes. Her hair was loose around her face and carefully applied makeup brought out the violet tones of her blue eyes.

On seeing her, both men had the immediate thought that

[144

in appearance and manner she would be the perfect choice to become wife of the Prime Minister.

Judith reached out her hand to shake Commissioner Barnes's. As he took it, he studied it quickly. Absolutely no scar. Maybe just the faintest trace of a long-ago injury, but nothing more. Certainly no raised skin or discoloration. He felt sharp relief—he didn't *want* this woman to be the culprit.

Commander Sloane observed Barnes's scrutiny of Judith's hand. At least we'll get *that* out of the way, he thought.

Barnes came directly to the point. Their one solid lead was that a construction worker had given an explosive to a woman who called herself Margaret Carew and who apparently bore a strong resemblance to Judith. "By any chance do you know anyone by that name?"

"Margaret Carew!" Judith exclaimed. "There was one who lived in the seventeenth century. I've come across her name in my research."

Both men smiled. "Not much of a help, that," said Barnes. "There are also ten in the London phone book, three in Worcester, two in Bath, six in Wales. Quite a popular name. Miss Chase, did you have any visitors on Tuesday night?"

"Last Tuesday night? No. I went to the hairdresser, had dinner in a pub, and went directly home. I was doing the final editing of my book. I just mailed it. Why do you ask?" Judith felt her palms go clammy. She had not been invited to stop here simply because she had been in the Tower the same day as the explosion.

"You did not leave your home?"

"Absolutely not. Commissioner, what are you implying?"

"Miss Chase, I'm implying nothing. The construction

145]

worker who we believe gave the explosive to the woman who has been setting the bombs noticed your picture on the back of your book and said that the person who called herself Margaret Carew resembles you. He emphatically said it was *not* you. In fact, this woman has a scar on her hand. The guard at the Tower, before he died, seemed to be saying that you had come back, so here again we have a woman who apparently resembles you. We have snapshots taken at the time of the bombing of the equestrian statue, and a woman in a cape and dark glasses, who again resembles you, is in one of them, placing the package containing the bomb at the base of the statue. That picture has been enlarged many times, and the scar is plainly visible. The point is—there is someone who *strongly* resembles you performing these crazed acts. Have you any idea who she might be?"

They know about Polly, Judith thought. She was absolutely sure of it. I've been under surveillance. "You mean someone who resembles me enough to be my twin, except that my twin is crippled? How long have you been following me?"

Barnes answered her question with another. "Miss Chase, have you been in touch with any other members of your birth family, especially one who strongly resembles you?"

Judith stood up. The scar, she was thinking, the scar. Lady Margaret Carew. The blank times she had told Patel about. "Sir Stephen was here a few days ago for a high-level meeting on the progress of the investigation. Did my name come up?"

"No, it did not."

"Why not? It would seem he should be informed of your concerns."

Sloane answered for Barnes. "Miss Chase, even at the

highest level meetings there are leaks to the press. For your sake, for Sir Stephen's sake, we don't want a whisper of your name to be heard in this matter. But you *can* help us. You have a dark green cape?"

"Yes. I don't wear it much. Frankly, the one I bought in Harrods has been copied so widely that it seems half the women in London are wearing it this season."

"We know that. You've never lent yours?"

"No, I have not. Is there anything more you want of me?"

"No," Barnes told her. "Please, Miss Chase, may I stress—?"

"Don't bother to stress anything." By an act of sheer will Judith managed to keep her voice steady.

Silently Jack opened the door for her. When he closed it behind her, he looked at his boss. "Under that makeup she went pale as a ghost when I mentioned the scar," Barnes told him. "Get an immediate tap on her phone."

When she got back to the apartment, Judith phoned Patel's office. There was no one there. The answering service told her that Doctors Patel and Wadley were at a two-day seminar in Moscow and would not be calling in until late in the evening at the earliest. "Have him phone me no matter what time he contacts you," Judith said.

She turned on the television and sat motionless in front of it. There was a segment showing Stephen voting in his district. The fatigue was evident on his face, but there was a confident expression in his eyes. For an instant he looked directly into the camera and it seemed to Judith he was looking straight at her. Oh God, she thought, I love him so.

She went to her desk and opened the calendar, meticulously checking the days of the bombings against her own schedule. With deepening despair, she realized that the bombings coincided with times she had either fallen asleep at her desk or not noticed the passage of many hours as she worked.

The week before the bombings began, she had experienced spells of loss of memory. She had told Dr. Patel about them. Why had Patel asked her about the exact date of the death of Margaret Carew? And why had that scar on her hand flared up?

She went back to the television and hungrily watched for glimpses of Stephen. She ached to be with him, to feel his arms around her. "I need you, Stephen," she said aloud. "I need you."

At three o'clock, he phoned. His voice was jubilant. "It's never over till it's over, darling, but all indications are that we've done it."

"*You've* done it." Somehow she managed to sound excited and happy. "When will you be sure?"

"The polls don't close until nine and the first results aren't in until nearly midnight. It will be the early hours of the morning before the general trend is known. The media is predicting a landslide victory for us, but we all know that upsets can happen. Judith, I wish you were with me now. The waiting would be easier."

"I know what you mean." Judith gripped the phone as she felt the break in her voice. "I love you, Stephen. Goodbye, darling."

She went into the bedroom, changed to a warm nightgown and flannel robe, and got into bed. Even with the blankets wrapped around her, she could not stop shivering. Profound despair made her body heavy and immobile. It was too much effort even to make a cup of tea. Hour after hour she lay staring up at the ceiling not noticing the light fade into darkness.

At six o'clock the next morning, Dr. Patel called her from Moscow. "Is anything wrong?"

[148

The question snapped the last of her self-control. "You know there is," she said. "What did you do to me?" Her voice became a shriek. "What did you do to me when I was under hypnosis? Why did you ask me about Margaret Carew?"

Patel interrupted her. "Judith, I am about to board a flight home. Come to my office at two o'clock. You must have with you the exact date when Margaret Carew died. Do you have that information?"

"Yes, but why? I want to know *why!*"

"It has to do with the Anastasia Syndrome."

Judith replaced the receiver and closed her eyes. *The Anastasia Syndrome.* No, she thought. It isn't possible.

Forcing herself to get out of bed, she showered, pulled on a heavy sweater and slacks, made tea and toast, and turned on the television.

Shortly before noon, Labour conceded defeat. Her eyes burning with anguish, Judith watched Stephen acknowledging his victory at the County Hall. His speech thanking his local supporters and his opponents for a fair fight was wildly cheered. From there he was driven to Edge Barton where a crowd of well-wishers awaited his arrival. He stood on the steps shaking hands, his face wreathed in smiles.

Judith stared at him, at the lovely stone mansion that she had expected to make her home again.

Again, she wondered?

Stephen gave a last wave to the crowd and went inside Edge Barton. A moment later Judith heard the peal of the phone. She knew it was Stephen. With a mighty effort, she managed again to sound excited and rejoicing. "I knew it, I knew it. I knew it!" she cried. "Congratulations, darling."

"I'm leaving for London now. At four-thirty I present myself to Her Majesty. Rory will pick you up at your flat at quarter to four and drive you to the house. We'll have a few private minutes before we leave for the Palace. I only wish I could bring you in with me, but it wouldn't be appropriate. We'll come to Edge Barton for the weekend and make our own announcement then. Oh, Judith, at last, at last."

Tears running down her cheeks, her voice breaking, Judith managed to convince Stephen that she was crying for joy. When she replaced the receiver, she began to search the apartment.

In Scotland Yard, Commissioner Barnes and Commander Sloane were in Barnes's office, hearing for the tenth time a recording of the conversation between Judith and Dr. Patel.

Barnes listened in astonishment as Sloane explained Patel's theory of the Anastasia Syndrome. "Bringing people back from other ages? What kind of rot is that? But is it possible he hypnotized Judith Chase and sent her on these bombing expeditions? Let's have a little talk with him before Miss Chase gets there."

When Judith arrived at Dr. Patel's office, her lips were ashen. Her eyes blazed from her deadly pale face. On her arm she was carrying the dark green cape. A bulging tote bag was in her hand. She was not aware that Commissioner Barnes and Commander Sloane were in the laboratory behind the one-way glass observing her and listening to her.

"I couldn't sleep last night," she told Patel. "I went over and over everything that has seemed unusual. Do you know something? I've been annoyed because the doors of the wardrobe Lady Ardsley reserved for her own use kept swinging open. The point is, they didn't swing open by themselves. Somebody opened them. *I* opened them. This is my cape. To my knowledge I haven't worn it more than once or twice, and only in good weather, but there's mud on the hem. The boots I wear with it are muddy." She tossed the boots and cape on a chair. "And look at this: powder, wires. You could put together a homemade bomb with all this." Carefully she laid the package on the antique table with the matching mirror near the door. "I'm afraid to get near this stuff. But why do I have it? *What did you do to me?*"

"Judith, sit down," Patel ordered. "When I showed you the videotape of your hypnosis, I did not show you all of it. You'll understand better if you see it now."

In the lab Rebecca Wadley watched the incredulous expressions on the faces of the Scotland Yard officers as they viewed the videotape of Judith's hypnosis.

"This is as far as I showed you before," Patel said at one point. "Here is the rest of it."

Disbelieving, Judith watched as the film showed the change in her manner, her desperate scream, her writhing on the couch.

"I gave you too much of the drug. It pulled you back to the period in history in which your mind was entrenched. Judith, you've proven my theory. It is possible to bring a presence back from the past, but it is not a power that can ever be used. When did Lady Margaret Carew die?"

This can't be happening to me, Judith thought. This can't be happening to me. "She was beheaded on the tenth of December, 1660."

"I'm going to regress you back to that moment again. You observed that execution. This time, turn from it. Do not witness it. Do not look into Lady Margaret's face. Eye contact would be extremely dangerous. Let her die, Judith. Be free of her."

Patel pushed the button on his desk, and Rebecca came out of the lab carrying a tray with an intravenous needle and a vial containing the litencum. Sloane and Barnes watched silently from behind the one-way glass, each busy with his own thoughts about the ramifications of what they were witnessing.

This time, Patel gave Judith the maximum strength of litencum immediately, and the monitors showed her to be in a sedation that reduced her body functions almost to the coma level.

Patel sat close to the couch on which she lay, his hand on her arm. "Judith, when you were here before, a very bad thing happened. You witnessed the execution of Lady Margaret Carew on December 10, 1660. You are going back, drifting back through the centuries to that date and to the place of the execution. When you were there before, you pitied Lady Margaret. You tried to save her. This time, remember you must turn your back to her. Let her go to her grave. Judith, tell me. It is December 10, 1660. Does a picture form in your mind?"

Lady Margaret ascended the steps to the platform where the executioner waited. She had almost managed to conquer Judith, to become her, and now they had brought her back to this terrible moment. To die now would be to betray Vincent and John. She looked about wildly. Where was Judith? She could not find her in the crowd of coarse peasant faces, all red with the excitement of the moment—a day's outing for them to see her head severed from her body. "Judith," she called. "Judith."

"There's such a crowd," Judith was saying softly. "All shouting. They're lusting for the execution. The King is in an enclosure. Oh, look at that man with him. He resembles

[152

Stephen. They're bringing Lady Margaret up. She just spat at the King. She's shouting at Simon Hallett."

She couldn't identify anyone unless Margaret Carew still has a link to her, Patel thought. "Judith, don't stay. Turn your back. Run."

Margaret saw the back of Judith's head. Judith was trying to push her way through the crowd but as the crowd strained forward, it was forcing her back to the platform. Margaret was at the block. Strong hands on her shoulders forced her to her knees. The white cap was jammed over her hair. "Judith!" she screamed.

"She's calling for me. I won't turn! I won't!" Judith cried out. Her hands flailed wildly in front of her. "Let me pass. Let me pass."

"Run," Patel ordered. "Don't turn around."

"Judith!" Margaret screamed. "Look. Stephen is here. They're going to execute Stephen." Judith whirled around and looked into the demanding, compelling gaze of Lady Margaret Carew. She began to scream, a frantic, terrified wail.

"Judith, what is it? What is happening?" Patel demanded.

"The blood. Blood gushing from her neck. Her head. They've killed her. I want to go home. I want Stephen."

"You *are* coming home, Judith. You will awaken now. You will feel peaceful and warm and refreshed. For the next few minutes you will remember everything that happened, and we will talk about it. And then you will forget it. Lady Margaret will be meaningless to you, other than as a character mentioned in your book. You will leave your cape and

153]

boots and the wires and powder you brought here. They and all records about this will be destroyed. You will marry Sir Stephen Hallett and know much happiness with him. Now wake up, Judith."

She opened her eyes and tried to sit up. Patel put an arm around her. "Very slowly," he cautioned. "You've taken a long and difficult trip."

"It was so awful," she whispered. "I thought I knew what they did to those people, but to see how crazed the crowd was . . . It was an excursion for them. But Doctor, she's gone now. She's gone. But have I any right to Stephen? I must tell him what happened."

"You won't remember what happened. Go to Stephen. Let him learn what he must about your sister. Then join her. I'm very sure she couldn't be your twin and not be like you."

Tears ran down her cheeks. Impatiently she brushed them away and hurried over to the mirror. "Why am I crying?" she asked. She was puzzled. "I guess it's just that I'm so happy." She walked slowly to the mirror.

"Judith is already forgetting," Rebecca Wadley told Commissioner Barnes and Commander Sloane.

"Do you expect us to believe what we just saw?" Barnes snapped. "These files will all be subpoenaed. We're sending a constable in to make sure nothing is touched. It isn't our job to decide the merits of this case."

Sloane was watching Judith. She was touching mascara to her eyes. He could see her reflection in the mirror over the antique table. Her smile was brilliant with happiness. "I shouldn't have taken so long," she told Patel. "I can't keep Stephen waiting. I'm riding with him to the palace when he presents himself to the Queen." Oh, Doctor, thank you for helping me find my sister."

With a wave of her hand she was gone. Sloane felt a

chill in his stomach. There was a scar glistening on her right hand. At the same moment, he realized that the bag she had brought in and placed on the antique table where she'd touched up her makeup was at a different angle. "Oh Christ!" he shouted. "Get out of here!" He threw open the lab door but it was too late. The bomb exploded with a thunderous blast. Bits of the bodies of Sloane, Barnes, Patel, and Wadley became entwined with pieces of the files, records, and tapes of the shattered office. Then flames leaped up and the entire building became a holocaust.

Lynch followed the quickly-moving figure through the streets. He heard the blast as he rounded the corner, started to run back, then realized that unlike other pedestrians, Judith Chase did not break stride, nor did she even turn her head in the direction of the sound. Instead, she hailed a taxi. Lynch grabbed another one and ordered it to follow hers. He reached in his pocket for his portable phone and called headquarters.

Judith was getting out of her taxi in front of her apartment house and stepping into a waiting Rolls-Royce when Lynch learned that the latest bombing had taken place at 79 Welbeck Street. *Patel's address!* He asked to be connected to Commander Sloane's office. The secretary told him that Commander Sloane and Commissioner Barnes had left together to see a Dr. Patel. Their driver? No, they didn't have one. They took one of the unmarked cars.

Oh God, no! Lynch thought. *They were in Patel's office when the bomb went off!*

There was a crowd of newspapermen and cameras outside Sir Stephen Hallett's home. It was always a historic moment when a new Prime Minister went to present himself to the Queen. Lynch waited across the street hidden by a parked BBC van. He realized that no one here seemed to know yet about the bombing of the Patel office.

A few minutes later the limousine drove slowly around the house. The driver parked at the curb. The dark windows protected the interior of the car from the intrusion of passersby looking in.

Lynch was sure that Judith Chase was in the car. There was a surge forward as the front door of the Hallett town house opened and Sir Stephen emerged surrounded by security officers. The chauffeur got out of the car and turned his back to it as he waited for the new Prime Minister to come down the walk.

Lynch saw his chance. Everyone was facing the house. Their backs were to the car. Turning up the collar of his coat and pulling his hat brim down, he rushed across the street and opened the door. "Miss Chase." And then he saw it. The vivid scar on her right hand, which she was now dabbing with makeup. "You *are* Margaret Carew," he said and reached into his pocket . . .

> *Lady Margaret looked up and saw the gun pointing at her. I've come so far, she thought. I tricked Judith by using Stephen's name. I killed her and I came back, and now it's over.*

> *She did not bother to close her eyes as Lynch pulled the trigger.*

The sound of the gun was lost in the cheers of the crowd as Stephen, shaking hands along the way, walked to the car. His bodyguard got into the front seat and Rory held the

[156

door open for him. "All set, darling?" Stephen asked, then cried, "Judith, Judith, *Judith.*"

Margaret felt arms go around her and lips graze her cheeks, heard a frantic shout for help. It is over, she thought. Then as the final darkness came, and she made her way to eternity to seek John and Vincent, she knew that she had achieved the ultimate revenge. She heard Stephen's sobs, felt his tears mingle with the blood pouring from her forehead. "Simon Hallett," she thought victoriously, "I have broken his heart just as you broke mine."

TERROR STALKS THE CLASS REUNION

He watched Kay from the corner of his eye. For these three days he'd been careful to stay away from her, never to be caught in a group picture with her. It hadn't been difficult. Nearly six hundred alumni had turned out for this reunion. For three days he'd had his nerves twisted as they'd launched into the tiresome memories of silly school kid nonsense from their days together at Garden State High in Passaic County, New Jersey.

Kay had finished eating a hot dog. She must have felt

[158

something on her lip because she brushed it with her fingertip, then laughed and poked the fingertip in her mouth.
Tonight he would hold those fingers in his own hands.

He was standing at the edge of a group. He knew that the
weight he had lost in these eight years, the beard he had
grown, the contact lenses instead of the heavy glasses, the
bald spot under his thinning hair, had changed his appearance a lot more than most of the students'. But some things
didn't change. Not one person had come up to him and said,
"Donny, great to see you." If anyone had recognized him,
they'd rushed past. Just like the old days. He could see again
the school cafeteria when he'd bring the sandwich in a paper
towel and go from table to table. "Sorry, Donny," they'd
mumble, "no room."

Finally he'd come to the point where he'd sneak onto the
fire escape stairs and eat his lunch there.

But now he was glad that in these three days no one had
slapped his back or clasped his arm or yelled, "Great to see
you." He'd been able to drift on the edges of groups, able
to watch Kay, able to plan what he would do. In exactly one
half hour more she would belong to him.

"What class were you?"

For a moment he wasn't sure that the voice was questioning him. Kay was sipping a soda. She was talking to a
student who had graduated in Donny's class, Virginia something or other. Kay's honey-colored hair was brighter than
he'd remembered. But she lived in Phoenix now. Maybe the
sun had streaked it. She'd cut it so that it curled around her
face. It used to lie on her shoulders. Maybe he'd make her
let it grow again. "Kay, let your hair grow. Your husband
is laying down the law." He'd be teasing but he'd mean it.

What was the stupid question this stupid person had
asked? Oh—the year he graduated. He turned. Now he

159]

recognized the man, the new principal. He'd made the opening remarks on Tuesday. "I graduated eight years ago," Donny said.

"That's why I don't know you. I've just been here four years. I'm Gene Pearson."

"Donny Rubel," he mumbled.

"It's been a fantastic three days," Pearson said. "Terrific attendance. Great school spirit. At a college you expect it. But high school . . . It's wonderful."

Donny nodded. He blinked and made it seem that he was moving because the sun was in his eyes. He could see that Kay was shaking hands with people. She was going to leave.

"Where do you live now?" Pearson seemed determined to keep up the conversation.

"About thirty miles from here." To forestall any more questions Donny said hurriedly, "I have my own fix-it business. My van is my workshop. Go anywhere up to an hour's drive to do repairs. Well, good to meet you, Mr. Pearson."

"Say, maybe you'd want to talk at our career day. Kids need to know there are alternatives to college . . ."

Donny raised one hand as though he hadn't heard. "Gotta run. Some of the guys from my class and I are pushing on to dinner." He didn't give Pearson a chance to answer. Instead he began to skirt the picnic area. He'd dressed carefully, khaki slacks, a blue polo shirt. Half the guys here had on practically the same thing. He'd wanted to blend into the crowd, be as inconspicuous as he'd been conspicuous in the years he'd spent in this school. The only kid in the class who wore an overcoat when everyone else had a school jacket.

Kay was walking through the grove of trees that separated the picnic area from the parking lot. The school adjoined the county park, so ideal for the reunion. And so

[160

ideal for Donny. He caught up with her just as she opened her car door. "Miss Wesley," he said. "I mean, Mrs. Crandell."

She looked startled. He knew that in a minute the parking lot would be crowded. He'd have to hurry. "I'm Donny Rubel," he said. "I guess you don't recognize me."

She looked unsure. Then that smile that he'd envisioned so many times lying awake at night began to form. "Donny. How good to see you. You look so different. Have you been here long? How come I haven't seen you?"

"Just made it here," he explained. "You're the only one I wanted to see. Where are you staying?"

He already knew. The Garden View Motel on Route 80. "That's perfect," he said when she answered. "A car is picking me up there in half an hour. I cabbed over. Is there any chance you could drop me? It would give us a chance to talk."

Did she suspect something? Was she remembering that last night when she told him she wasn't coming back next term, that she was going to be married, and he'd started to cry? She hesitated, then said, "Of course, Donny. It will be good to catch up. Hop in."

He managed to bend down and yank his shoelace open as he hurried around to the passenger side. When he got into the car he leaned over and made a big thing of tightening the shoelace. Anyone who noticed the car at all would swear Kay had left the picnic area alone.

Kay drove swiftly. She tried to push down her faint irritation at the presence of the young man beside her. Mike would be home from New York in an hour, and after the way she'd been so rotten to him on the phone last night, she was desperately anxious to straighten things out between them. This school reunion had been good for her. It had been fun to see the teachers she'd worked with the two years she'd taught there, fun to catch up with her students. She'd loved teaching. That was one of the problems between her and Mike. His job of setting up new plants for his company meant they never stayed anyplace more than a year. Twelve moves in eight years. She'd told him when he'd left her at the motel to tell the company that he wanted a permanent assignment.

"That sounds like an ultimatum, Kay," he'd told her.

"Maybe it is, Mike," she'd answered. "I want roots. I want to have a baby. I want to be in a place long enough that eventually I can get back into teaching. I can't keep moving like this. I just can't."

Last night he'd started to tell her that the company had promised him a partnership and a permanent spot in the New York office if he would just do one more on-location job. She'd hung up on him.

She was so concerned with her own thoughts that she didn't notice the silence of her passenger until he announced, "Your husband's been at a company meeting in New York. He's due back tonight."

"How did you know?" Kay looked quickly at the impassive profile of Donny Rubel, then glued her eyes to the road.

"I talked to people who talked to you."

"I thought you just got to the picnic."

"You thought that. That's not what I said."

The vent was blowing cool air into the car. Kay's skin went suddenly cold as though the pleasant June evening had chilled. They were less than a mile from the motel. Her foot went down on the accelerator. Something warned her not to ask questions. "It worked out so well," she said. "My husband had a business meeting in New York. I got the notice about the reunion and . . ."

[162

"I read the *Alumni News*," Donny Rubel told her. "It said 'Garden State High's favorite teacher to come to reunion.' "

"That was generous." Kay tried to laugh.

"You didn't recognize me." Donny sounded pleased. "But I bet you didn't forget you went to the prom with me."

She'd taught English and choir. The guidance counselor, Marian Martin, had suggested that Donny Rubel join the choir. "He's one of the saddest kids I've ever seen," she told Kay. "He's a klutz at sports, he has no friends, I'm sure he's bright but he just gets by academically, and God knows the poor kid was behind the gate when looks were given out. If we can get him in an activity where he might make friends . . ."

She remembered his earnest efforts, the snickers of the others in the group until one day when Donny was out, she'd talked to them. "I have news for you guys. I think you're rotten." They'd let up on him, at least during choir. After the spring concert he used to drop in to talk with her. That was when she'd learned he wasn't going to the prom. He'd invited three girls and they'd all turned him down. On impulse, she'd suggested that he come anyhow and sit with her at dinner. "I'm one of the chaperons," she said. "It will be nice to have you with me." Uneasily she remembered how Donny had started to cry at the end of the evening.

The motel sign was on the right. She chose not to notice that Donny's hand had moved and was brushing her leg.

"Remember at the prom I asked if I could see you over the summer? You told me you were getting married and moving away. You've lived in a lot of places. I've tried to find you."

"You have?" Kay tried not to sound too nervous.

"Yes. I looked you up in Chicago two years ago but by then you'd moved to San Francisco."

163]

"I'm sorry I missed you."

"Do you like to move around so much?" Now his hand was resting on her knee.

"Hey, fellow, that's my knee." She tried to sound amused.

"I know it. You're really sick of moving around so much, aren't you? You don't have to anymore."

Kay glanced at Donny. The heavy, dark sunglasses covered his eyes and half his face, but his mouth was pursed and partly open. He was exhaling through it now, an almost soundless whistling note that had an eerie echo.

"Drive to the end of the lot and turn left behind the main building," he told her. "I'll show you where to park."

His hand tightened on her knee. She felt before she saw the gun that he pressed against her side. "I'll use it, you know," he whispered.

This couldn't be happening. She should never have given him a ride. Her hands trembled as she turned the wheel in obedience to his directions. There was a cold chill in the pit of her stomach. Should she try to attract attention, to crash the car? She heard the click of the safety catch on the gun.

"Don't try anything, Kay. There are six bullets in this gun. I only need one for you, but I won't waste the others. Pull in beside that van, on the other side. The last spot."

She obeyed him, then realized immediately that her car was totally hidden from the windows of the motel by the dark gray van on the left. "Now slide out your door and don't scream." His hand was on her arm. He slipped out behind her. She heard him pull the key ring from the starter and drop it on the floor. In one quick movement he pushed her forward and slid open the side door of the van. With one arm he lifted her inside and climbed in behind her. The door slid closed. Almost total darkness replaced the late afternoon sun. Kay blinked.

[164

"Donny, don't do this," she pleaded. "I'm your friend. Talk to me but don't . . ."

She felt herself being pushed forward, stumbled and fell onto a narrow cot. Something was covering her face. A gag. Then with one hand he held her down, with the other snapped handcuffs on her wrists, shackles on her ankles, and joined them with a heavy metal chain. He slid open the side door of the van, jumped down, and snapped it closed. She heard the driver's door slam shut and an instant later the van began to move. Her desperate efforts to attract attention by pounding her chained legs against the side of the van were defeated by the clicking of the tires against the macadam.

Mike bit his lip impatiently as the cabdriver slowed to allow a van to cross in front of them at the turnoff to the motel. His lean, disciplined body vibrated with tension as he willed the cab to move faster.

He felt lousy about the way he and Kay had left it last night. He'd almost called her back when she hung up on him. But he knew Kay—she never stayed angry long. And now he could give her what she wanted. *Just one more assignment, honey. A year at most . . . maybe even six months. Then they'll bring me into the New York office permanently as a partner.* If she wanted, they could buy a house in this area. She liked it here.

The driver pulled up to the lobby entrance.

Mike jumped out of the cab. Long strides took him through the lobby.

He and Kay were in room 210. His first reaction when he turned the key and pushed the door open was keen disappointment. It was a little early for Kay to be back but somehow he'd expected to find her. The room was typical motel: shaggy carpeting, beige and brown bedspread, heavy oak-veneer double dresser, television camouflaged in an armoire, windows overlooking the parking lot. The other night he had simply dropped Kay here and rushed off to New York for the first sales meeting. Reluctantly he remembered how Kay had wrinkled her nose and said, "These rooms. They're all alike and I've been in so many of them."

And yet, as usual, she had managed to add a touch of homeyness to the place. There were fresh flowers in a vase and next to it three small silver picture frames. One showed him holding a freshly caught striped bass; another was a snapshot of Kay in front of their Arizona condo; the third, a Christmas-card picture of Kay's sister's family.

The books Kay had brought to read were on the night table. The mother-of-pearl comb, brush, and hand mirror that had been her mother's were neatly placed on the dresser. When he opened the door of the closet, there was the faint scent of the sachet bags on her satin hangers.

Unconsciously Mike smiled. Kay's exquisite neatness was a continuing source of joy to him.

He decided that a quick shower would feel good. When Kay got back, they'd talk it out and he'd take her for a festive dinner. *A full partner, Kay. Within the year. It's been worth all the moving. I promised you it would happen.* As he hung up his suit and stuffed his underwear and socks and shirt in the laundry bag, the thought struck him that the constant moving had never bothered him because Kay had managed to make a home out of every motel unit or rented apartment they'd ever stayed in.

At six-fifteen, he was sitting at the round table overlooking the parking lot, watching the news and listening for the turn of the key in the lock. He'd set out a bottle of wine from the room bar-refrigerator. At six-thirty, he opened the wine and poured a glass. At seven, he began watching Dan

[166

Rather, who was reporting a new outburst of terrorist activity. At seven-thirty, he had worked up a self-justifying annoyance. . . . All right, so Kay's still mad at me. If she's having dinner with friends, she could have left a message. At eight o'clock, he called the desk for the third time and was again assured by a testy operator that *there were absolutely no messages for Mr. Crandell in room 210.* At nine o'clock, he began going through Kay's address book and managed to find the name of a former student he knew Kay kept in touch with. Virginia Murphy O'Neil. She answered on the first ring. Yes, she had seen Kay. Kay left the picnic just when it was breaking up. As a matter of fact, Virginia had seen Kay drive away. That would have been between five-fifteen and five-thirty. She was absolutely sure Kay was alone in the car.

When he finished speaking to Virginia O'Neil, Mike called the police to ask about accidents between the school and the motel and on learning there were none, reported Kay missing.

The handcuffs dug into her wrists; the shackles were bruising her ankles; the gag was choking her.

Donny Rubel? Why was he doing this to her? She suddenly thought of Marian Martin, the guidance counselor who had asked her to take Donny into the choir. That last week she'd told Marian that she'd invited Donny to sit at her table at the prom. Marian had been troubled. "I've already heard about it," she said. "Donny bragged to someone that you asked him to be your date. I suppose it's understandable, the way the kids make fun of him, but even so . . . But, really, what difference? You're leaving, you're getting married in two weeks."

But he's kept track of me all these years. Kay felt herself panicking. She strained her eyes but could not see him through the partition. The van seemed unusually wide and in the near darkness she could begin to make out the outlines of a worktable opposite the cot. Over it a corkboard held a variety of tools. What did Donny do with them? What was he planning to do to her? *Mike, help me, please.*

The road seemed to climb and twist and curve. The narrow cot swayed, bumping her shoulder against the side of the van. Where were they going? Finally she sensed that they were descending. More curves, more bumps, and the van stopped.

She heard the whirring of the panel being lowered. "We're home." Donny's voice was high-pitched and triumphant. An instant later the side door of the van rumbled open. Kay cringed as Donny bent over her. His breath was rapid and warm on her cheek as he released the gag. "Kay, I don't want you to scream. There's no one for miles around to hear you and you'll only make me very nervous. Promise."

She gulped in the cool air. Her tongue felt thick and parched. "Promise," she whispered. He removed the shackles and rubbed her ankles solicitously. The handcuffs were unsnapped from her wrists. He put an arm around her and lifted her from the cot. Her legs were numb. She stumbled and he half carried her down the high step to the ground.

The place where he had taken her was a shabby frame house in a small clearing. A sagging porch held a rusty swing. The windows were shuttered. The thick trees around the clearing almost blotted out the last slanting rays of the sun. Donny steered her toward the house, unlocked the door, pushed her inside, and snapped on the overhead light.

The room they were in was small and grimy. An upright piano had long ago been painted white, but peeling patches showed the original black finish. Several keys were missing. An overstuffed velour couch and a chair must have at one

[168

time been bright red. Now they were faded into shades of purple and orange. A stained hooked rug covered the center of the uneven floor. A bottle of champagne in a plastic ice bucket and two glasses were laid out on a metal table. Next to the couch a crudely made bookcase was stuffed with student notebooks.

"Look," Donny said. He turned Kay around so she was facing the wall opposite the piano. It was covered with a poster-sized picture of her sitting with Donny at the prom. From the ceiling a crudely printed banner hung motionless. It read, "WELCOME HOME, KAY."

Detective Jimmy Barrott was assigned to follow up the call from Michael Crandell, the guy who had reported his wife missing. On the way to the Garden View Motel he stopped at a fast-food place and ordered a hamburger and coffee.

He ate as he drove and by the time he got to the motel, his slight headache had disappeared and he was his usual cynical self. After twenty-five years in the prosecutor's office he felt he had seen it all.

Jimmy Barrott's instinct told him that this was a waste of time. A thirty-two-year-old woman goes to a reunion and doesn't get home right on the button. And the husband panics. Jimmy Barrott knew all about getting home late and not phoning. That was the primary reason he'd been divorced twice.

When the door to room 210 was opened, he had to admit that the young fellow, Michael Crandell, looked sick with worry. Nice-looking guy, Jimmy Barrott thought. About six feet one. The kind of rugged looks the girls go for. But Mike's first question got Jimmy's goat. "What kept you so long?"

Jimmy settled himself in a chair at the table and opened

his notebook. "Listen," he said, "your wife is a couple of hours late getting back here. She's not officially missing for at least twenty-four hours. Did you two have a fight?"

He did not miss the guilty expression on Mike's face. "You had a fight," he pressed. "Why don't you tell me about it and then let's figure where she'd go to cool off."

To Mike's ears, he was telling it badly. Kay had been upset when they talked on the phone last night. She'd hung up on him. But it wasn't the way it seemed. Quickly he sketched their background. Kay had taught at Garden State High for two years. They'd met in Chicago at her sister's and been married from there. He'd never known her New Jersey friends. There was no point calling her sister. Jean and her husband and kids were in Europe on vacation.

"Give me a description of the car," Jimmy Barrott ordered. White 1986 Toyota. Arizona license plate. He scribbled the numbers. "Pretty far to drive," he observed.

"I had vacation coming. We decided to wind it around the company meeting and the alumni reunion. We're supposed to start driving back to Arizona tomorrow."

Jimmy closed his notebook. "My hunch is she's having dinner and a drink by herself or with some old friends and will be back in the next couple of hours." He glanced at the framed pictures on the table. "One of those your wife?"

"That one." He'd snapped the picture in front of the condo. It had been a hot day. Kay was wearing shorts and a T-shirt. Her hair was held back by a band. She looked about sixteen. With the T-shirt clinging to her breasts, and her long, slender legs in open sandals, she also looked damn sexy. Mike sensed that that was the reaction this detective had.

"Why don't you let me have this picture?" Jimmy Barrott suggested. Deftly he slipped it from the frame. "If she isn't

[170

home in the next twenty-four hours, we'll make up a missing person's report."

Some instinct made Jimmy Barrott walk around the parking lot before he went to his own car. By now the lot was almost full. There were a couple of white Toyotas in it but none with Arizona plates. Then one car at the end of the lot, off by itself, caught his eye. He sauntered over to it.

Five minutes later he was rapping sharply at the door of room 210. "Your car is in the parking lot," he told Mike. "The keys were on the floor. Looks as though your wife left them for you."

As he studied the incredulous look on Mike's face, the telephone rang. Both men rushed to answer it. Jimmy Barrott reached it first, picked up the receiver, and held it so that he could hear what was said.

Mike's "hello" was almost inaudible. And then the men listened as Kay said, "Mike, I'm sorry to do this to you but I need time to think. I left the car in the lot. Go back to Arizona. It's all over for us. I'll be in touch with you about a divorce."

"No . . . Kay . . . please . . . I won't leave without you."

There was a click. Jimmy Barrott felt reluctant sympathy for the shocked and bewildered young man. He took Kay's picture and laid it on the table. "That's just the way my second wife took off," he told Mike. "The only difference is while I was at work she had the movers in. Left me with a beer mug and my laundry."

The remark cut through the numbness. "But that's it," Mike said. "Don't you see?" He pointed to the dresser. "Kay's toilet articles. She wouldn't leave without them. Her makeup is in the bathroom cabinet. The book she was reading." He opened the closet door. "Her clothes. What woman doesn't bring anything personal with her?"

171]

"You'd be surprised how many," Jimmy Barrott told him. "I'm sorry, Mr. Crandell, but I have to write this up as a domestic affair."

He went back to the office to file his report, then drove home. But even when he'd gone to bed, Jimmy Barrott couldn't sleep. The neatly hung clothes, the toilet articles so carefully laid out. Something in his gut was telling him Kay Crandell would have taken them with her. But she'd phoned.
Had she?
Jimmy sat bolt upright. Some women phoned. He had only Mike Crandell's word that it was his wife's voice. And Mike Crandell and his wife had had a fight just before she disappeared.

Hours passed as Mike sat by the phone. She'll call again, he told himself. She'll change her mind. She'll come back.
Would she?
At last Mike got up. He stripped and fell onto the bed, the side nearest the phone, ready to grasp the receiver at the first ring. Then he closed his eyes and began to cry.

Kay bit her lip, trying not to scream in protest as Donny broke the phone connection. Donny was smiling at her solicitously. "That was very good, Kay."
Would he have carried out his threat? He'd warned her that if she did not say exactly what he'd written and say it convincingly, he would go to the motel tonight and kill Mike. "I was in your room twice this past week, you know," he told her. "I do odd jobs at the motel. It was easy to make a key." Then he had led her into the bedroom. The furniture here consisted of a sagging double bed covered with a cheap chenille spread, a card table nightstand, and a battered

[172

dresser. "Do you like the bedspread?" Donny asked. "I told the woman it was a present for my wife. She said most women like white chenille." He pointed to the comb and brush and mirror on top of the dresser. "They're almost exactly the same color as yours." He opened the closet. "Do you like your new clothes? They're all size eight just like the ones you had in the motel." There were a couple of cotton skirts and T-shirts, a raincoat, a robe, a flowered print dress. "There's some underwear and a nightgown in the drawers," Donny told her proudly. "And look, the shoes are your size too, seven medium. I got you sneakers and loafers and heels. I want my wife to be well dressed."

"Donny, I can't be your wife," she'd whispered.

He'd looked puzzled. "But you're going to be. You always wanted to marry me." It was then she'd noticed the chain neatly folded in the corner by the bed and attached to a metal plate on the wall. Donny had seen her horrified expression. "Don't worry, Kay. I have one in every room. It's just that at night I'll be sleeping in the living room and I don't want you to try to leave me. And during the day I have to go to work so I have it fixed that you'll be comfortable in the living room."

He'd taken her back to the living room and ceremoniously uncorked the champagne. "To us."

Now as Kay watched him put the receiver in place, her mouth felt sour remembering the taste of the warm, sugary champagne, the greasy hamburgers Donny had cooked.

All through the meal he'd said nothing. Then he'd told her to finish her coffee, that he'd be right back. When he returned he was clean-shaven. "I only grew the beard so people wouldn't recognize me at the school," he said proudly.

After that he made her finish the champagne with him and call Mike. Now he sighed. "Kay, you must be tired. I'll let you go to bed soon. But first I'd like to read you a couple of

173]

chapters of my first book about you." With almost a swagger, he walked over to the bookcase and took out one of the notebooks.

This isn't real, Kay thought.

But this was real. Donny settled himself in the overstuffed chair opposite her. The room was chilly now but sweat glistened on his face and arms and stained his polo shirt. His unnaturally pale skin was accentuated by dark circles under his eyes. When he'd taken off his sunglasses, she'd been surprised to see how blue his eyes were. She'd remembered them as being brown. They *are* brown, she told herself. He must be wearing colored contacts. Everything about him is fantasy, she thought. He looked up at her almost shyly. "I feel like I'm a kid back in school," he said.

A tiny whisper of hope told Kay that she might be able to establish some authority over him, teacher to student. But when he began to read, her throat closed in near-panic. "June third. Last night I went to the prom with Kay," he intoned. "We danced every dance. When I drove her home, she cried in my arms. She said her family was forcing her to marry a man she did not love and that she wanted me to come for her when I am able to take care of her. My beautiful Kay, I promise you that one day I shall claim you as my wife."

A sleepless night and the fact that he had absolutely no coffee in his apartment made Jimmy Barrott unusually grumpy. After a stop for coffee, he headed for the office. When the prosecutor's office was cleared, Jimmy sauntered in.

"Something stinks," he told his boss, "about that domestic affair report I filed last night. I want permission to look into the husband." Tersely he related the interview with Mike, the finding of the car, the telephone call.

[174

The prosecutor listened and nodded. "Start digging," he said. "Let me know if you want any help."

At the first sign of dawn, Mike got up, shaved and showered. He hoped that the hot, then cold needles of water would wash away the sluggishness from his brain.

Somewhere during the dark hours of the night, his despair at Kay's disappearance had hardened into certainty that she would not have abandoned him that way. He pulled a notebook from his briefcase and between gulps of coffee began to jot down the possible actions he could take. Virginia Murphy O'Neil. She'd been with Kay right at the end of the picnic. She'd seen Kay leave. Maybe Kay had told her something that didn't seem important then. He'd go to Virginia's home and talk to her. Detective Barrott had spotted the car at ten o'clock. But no one knew what time it had been left there. He'd talk to the motel employees. Maybe someone had seen Kay alone or with someone.

He wanted to sit by the phone, to wait because Kay might call again, but that was crazy. Mike's blood chilled at the thought that maybe she wouldn't be able to call again.

His first stop was at the motel telephone operator's station. The operator assured him that she was much too busy to give messages to people who called in but she was very happy to take any that he might receive. He made his voice confidential. "Look, you ever had a fight with your boyfriend?"

She laughed. "Like every night."

"Last night I had a row with my wife. She walked out on me. I have to go out now, but I'm pretty sure she'll call. Please, can you plug the line or something so you won't forget to give her this message?"

The operator's heavily mascaraed eyes sparkled with curiosity. She read the note aloud. In block letters Mike had written. "If Kay Crandell phones, tell her Mike has to talk to her. He'll go along with anything she wants but please leave a phone number or time when she'll call back."

The operator's look was filled now with sympathy and a certain coyness. "I don't know why any woman would be dope enough to walk out on you," she told him.

Mike slipped a twenty-dollar bill in her hand. "I'm counting on you to play Cupid."

Talking to employees who might have seen the white Toyota come into the parking lot was hopeless. There was no parking lot attendant. The one security guard had been inside the motel most of the evening. "Just started today," he told Mike. "Otherwise I wouldn't be here either. Nope. Not a wink of trouble." He scratched his head. "Come to think of it, they did have one car grabbed last year but it was abandoned two miles away. The owner said even a crook could tell it was a lemon." He chuckled.

Two hours later, Mike was thirty miles away sitting across the table in Virginia O'Neil's house. She was a small, trim young woman who had been in Kay's choir the last year Kay taught at Garden State High. The kitchen was large and cheerful and opened into an airy recreation room cluttered with toys. Virginia's two-year-old twins were playing there with noisy, unrestrained energy.

Mike did not attempt to concoct a story about why he was looking for Kay. He liked Virginia and instinctively trusted her. By the time he had finished, he saw his own sick worry mirrored in Virginia's eyes. "That is *weird*," she told him. "Kay wouldn't pull that kind of stunt. She's just too considerate."

"How much of her did you see at the reunion?"

A teddy bear went flying past Mike's foot. An instant later a small figure hurtled by him and tackled it.

[176

"At ease, Kevin," Virginia ordered. She explained to Mike, "My aunt gave the kids teddy bears yesterday. Dina is cuddling hers. Kevin is tackling his."

This is what Kay wanted, Mike thought. A house like this, a couple of kids. The thought gave him a new and disquieting possibility. "Did most people bring their children to the reunion?"

"Oh, there were loads of kids around." Virginia's face became contemplative. "You know, Kay did look a little wistful when she was holding Dina the other day, and she said, 'All my students have families. I never expected it would turn out like this for me.'"

Mike rose to leave a few minutes later. "What are you going to do?" Virginia asked. He took Kay's picture from his pocket. "I'm going to get posters made and just hand them out. It's the only thing I can think of."

When Donny finally decided it was time to go to bed, he told Kay to change in the tiny bathroom. It held a small sink, a commode, and a makeshift shower. He handed her the nightgown he'd bought, a low-cut, transparent scrap of nylon edged with imitation lace. The robe matched. As she changed, Kay frantically tried to decide how to deal with him if he tried to attack her. He could certainly overpower her. Her only hope was to try to take charge, to establish a teacher-student relationship.

But when she emerged he didn't attempt to touch her. "Get into bed, Kay," he said. He turned down the spread. There were blue-flowered muslin sheets and pillowcases on the bed. They looked stiff and new. She walked firmly to the bed. "I'm very tired, Donny," she said crisply. "I want to get to sleep."

"Oh, Kay, I promise you, I won't touch you till we're

married." He covered her, then said, "I'm sorry, Kay, but I can't take a chance that you'll try to get away while I'm asleep." And then he shackled her foot to the chain.

All night she'd lain awake, trying to pray, trying to plan, only able to whisper *Mike, help me, Mike, find me.* Toward dawn she fell into an uneasy sleep. She awakened to find Donny staring at her. Even in the semidark, there was no mistaking the urgency in his stance. Through clenched teeth, he whispered, "I just wanted to make sure you were comfortable, Kay. You look so pretty when you're asleep. I can hardly wait till we're married."

He wanted her to cook breakfast for him. "Your future husband has a good appetite, Kay." At eight-thirty, he settled her in the living room. "I'm sorry to close the shutters again but I can't risk having someone walk by and look in. Not that it ever happens, but you'll understand." He shackled her leg to the chain in the living room. "I measured it," he told her. "You can get into the bathroom. I'm leaving stuff for sandwiches and a pitcher of water and some sodas right here on the table. You can reach the piano. I want you to practice. And if you want to read, you can read all my books. They're all about you, Kay. I've been writing about you for these whole eight years."

He left the recorder-phone in the padlocked wire cage near the ceiling. "I'll leave the conference call on, Kay. You'll hear people phoning jobs in for me. I beep my messages from the phone in the van every hour or so. I'll talk to you then, but you won't be able to talk to me. I'm sorry. It's a real busy day, so I may not get back till six or seven." As he left, he lifted her chin in his hand. "Miss me, won't you, sweetheart?"

His kiss on her cheek was prim. His arm around her waist tightened convulsively.

He had bolted the shutters before he left and the dim

[178

overhead light cast shadows throughout the room. She stood on the couch, straining the chain until the shackle ripped her ankle, but it was impossible to get at the wire cage and, even so, it was padlocked. There was no chance of making a phone call.

The chain was attached to a metal plate on the wall. There were four screws holding the plate in place. If she could somehow undo those screws, she could get out. How near was it to the highway? How fast could she move with the shackle on her ankle and carrying the chain? What could she use to undo the screws?

Feverishly, Kay searched the living room. The plastic knife he'd left snapped when she tried to twist it into the head of a screw. Frustrated tears filled her eyes. She pulled the cushions from the couch. The upholstery was ripped and she could see the wires but there was no way she could break one loose.

She dragged herself over to the piano. If she could reach into the strings maybe there was something sharp she could pull loose.

There wasn't.

There was no way to loosen the metal plate. Her only hope would be if someone happened to come by while he was away. But who? There was some mail on top of the bookcase. Most of it was addressed to a box number in Howville. A few pieces had the address of this place, 4 Timber Lane, Howville. Each of them had the box number penciled on the envelope, so Donny did not have postal delivery.

Her eye fell on the rows of black-and-white student notebooks. He had told her to read them. She pulled out a half dozen of them and dragged herself over to the couch. The light was dim and she frowned in concentration. She'd put on the dress she'd been wearing yesterday at the picnic, wanting to keep some sense of her own identity. But the dress was wrinkled now and she felt soiled. Soiled by her presence in this place, by the memory of his hands convulsively gripping her waist, by her sense of being a caged animal with a berserk keeper. The thought brought near hysteria. Get a grip on yourself, she said aloud. Mike is trying to find you. He will find you. It was as though she could feel the intensity of his love. Mike. Mike. I love you. She didn't want to move around anymore. She wanted to stay in one place. Even Donny Rubel had known that. And he was granting that wish. Kay realized she was laughing aloud, a shrieking, sobbing laugh that ended in a frenzy of tears.

But at least it brought a certain release. After a few minutes, she dried her face with the back of her hand and began to read.

The books were all alike. A day-by-day odyssey of a fantasy life starting with that night at the prom. Some of the entries were written as future plans. "When Kay and I are together, we will take a camping trip to Colorado. We will live in a tent and share the rustic, outdoor life of our forefathers. We will have a double sleeping bag and she will lie in my arms because she is a little afraid of the sounds of the animals. I will protect her and comfort her." Other times he wrote as though they had been together. "Kay and I had a wonderful day. We went into New York to the South Street Seaport. I bought her a new blouse and blue high-heeled shoes. Kay likes to hold my hand when we are walking. She loves me very much and never wants to be away from me. We have decided that if one or the other ever gets sick, we will not risk being separated. We are not afraid to die together. We will be in heaven for all eternity. We are lovers."

[180

At times it was almost impossible to make out the nearly illegible scrawl. Kay ignored her growing headache as she read book after book. The depths of Donny's madness brought her to the edge of panic. She must finish reading every one of the books. Somehow, some way, she might get a clue as to how she could persuade him to release her, to take her somewhere in public. He constantly wrote about sharing outings with her.

From about ten o'clock on, the phone began to ring. She could hear the messages that were left for Donny. Every nerve in her body vibrated at the sound of the impersonal voices. *Listen to me,* she wanted to shriek. *Help me.*

Donny apparently had an active repair service. A pizza parlor call—could he get over as soon as possible? One of the ovens wasn't working. Several housewives—could he take a look at the television? The VCR? A windowpane was broken. Every hour or so, Donny beeped in for messages, then left a message for her. "Kay, darling, I miss you very much. Do you see how busy I am? I've already made two hundred dollars this morning. I'll be able to take very good care of you."

After each call, she went back to reading. Over and over, in all the books, Donny kept referring to his mother. "When she was eighteen she let my father go too far and she got pregnant with me and had to get married. My father walked out on her when I was a baby and he blamed her for everything. I will never be like my father. I will not put a finger on Kay until we are married. Otherwise she might grow to hate me too and dislike our children."

In the next-to-last book she learned his plans. "On television I heard a preacher say that marriages have the best chance when people have known each other for four seasons. That there is something in the human spirit just as there is in nature that needs that cycle. I was in Kay's class in the fall and winter. I will take her away during the reunion. It will still be spring. We will exchange our vows together with only God as our witness on the first day of summer. That will be on Sunday, June 21. We will then leave and tour the country together, the two of us, lovers."

Today was Thursday, June 18.

At four o'clock a call came in from the Garden View Motel. Could Donny stop by this afternoon? A couple of television sets weren't working.

The Garden View Motel. Room 210. Mike.

Donny phoned a few minutes later. His voice had an echoing, hollow sound. "See what I mean, Kay. I do a lot of work over at the motel. I'm glad they called. It will give me a chance to see if Mike Crandell is going to clear out. I hope you've been practicing our songs. I really want to sing with you tonight. Good-bye for now, my darling."

There was anger in his voice when he said Mike's name. He's afraid, Kay thought. If anything upsets his plans, he'll go crazy. She must not antagonize him. She put the books back in the shelves and dragged herself over to the piano. It was hopelessly out of tune. The missing keys meant that everything she attempted to play was riddled with discordant sounds.

When Donny came in, it was nearly eight o'clock. His face was set in grim, angry lines. "Crandell isn't going home," he told Kay. "He's asking a lot of questions about you. He's passing out your picture."

Mike was at the motel. Mike had known there was something wrong. Oh, Mike, Kay thought. Find me. I'll go anywhere, anyplace. I'll have a baby in Kalamazoo or Peoria. What does it matter where we live as long as we're together?

[182

It was as though Donny could read her thoughts. He stood in the doorway glowering at her. "You didn't make him believe you when you talked to him last night. It's your fault, Kay."

He started across the room toward her. She shrank back on the couch and the chain yanked the shackle on her ankle. A thin trickle of blood, warm and slippery, dripped from her bruised flesh.

Donny noticed. "Oh, Kay, that hurt you, I can tell." He went into the bathroom and returned with a warm, wet cloth. Tenderly he lifted her leg from the floor and laid it across his lap. "It will feel much better now," he assured her as he wrapped the cloth around it, "and as soon as I'm sure you've fallen in love with me again, I'll take these off." He straightened up and his lips grazed her ear. "Should we call our first baby Donald Junior?" he asked. "I'm sure it will be a boy."

On Thursday afternoon, Jimmy Barrott went into the office of Michael Crandell's employers, the engineering firm of Fields, Warner, Quinlan, and Brown. Upon showing his badge, he was ushered into the office of Edward Fields, who was shocked to learn that Kay Crandell was missing. No, they hadn't heard from Mike today but that wasn't unusual. Mike and Kay were planning to drive back to Arizona. Mike was taking a week's vacation. Mike Crandell? Absolutely top drawer. The best. In fact, he'd just been voted into the partnership as of his completing a job that would begin next month in Baltimore. Yes, they knew Kay was upset about all the moves. Most of the wives felt that way. Would Jimmy know where Mike was staying?

Jimmy Barrott cautiously said that it was all probably a misunderstanding.

Edward Fields suddenly became very formal. "Mr. Barrott," he said, "if this is double-talk and you mean you're checking up on Mike Crandell, do yourself a favor and don't waste your time. I stake my own reputation and our firm's reputation on him."

Jimmy phoned the office for messages. There were none and he went directly home. There wasn't much food in the refrigerator and he decided to go to a take-out Chinese joint. But somehow he found his car steering toward the Garden View Motel.

It was nine-thirty when he arrived there. He learned from the desk clerk that Mike had been handing out pictures of his wife to all the employees, that he had given the switchboard operator twenty dollars to give his wife a message if she called. "There was absolutely no trouble around here last night," the clerk said nervously. "I couldn't refuse to allow him to pass out those pictures, but this isn't the kind of publicity we want." At Jimmy's request, the clerk produced one of the pictures, a blowup of the snapshot and underneath in large, block lettering: KAY CRANDELL IS MISSING. SHE MAY BE ILL. SHE IS 32 YEARS OLD, FIVE FEET FOUR INCHES, 115 POUNDS. SUBSTANTIAL REWARD FOR INFORMATION ABOUT HER WHEREABOUTS. Mike's name and the phone number of the motel followed.

At ten o'clock Jimmy knocked on the door of room 210. It was yanked open instantly and Jimmy noted the keen disappointment on Mike's face when he saw who was there. Reluctantly Jimmy conceded that Mike Crandell looked like a very worried guy. His clothes were rumpled as though he'd gotten most of his sleep in catnaps. Jimmy sauntered past him and saw the stack of photocopied pictures of Kay on the table. "Where have you passed these out so far?" he asked.

"Mostly around the motel. Tomorrow I'm going to deliver them to train stations and bus stops in the towns around here and ask people to put them in store windows."

"You haven't heard anything?"

Mike hesitated.

"You have heard something," Jimmy Barrott told him. "What is it?"

Mike pointed to the phone. "I didn't trust the operator to remember. I put in a recorder this afternoon. Kay phoned back while I was picking up a hamburger. It must have been about eight-thirty."

"Were you planning to let me in on that?"

"Why should I?" Mike asked. "Why should you be bothered with . . . what did you call it, a domestic affair?" There was a thin edge of hysteria in his voice.

Jimmy Barrott walked over to the recorder, rewound the tape and pressed the "play" button. The same woman's voice he had heard yesterday came on. "Mike, I'm really fed up. Go home and don't leave those pictures of me around. It's humiliating. I'm here because I want to be here." There was the sound of the receiver being slammed down.

"My wife has a soft, pretty voice," Mike said. "What I hear is stress, nothing else. Forget what she's saying."

"Look," Jimmy said in what for him was a kindly tone. "Women don't walk out of a marriage without some stress. I should know. Even my first wife cried at the divorce hearing and she was already pregnant by some other guy. I talked to the people you work with. They think a lot of you. Why don't you get on with your job and count your blessings? There isn't a dame worth it."

He watched as Mike's face whitened. "My office called," Mike told him. "They've offered to get a private investigator to help me. I may take them up on it."

Jimmy Barrott leaned over and took the cassette out of the

recorder. "Can you give me the name of someone who might be able to identify your wife's voice?" he asked.

All through the night, Mike sat with his head in his hands. At six-thirty, he left the motel and drove to the train stations and bus stops in the neighboring towns. At nine o'clock, he went to Garden State High. Classes were over for the summer but the office staff was still working. He was taken to the office of the principal, Gene Pearson. Pearson listened intently, his thin face frowning and thoughtful. "I remember your wife well," he said. "I told her that if she ever wanted a job here again, it was hers. From everything her former students told me, she must have been a very good teacher."

He'd offered Kay a job. Had she decided to take it?

"How did Kay respond to that?"

Pearson's eyes narrowed. "As a matter of fact, she said, 'Be careful, I may take you up on that.' " His attitude suddenly became formal. "Mr. Crandell, I can understand your concern, but I don't see how I can help you." He stood up.

"Please," Mike begged. "There must have been pictures taken at the reunion. Did you have an official photographer?"

"Yes."

"I want his or her name. I've got to get a full set of pictures right away. You can't refuse me that."

His next stop was the photographer on Center Street—six blocks from the school. At least here the only issue was cost. He placed the order and went back to the motel to hear the recorder. At eleven-thirty he returned to the photographer who had made a stack of 8 × 10 pictures for him from all the rolls that had been shot at the reunion—over two hundred prints in all.

[186

The pictures under his arm, Mike drove to Virginia O'Neil's house.

All Thursday night Kay lay awake on the lumpy mattress with its harsh new sheets. Her sense that something in Donny was building up to an explosive level was all-pervasive. After she phoned and left the message for Mike, she'd cooked dinner for Donny. He had brought in cans of hash and frozen vegetables and wine. She'd gone along with him, pretending it was fun to work together.

At dinner she'd gotten him to talk about himself, about his mother. He'd shown her a picture of his mother, a slender blonde in her forties in a bikini that belonged on a teenager. But Kay had felt her skin prickle. There was a definite resemblance between Donny's mother and herself. They were a type, as far apart as A and Z, but a type in size and features and hair.

"She got married again, seven years ago," Donny told her, his voice expressionless. "Her husband works for one of the casinos in Las Vegas. He's a lot older than she is but his kids are crazy about her. They're her age." Donny produced another picture of two men in their forties with their arms around his mother. "She's crazy about them too."

Then he turned his attention to the food on his plate. "You're a very good cook, Kay. I like that. My mother didn't like to cook. Most of the time I just had sandwiches. She wasn't home much."

After dinner she played the piano and sang with him. He remembered the words to all the songs she used to teach in choir. He had opened the shutters to let in the cool night air but clearly had no fear of being heard. She asked him about that. "Nobody comes here anymore," he told her. "The lake doesn't have any fish. It's too polluted for swimming. All the other houses are just rotting away. We're safe, Kay."

When he decided it was time to go to bed, he removed the leg chain and again waited for her outside the bathroom door. When she stepped out of the shower she heard the door begin to open, but when she slammed it shut, he didn't touch it again. Then as she was walking rapidly into the bedroom, Donny asked, "What do you want for a wedding supper, Kay? We should plan something special."

She pretended to be seriously considering the question, then shook her head and said firmly, "I absolutely cannot make plans to get married until I have a white gown. We'll have to wait."

"I didn't think about that, Kay," he said as he tucked her into bed and fastened the shackle on her ankle.

She drifted in and out of sleep. Each time she woke up, it was to see Donny standing at the foot of the bed, staring at her. Her eyes would begin to open and she'd force them shut, but it was impossible to deceive him. The dim light he left on in the living room shone on the pillow. "It's all right, Kay. I know you're awake. Talk to me, darling. Are you cold? In a few days when we're married, I'll keep you warm." At seven o'clock he brought coffee to her. She pulled herself up, careful to tuck the sheet and blanket under her arms. Her murmured "thank you" was stilled by a kiss.

"I'm not going to work all day," Donny told her. "I was thinking all night that you said you didn't have a gown to wear to our wedding. I'm going to buy you a dress today."

The coffee cup in her hand began to tremble. With a mighty effort, Kay managed to stay calm. This might be her only chance. "Donny, I'm sorry," she said. "I really don't want to seem ungrateful but the clothes you bought for me

[188

really don't fit properly. Every woman wants to select her own wedding gown."

"I didn't think about that," Donny said. Again he looked puzzled and thoughtful. "That means I'd have to take you to the store. I'm not sure if I want to do that. But I'd do anything to make you happy."

On Friday morning at six-thirty, Jimmy Barrott gave up trying to sleep and stomped into the kitchen. He made a pot of coffee, fished for a ballpoint pen on the table and started making notations on the back of an envelope.

1. Did Kay Crandell make those phone calls? Ask Virginia O'Neil to identify the voice.

2. If voice is that of Kay Crandell, check stress level with lab.

3. If Kay Crandell did make phone calls, she knew about the posters a few hours after Mike Crandell started distributing them in the motel. How?

The last question vanquished any final vestiges of sleepiness in Jimmy's brain. Could this be some kind of crazy hoax cooked up by Mike and Kay Crandell?

At ten-thirty, Jimmy Barrott was the unwilling recipient of a game of catch with two-year-old Kevin O'Neil. He tossed the ball to Kevin who caught it with one hand, but as he threw it back, Kevin yelled, "scravits." Jimmy missed the easy catch.

" 'Scravits' is his way of putting a hex on you," Virginia explained. She had absolutely no doubt about identifying Kay's voice. "Except that it doesn't really sound like her," Virginia said. "Miss Wesley, I mean Mrs. Crandell, oh, blazes, she kept telling me to call her Kay . . . Kay has such a lilt in her voice. She always sounds warm and up. That's her voice but it *isn't* her voice."

"Where's your husband?" Jimmy asked.

189]

Virginia looked startled. "He's at work. He's a trader in the Mercantile Exchange."

"You happy?"

"Of course I'm happy." Virginia's tone was frosty. "May I ask why that question?"

"How would you sound if you were taking off with or without your kids and dumping your husband? Stressed?"

Virginia grabbed Kevin just before he tackled his twin. "Detective Barrott, if I were going to leave my husband, I'd sit across the table from him and tell him when and why I was leaving. And you want to know something? Kay Wesley Crandell would do it exactly the same way. It's obvious that you're projecting the way you *think* women like Kay and I act. Now if you have no further questions, I'm pretty busy." She stood up.

"Mrs. O'Neil," he said. "I spoke to Mike Crandell just before I came here. I understand he's ordered copies of the pictures taken at the reunion and that he'll be over here about noon with them. I'll be back at noon. In the meantime, try to remember if Kay dated anyone from around here. Or give me the names of the faculty members she was friendly with."

Virginia separated the twins, who were now fighting over custody of the available teddy bear. Her manner changed. "I'm beginning to like you, Detective Barrott," she told him.

The same thought that had occurred to Jimmy Barrott, that Kay knew he was showing her picture only hours after he'd passed it out at the motel, struck Mike as he drove to Virginia O'Neil's house with the stacks of pictures of the reunion.

When Virginia answered the doorbell, Mike was on the raw edge of hysteria. The sight of Jimmy Barrott's glum face was like another turn to the already taut wire that was his nervous system.

[190

"What are you doing here?" His blunt inquiry was almost a shout.

He was aware of Virginia O'Neil's hand on his arm, of the fact that the house seemed unnaturally quiet. "Mike," Virginia said, "Detective Barrott wants to help. A couple of the other women from our class are here; we've got some sandwich makings; we'll go over the pictures together."

For the second time in as many days, Mike felt tears welling in his eyes. This time he managed to force them back. He was introduced to the other young women, Margery, Joan, and Dotty, all students of Garden State High in the years Kay had taught there. They sat together and studied the pictures Mike had brought. "That's Bobby . . . he lives in Pleasantwood. That's John Durkin Kay's talking to in that picture. His wife is with him. That's . . . ."

It was Jimmy Barrott who taped each picture to a poster-sized cardboard, marked the heads of the people in each with a number, and then had the young women identify anyone they knew. It was soon obvious that there were too many no one could remember in groups surrounding Kay.

At three o'clock, Jimmy said, "Sorry, but we're not getting anywhere. I know you have a new principal at the school. He won't be any help to us, but is there any teacher who's been around a long time, who might be able to identify former students you people don't know?"

Virginia and her friends exchanged long, thoughtful stares. Virginia spoke for all of them. "Marian Martin," she said. "She was at Garden State from the day it opened. She retired two years ago. She lives in Litchfield, Connecticut, now. She was supposed to come to the reunion but had other commitments she couldn't break."

"She's the one we need," Jimmy Barrott said. "Does anyone have her phone number or address?"

191]

The flicker of hope that had begun in Mike when he realized that Jimmy Barrott was on his side now leaped into a flame. People were working with him, were trying to help. *Kay, wait for me. Let me find you.*

Virginia was looking through her phone book. "Here's Miss Martin's number." She began dialing.

Vina Howard had accomplished a lifelong ambition when she opened the Clothes Cartel shop in Pleasantwood, New Jersey. She had been an assistant buyer at J. C. Penney before her relentlessly unhappy marriage. When after eighteen years she'd finally left Nick Howard, she'd returned to the family home in time to nurse her two aging parents through a series of heart attacks and strokes. After they died, Vina had sold the old house, bought a small co-op, and realized her heart-hunger dream, to open a dress shop that would cater to the modern suburbanite on a budget. As an afterthought she'd added a line that would appeal to the modern suburbanite's teenage daughter. And it was that mistake that had become a daily vexation.

On Friday morning, June 19, Vina was straightening the dresses on the rack, polishing the glass over the costume jewelry counter, giving a push and tug to the chairs near the curtained-off dressing-room area and muttering to herself. "Horrible kids. Come in here and try on every stitch in the place. Get makeup all over the collars. Leave everything on the floor. This is the last season I cater to those slobs."

Vina had genuine reason to be upset. She'd just had expensive new wallpaper put in the minuscule changing area, and some fresh kid had written the usual four-letter word all over one wall. She'd finally scrubbed it clean but the paper was blotched and shredded.

Nevertheless the day started pleasantly enough. By ten-

[192

thirty, the time her assistant, Edna, arrived, the store was bustling and the cash register jingling.

At three-fifteen there was a lull and Vina and Edna managed to have a peaceful cup of coffee. Edna promised that her husband would surely be able to stretch the leftover wallpaper to replace the damaged area in the dressing room. A visibly cheered Vina had a warm smile on her face when the door of the shop opened and a couple came in, a pretty young woman of about twenty-six or -eight in a cheap-looking T-shirt and skirt and a gaunt-looking man about the same age whose arm was tightly around her. His dark red curly hair looked as though he'd just left a hairdresser. His china-blue eyes glittered. There was something spacey about the two of them, Vina thought. Her smile tightened. There'd been a series of drug-related robberies in the area lately.

"We want a long white dress," the man told her. "Size eight."

"The prom season is over," Vina said uneasily. "I don't have much of a selection in long dresses."

"This one should be suitable for a wedding."

Vina addressed herself to the young woman. "Have you any particular style in mind?"

Desperately Kay tried to find a way to communicate with this woman. From the corner of her eye she could see that the clerk at the cash register was sensing something odd about Donny and herself. That wild-looking red wig he was wearing. She also knew that Donny's right hand was touching the gun in his pocket and that any slight effort on her part to alert these women would become their death sentence.

"Something in a cotton," she said. "Do you have eyelet? Or maybe a sheer jersey?" She had spotted the curtained-off dressing area. She would have to go in there alone to change. . . . Maybe she could leave a message. The more dresses she tried on, the more time she would have.

But they had only one size-eight long white eyelet dress. "We'll take it," Donny said.

"I want to try it on," Kay said firmly. "The dressing room is right there," she pointed out. She walked over and pulled back the curtain. "See."

It was barely large enough for one person. The privacy curtain did not go down to the floor. "All right, you can try it on," Donny said. "I'll wait right outside." He firmly vetoed Vina's offer to assist Kay. "Just hand the dress in to her."

Kay whipped off the T-shirt and skirt. Frantically she glanced around the small cubicle. A narrow shelf held a box with a couple of straight pins. But no pencil. No way to leave a message. She pulled the dress over her head, then grabbed a pin. The wallpaper on one side of the cubicle was stained and shredded. On the other side she tried to scratch the word HELP. The pin was light. It was impossible to move it quickly. She managed a large jagged H.

"Hurry up, sweetheart."

She shoved aside the curtain. "I can't reach these buttons in the back," she told the salesclerk.

As she fastened the buttons, Vina glanced nervously at the cash register. Edna shook her head slightly. Get rid of them was what she was saying.

Kay studied herself in the floor-length mirror. "I don't think it's quite right," she said. "Have you anything else?"

"We'll take this one," Donny interrupted. "You look beautiful in it." He pulled out a wad of bills. "Hurry up, honey," he ordered. "We're running late."

Inside the cubicle, Kay stepped out of the dress, handed it around the curtain, yanked on her T-shirt and skirt, and grabbed another pin. With one hand, she pretended to be

[194

fussing with her hair; with the other, she tried to begin the
letter *E* on the wallpaper but it was impossible. She whirled
around when she heard Donny pull open the curtain.
"What's taking you so long, sweetheart?" he asked. Her
back was to the wall where she'd begun to write. She
continued to run her fingers through her hair as though
trying to smooth it. She let the pin drop behind her and
watched as Donny's eyes took in the tiny cubicle. Then,
apparently satisfied, he took her hand and with the box
under his arm hurried her from the store.

Marian Martin had just completed planting her new
azaleas when the pealing of the phone summoned her into
the house. She was a tall, sixty-seven-year-old woman with
a trim, disciplined body, close-cropped hair that curled
around her face, lively brown eyes, and a kind, no-nonsense
manner. In the two years since she had retired from
her position as head guidance counselor at Garden State
High and moved to this quiet Connecticut town, she'd
joyfully indulged herself in the avocation she'd never had
enough time for. Now her English garden was her un-
abashed pride. The telephone call that Friday afternoon
was therefore not a welcome interruption, but after she
finished listening to Virginia O'Neil, Marian forgot about
her unplanted dahlias.

Kay Wesley, she thought. A born teacher. She'd always
been willing to take on kids who weren't doing well. All her
students were crazy about her. Kay, *missing*. "I have a
couple of errands," she told Virginia. "But I can be on my
way by six. It should take about two hours. Have the
pictures ready. There isn't a kid who went to Garden State
whose face I don't know."

As she hung up, Marian was struck by the memory of
Wendy Fitzgerald, the Garden State senior who twenty

years ago had vanished during a school picnic. Her murderer had been Rudy Kluger, the school handyman. Rudy must be due out of prison around now. Marian's mouth went dry. Not that, please.

At five-forty-five, her overnight bag tossed in the back of her car, she was on her way to New Jersey. Details of that horrible time from the moment Wendy Fitzgerald was reported missing to the day her body was found filled Marian's mind. So engrossed was she in her apprehension about Rudy that she pushed deep into her subconscious the fleeting thought that some incident involving Kay was eluding her.

Virginia put the receiver down. "Miss Martin should be here around eight," she said.

Jimmy Barrott pushed back his chair. "I've gotta check in at the office. If this guidance counselor comes up with anything tonight, anything at all, call this number. Otherwise, I'll be back in the morning." He handed Virginia a somewhat dog-eared card.

The other young women stood up as well. They too would come back to work with Miss Martin tomorrow.

Mike stood up. "I'll get more flyers around. Then I'll go back to the motel. There's always the chance Kay will phone again."

This time he tacked Kay's pictures on telephone poles in the main streets of the towns he drove through and in the large shopping malls in the area. In Pleasantwood he had a near brush with a van that hurtled past him as he drove into the municipal parking lot. Damn fool, Mike thought. He'll kill someone.

Donny had parked the van in the municipal lot behind the Clothes Cartel. When they left the store, he kept his arm tightly around Kay until they reached the van, then he opened the side door and nudged her forward. Frantically, Kay looked at the burly young man about to start his car two parking spaces away. For an instant she made eye contact with him, then felt the tip of the gun pressed against her side. "There's a little kid in the back of that car, Kay," Donny said softly. "You make a sound and that guy and the kid are dead."

Her legs turned to rubber as she stumbled up the step. "Here's the package, honey," Donny said loudly. He watched as the nearby car passed them, then jumped into the van and yanked the door shut.

"You wanted to signal that guy, Kay," he hissed. The gag that he shoved in her mouth was cruelly tight. His hands were rough as he snapped on the handcuffs, shackled her feet and looped the chain through them. He dropped the box beside her on the cot. "Just remember why we bought that dress, Kay, and don't make eyes at other men." He opened the door a crack, looked around, then pushed the door a little wider and slipped out. In the moment that light filtered into the van, Kay's glance fell on a long, thin object on the floor beneath the worktable.

A screwdriver.

If she had the screwdriver, she might be able to unfasten the metal plate from the wall in the cottage, might have a chance to get away while Donny was at work.

The van leaped forward. Donny had to be at the breaking point to drive this fast. Let the police see him, she prayed, please. But then the van slowed perceptibly. He must have realized he was driving too fast.

She turned on her side, slowly dropped her manacled hands and with her fingertips tried to reach the screwdriver. Angry, frustrated tears blurred her eyes and impatiently she shook them away. In the near dark, she could barely make out the long, thin outline of the tool, but no matter how desperately she tried, until the handcuffs burned her wrist bones, it was beyond her reach.

She rolled onto her back and dragged her hands up until they rested on her knees. The cot creaked as she worked her way to a sitting position, swung her legs down, wiggled her body until she was at the very edge of the cot and stretched her legs toward the screwdriver. It was less than an inch beyond her reach. Ignoring the searing pain as the shackles bit into her legs, she pointed the toes of her sandals until she felt the thin blade, then grasped it between the soles of her sandals and pulled the screwdriver back toward the cot. Finally it was directly below her. She swung her legs up, fell onto her back, and again dropped her hands over the side toward the floor. The bruised flesh sent angry pain signals that she no longer felt because her fingers were closing around the handle of the screwdriver, closing around it, holding it, lifting it up.

For a moment she rested, gasping from the effort, exulting in her victory. Then her fingers tightened on the tool as a new thought struck her. How could she get it into the house? There was no place to hide it on her person. The cheap T-shirt clung to her body; the cotton skirt had no pockets; the sandals were open.

They were nearly at the cabin. She could feel the movement of the van as it twisted and turned and bumped along the dirt road. The dress box flipped over and brushed her arm. *The dress box*. The clerk had tied the string around the box with a double knot. She couldn't possibly undo it. Carefully, Kay slipped her fingers between the lid and the bottom of the box, then slowly began to work the screwdriver into the opening her fingers had made. She felt the lid tear at the side.

The van stopped. Desperately she pushed the screwdriver

[198

in, trying to force it between the folds of the dress, and managed to flip the box on its side before the door opened. "We're home, Kay," Donny said tonelessly.

She prayed that he wouldn't notice the angry new marks on her wrists and ankles, the tear in the box. But his movements when he unlocked the chain and cuffs were automatic. He slung the box under his arm without glancing at it, unlocked the cabin door and pushed her inside quickly as though he was afraid of being followed. The inside of the cabin was stifling.

Every instinct told Kay that somehow she must try to calm him. "You're hungry," she told him. "You haven't eaten for hours." She'd fixed lunch when he returned to the cabin at one o'clock but he was too agitated to eat. "I'll make a sandwich for you and some lemonade," she said. "You need it."

He dropped the dress box on the couch and stared at her. "Tell me how much you love me," he ordered. His eyes were wide-pupiled now, his grip on her wrists tighter than the handcuffs had been. His breath came in short, uneven gasps. Terrified, Kay stepped back until the rough velour of the couch touched her legs. He was about to come apart. He would know immediately if she tried to placate him with lies. Instead she said crisply, "Donny, I'd like to hear more about why *you love me*. You say you do, but you always get angry at me. How can I believe you anymore? Read to me from one of your books while I get us something to eat." She forced a note of cold authority into her voice. "Donny, I want you to read to me *now*."

"Of course, I'll read, Miss Wesley." His voice lost the hard edge of anger, became higher-pitched, almost adolescent. "But first I have to check my messages."

He had left the phone on the table by the couch when they went out. Now he took a notebook and pencil from his pocket and pressed the "play" button. There were three messages. One from a hardware store: Could Donny come in tomorrow? Their repairman was out sick. One from the Garden View Motel: They needed extra help installing some electronic equipment for a seminar. They really needed him to work through the evening.

The last call was obviously from an elderly man. There was a distinct wheeze in his halting voice as he identified himself. Clarence Gerber. Could Donny stop by and take a look at the toaster? It wouldn't heat up and the wife was burning all the bread trying to make toast in the oven. A labored laugh followed and "Put us on the top of the list, Donny. Call and let me know when you're coming."

Donny put his notebook away, rewound the tape and this time stood on the couch to set the recorder in the wire box. "I can't stand that old guy, Gerber," he told Kay. "No matter how many times I tell him not to—when I'm fixing something of his—he gets in the van and keeps talking to me while I work. And I have to go to the motel first. They pay me on the spot. I've saved a lot of money for us, Kay." He got down from the couch. "And now I'll read to you. Show me which books you haven't seen yet."

"I sensed from that first day in choir, when Kay put her hands on my chest and told me to sing, that there was something special and beautiful between us," Donny read as he sipped the lemonade. His voice calmed as he spoke of the many times she had phoned him and asked him to come to her. As she sat opposite him, Kay found it almost impossible to swallow. Over and over he repeated how happy he would be to die with her, how glorious it would be to die defending his right to her.

He finished reading and smiled. "Oh, I forgot," he said. Reaching up, he pulled off the curly red wig, revealing his balding head of skimpy brown hair. He leaned down and for the first time removed the blue contact lenses. His own pupils, muddy brown with odd flecks of green, stared at her. "Do you love me best when I'm the real me?" he asked. Without waiting for an answer he came around the table and pulled her up. "I've got to go to the motel. I'll get you settled in the living room, Kay."

At the Clothes Cartel, Vina Howard and her assistant, Edna, spent a gossipy five minutes discussing the couple who had bought the white eyelet dress. "I swear the two of them were on drugs," Edna volunteered. "But listen, we both agreed that dress was a mistake. You were about to reduce it, right? So now you got full price. And cash at that."

Vina agreed. "But I still say he was weird-looking. He dyes his hair. I could swear it." The door opened and a new customer came in. Vina helped her select several skirts, then led her to the dressing area. Her burst of indignation startled both Edna and the customer. "Look," Vina exploded. With a trembling finger she pointed to the jagged *H* on the wall. "She was worse than he was," she fumed. "Now we won't have enough paper to fix both walls. I wish I had my hands on her." Even the customer's sympathetic exclamations and Edna again pointing out that she had sold the eyelet dress full price did not placate Vina's sense of outrage.

Vina continued to churn inwardly, to the point that at six o'clock when she closed the shop and started to walk the three blocks home, she stared straight at the poster dangling from the telephone pole and it did not register on her consciousness that the woman whose face she was seeing was the same miserable creature who had wrecked the rest of her wallpaper.

It was nearly nine o'clock when Mike arrived back at the Garden View Motel. The night had become hot and muggy, and beads of perspiration formed on his forehead as soon as he left the air-conditioned car. He began walking toward the motel. A wave of dizziness made him stop and steady himself against the car he was passing, a dark gray van. He realized that he'd eaten nothing since the sandwich at Virginia's home. He went directly to the room and checked the recorder. There were no messages.

The coffee shop was still open. Only three or four booths were occupied. He ordered a sliced-steak sandwich and coffee. The waitress offered a sympathetic smile. "You're the one whose wife is missing. Good luck. I'm sure it will turn out fine. I have a feeling."

"Thank you." I wish to God I had that feeling, Mike thought. On the other hand, at least people were noticing Kay's picture.

The waitress left him and returned with a take-out bag and a check for the man seated two booths away. "Working late tonight, aren't you, Donny?" she asked.

It was after six o'clock when Donny pulled away in the van. As soon as the sound of the engine faded, Kay worked her hand into the dress box for the screwdriver. If she could free the metal plate from the wall, she might be able to get to the phone. But as she studied the thick padlock on the cage, she knew that would be hopeless. It was the metal plate or nothing.

She pulled herself over to the plate and crouched on the floor. The screws were so tightly in place they might have been welded to the plate. The screwdriver was small. Minutes passed, a half hour, an hour. Unaware of the heat, of the perspiration that soaked her body, of the exhaustion in her fingers, she worked on. Finally she was rewarded. One of the screws began to turn. With paralyzing slowness, it yielded. Finally it was completely loose. Carefully she tight-

[202

ened it just enough to keep it from wobbling and began on the next screw. How much time had passed? How long would Donny be gone?

After a while numbness took over. She worked like a robot, heedless of the pain shooting through her hands and arms, the cramps in her legs. She had just felt the second screw begin to move when she realized that the faint sound she had heard was the van. Frantically she dragged herself to the couch, slipped the screwdriver into the springs, and picked up the book Donny had left on the couch.

The door creaked open. Donny's heavy footsteps resounded across the floorboards. He was holding a bag in his hand. "I brought you a hamburger and a soda, Kay," he told her. "I saw Mike Crandell in the coffee shop. Your picture is all over the place. It wasn't a good idea for you to make me take you shopping. We're going to move up our wedding a day. I have to go to the motel in the morning—they'll think it's funny if I don't show up. And they owe me money. But when I come back, we'll get married and clear out of here."

The decision seemed to have made him calm. He walked over to her and put the bag on the couch. "Aren't you glad that whenever I get something for myself, I think of you?" His kiss on her forehead was lingering.

Kay tried not to show revulsion. At least in the dim light he wouldn't notice how swollen her hands were. And he was going to the motel to work tomorrow morning. That meant she had just a few hours left before she disappeared with him.

Donny cleared his throat. "I'm going to be such a nervous bridegroom, Kay," he said. "Let's practice our wedding vows now. 'I, Donald, take thee, Kay . . .' "

He had totally memorized the traditional marriage service. Kay's mind was filled with the memory of saying, "I,

203]

Katherine, take thee, Michael." Oh Mike, she thought, Mike.

"Well, Kay?" The edgy tone was returning to Donny's voice.

"I don't have as good a memory as you," she said. "Maybe you'd better write the words down so I can practice tomorrow when you're at work."

Donny smiled. In the dim, shadowy light, his eyes seemed deep in their sockets, his face thin to the point of being skeletal. "I think that would be nice," he said. "Now, why don't you eat your hamburger?"

That night Kay kept her eyes resolutely closed, forced her breathing to sound even. She was aware of Donny drifting back and forth and watching her, but her mind was focused only on the fact that even if she did manage to get the metal plate loose before he came back, there was no guarantee that she could escape him. How far could she go in these unfamiliar woods, with one foot shackled and carrying the weight of the plate and the chain?

The traffic was heavy on Route 95 South. At six-thirty, Marian Martin realized that the slight persistent headache she was developing was probably the result of having eaten only a small sandwich for lunch. A cup of tea and a roll, she thought longingly. But the sense of urgency that was steadily building within her kept her foot on the accelerator until at seven-fifty she pulled into the driveway of Virginia O'Neil's home in Jefferson Township.

Virginia had cheese and crackers and a chilled decanter of wine waiting in the living room. Gratefully Marian nibbled the brie, sipped Chablis, and absorbed the pleasantly furnished room with its grand piano covered with sheet music in one alcove.

[204

The sheet music triggered Marian's memory. "You played the piano in Kay Wesley's choir class, didn't you?"

"Not for the whole year. Just the last semester Kay taught."

"*What am I trying to remember about that class?*" Marian wondered aloud, impatiently.

Dinner was a lemon chicken casserole with a wild rice mix and a salad, but hungry as she was, Marian barely knew what she was swallowing. She insisted on studying the reunion pictures while she ate. Rudy Kluger had been tall and thin. He'd been in his early thirties when he murdered Wendy Fitzgerald. That means he'd be in his fifties now. Marian skimmed the pictures quickly. The earliest graduates would be about forty. There shouldn't be too many older men in the photos.

There weren't. The few she saw did not remotely resemble Rudy. As she went through the pictures, Virginia filled her in on the fact that Mike was distributing Kay's picture in local towns, that the detective on the case at first seemed to doubt this was a legitimate disappearance but now was actively helpful. "He'll be at his office till pretty late tonight, I gather," Virginia said. "He told me to phone if we think we've come across anything." She moved her chair to sit next to Marian as Jack cleared the table and set out coffee cups. Virginia picked up one picture. "You see," she said, "this was right at the end. Kay had just finished a hot dog. She started saying good-bye to the people around her. I was the last one she spoke to. Then she walked through the path to the parking lot."

Marian studied the picture. Kay was standing very near the path. But something caught Marian's eye in the woods leading to the parking lot. "Have you a magnifying glass?" she asked.

A few minutes later, they were in agreement. Almost hidden behind a big elm tree near the parking lot was something that might be a man trying to avoid being seen. "This probably means absolutely nothing," Marian said, trying to keep her voice steady. "But maybe it would be a good idea for me to talk to that detective now."

Jimmy Barrott was at his desk when the call came. He was as a matter of fact studying the files of one Rudy Kluger who twenty years ago had "killed and murdered" a sixteen-year-old student at Garden State High after waylaying her in the woods near the picnic area. Rudy Kluger had been released from Trenton State Prison six weeks ago and had already violated his parole by not reporting to his parole officer.

Jimmy Barrott felt a weight settle in his chest as he listened to the former guidance counselor tell him that in one picture she thought she saw someone lurking in the woods just as Kay Crandell was leaving and that she had this horrible worry about Rudy Kluger.

"Miss Martin," Jimmy Barrott said. "I'll tell you straight. Rudy Kluger is out of jail. We've got an alert out for him now. But will you do me a favor? Pretend that Kluger doesn't exist. Go over those pictures with an open mind. I don't know why, but I have a feeling you're going to come up with something that will help us."

He was absolutely right about having an open mind, she knew. Marian hung up the phone and began studying the pictures again.

At eleven-thirty, she could not keep her eyes open. "I'm not as young as I used to be," she said apologetically.

The guest room was at the other end of the second floor from the nursery. Even so, Marian vaguely heard one of the twins wailing in the middle of the night. She fell back to sleep but in that brief wakening time realized that something was bothering her, something she had seen in the photos that was absolutely vital to remember.

Clarence Gerber did not sleep well that Friday night. There was nothing Brenda enjoyed more for breakfast than toaster waffles and the toaster hadn't worked for two days. As Brenda said, there was no use buying a new one when Donny Rubel could fix the old one good as new for ten dollars.

On that restless night, Clarence reflected that the real problem with retirement was you didn't have anything to do when you woke up and that meant you had nothing to talk about. Now Brenda's two sisters hung around the house so much he never could get a word in edgewise. They always cut him off when he began to talk.

At five in the morning as Brenda rumbled and snorted next to him, as far removed from his body on the double bed as she could be without falling off it, Clarence conceived his plan. Maybe it wasn't worth Donny's time to drive around for a ten-dollar job. But Clarence had worked up a solution. Once or twice, he hadn't had any cash when Donny fixed something, so he'd mailed a check to Donny. He had his address. Someplace in Howville. Timber Lane. That was it. Near those lakes where Clarence used to go swimming when he was a kid. Later in the morning, he'd find Donny's house, leave the toaster if Donny was out and a note saying he'd pick it up as soon as Donny had it ready.

Sleep made Clarence's eyelids begin to droop. He had a half-smile on his face as he dozed off. It was good to have a plan, to have something to do when you woke up.

Long before dawn, Kay heard the sounds of noisy activity in the living room. What was Donny doing? The thump of objects being dropped. Donny was packing. The inevitability of what those pulling and tugging sounds meant caused Kay to clamp her hands in fists over her mouth. If ever she needed to stay calm to keep him from becoming suspicious, it was in these next few hours. The only chance she had to escape him would be when he completed his final jobs and deliveries this morning. If he suspected anything, he would leave with her immediately.

She was able to pretend a drowsy smile when he handed her a cup of coffee at seven o'clock. "You're so thoughtful, Donny," she murmured as she sat up, again careful to tuck the blankets high under her arms.

He looked pleased. He was wearing dark blue trousers and a short-sleeved white shirt. Instead of his usual sneakers he had on highly polished light brown shoes. He had obviously taken special pains with his hair. It was plastered close to his skull as though he'd used hairspray. His mud-colored eyes smoldered with excitement. "I have it all figured out, Kay," he told her. "I'll pack most of the stuff in the van before I leave. That way, the minute I get back we can be married and have our wedding brunch. It has to be brunch because I don't want to wait until tonight. Then we'll just take off. I'm going to leave a message on the recorder right now that I'm on an extended vacation. I'll tell my best customers this morning that I'm getting married. That way, nobody will think it funny if we don't come back for a long time."

He was obviously pleased with his plans. He bent over and kissed the top of Kay's head. "Maybe when you have a baby, we'll go visit my mother. She always laughed at me when I told her I never got anywhere with girls. She used to say that the only way I'd ever get a girl was to tie her up. But when she sees how pretty you are and how much we love our baby, I bet she apologizes."

He would not let Kay dress before breakfast. "Just put on

[208

your robe." The intensity in his body was approaching fever pitch. She did not want to walk around in the sheer, clinging nightgown and robe.

"Donny, it's awfully chilly. Lend me your raincoat while we wait."

He had left out a few utensils and the coffeepot, toaster, two plates. Everything else was packed. "Most of the time we'll be staying in tents and cabins until we get to Wyoming, Kay. You like roughing it, don't you?"

She had to bite her lips to hold back shrieks of hysterical laughter. She had considered furnished condos, many of them very attractive, as "roughing it." Mike. Mike. The thought of his name changed the approaching laughter into a flood of tears. Don't, she warned herself, don't.

"Are you crying, Kay?" Donny leaned across the table and peered at her. Somehow she swallowed back the need to weep.

"Of course not." She managed to sound breathless and teasing. "Every bride gets the premarital jitters."

The broad separation of his lips from his teeth was a caricature of a smile. "Finish your breakfast, Kay. You've got to do your packing."

He produced a bright red suitcase. "Surprise! I bought it for you." But he refused to allow her to put on jeans and a T-shirt. "No, Kay. Pack everything except your wedding dress."

At nine-thirty he left, promising he wouldn't be gone more than two or three hours. In the living room his two old suitcases surrounded her new red one. Only the poster with them in the prom picture remained on the wall. "We'll exchange our vows in front of it," Donny had said.

The eyelet dress was too tight at the shoulders. It pulled and then tore as she reached deep into the springs of the couch for the screwdriver. Kay grasped the screwdriver in her hand, then laid it down and carefully shredded the scrap of paper on which Donny had written the marriage vows for her. He was going to kill her anyhow. She might as well defy him here, where at least her body might someday be found and Mike would be free to stop looking for her.

With the calmness of desperation, she picked up the screwdriver, got up from the couch, and walked to the metal plate, the heavy chain dragging with her. She crouched down, undid the already loosened screw, dropped it onto the floor, and put the head of the screwdriver into the second screw, the one that had already begun to loosen last evening.

Mike arrived at the O'Neil home at nine o'clock.

It was a beautiful June day, brilliant with sunlight. Incongruous that anything could be wrong on a day like this, Mike thought. As though in a dream, he saw a young man on the neighboring lawn turning on a sprinkler. All around him, people were doing ordinary Saturday morning chores, or going to play golf, or taking their kids on outings. For the last three hours, *he'd* been nailing more copies of Kay's picture to telephone poles around local swim clubs.

He rapped on the screen door, then let himself in. The others were already around the kitchen table. Virginia and Jack O'Neil, Jimmy Barrott, Virginia's three classmates. Mike was introduced to Marian Martin. He immediately sensed the additional tension in the room. Dreading to ask, he looked squarely at Jimmy Barrott. "Tell me what you know."

"We don't *know* anything," Jimmy Barrott told him. "We *think* Miss Martin may have spotted someone hiding on the path just when Kay was leaving the picnic. We're having that print blown up now. We're not even sure that it isn't a tree branch or something." He hesitated as though

[210

he was about to go on, then said, "I suggest we don't waste time. Let's keep on identifying the people in these pictures."

Minutes passed. Mike sat helplessly. There wasn't any way he could help. He thought about driving to towns farther away that he hadn't yet covered with Kay's picture, but something held him here. He had the sense of time running out. He was sure everyone did.

At nine-thirty, Marian Martin shook her head impatiently. "I thought I'd know every face, fool that I was. People change so. What I need is a list of the students who signed up for the reunion. That will help."

"It's Saturday," Virginia said. "The office is closed. But I'll call Gene Pearson at home. He lives four blocks from the school. He's the principal at Garden State," she told Mike.

"I've met him." Mike thought of Pearson's earlier reluctance.

But when he arrived a scant thirty minutes later, it was obvious that, like Jimmy Barrott, Gene Pearson had changed his attitude. He was unshaven; he looked as though he had thrown on the clothes nearest at hand; he apologized for taking so long.

Pearson handed Marian the list of people who had attended the reunion. "How can I help?" he asked.

The phone rang. They all jumped. Virginia picked up the receiver. "It's for you," she told Jimmy Barrott.

Mike tried to decipher Jimmy's expression but could not. "Okay. Read him his stinking Miranda warnings and make sure he signs the statement," Jimmy said. "I'll be right down."

The room was deathly quiet. Jimmy replaced the receiver and looked at Mike. "We've been trying to track down a guy named Rudy Kluger who's just been released from prison. He served twenty years for murdering a girl whom he abducted from the picnic area near Garden State High."

Mike's chest tightened as he waited.

Jimmy moistened his lips. "This may have nothing to do with your wife's disappearance, but they just picked up Kluger in those same woods. He tried to waylay a young woman jogger."

"And he may have been there on Wednesday," Mike said.

"It's possible."

"I'll go with you." *Kay*, Mike thought, *Kay*.

As if suddenly feeling their task was hopeless, everyone at the table laid down the pictures. One of Virginia's classmates began to sob.

"Mike, Kay *did* phone you night before last," Virginia reminded him.

"But not last night. And now Kluger is trying to pick up someone else."

Mike walked behind Jimmy Barrott to the car. He was aware that he must be having a shock reaction. He felt absolutely nothing, not pain nor sorrow nor anger. Again he whispered Kay's name but it evoked no emotion.

Jimmy Barrott was backing the car from the driveway when Jack O'Neil dashed out of the house. "Hold it!" he shouted. "Your office is on the phone. A woman named Vina Howard saw one of those posters with Kay's picture and swears Kay was in her dress shop in Pleasantwood yesterday afternoon."

Jimmy Barrott slammed on the brakes. He and Mike jumped from the car and rushed into the house. Jimmy grabbed the phone. Mike and the others crowded around him. Jimmy asked questions and barked instructions. He hung up and addressed Mike.

"This Howard woman and her assistant both swear it was Kay. She was with some guy in his twenties. The Howard woman thought they were high on something, but after she talked to my people, she realized Kay was probably terrified. Kay scratched the letter *H* on the wall in the dressing room."

"A guy in his *twenties*," Mike exclaimed. "That means it can't be Kluger." Relief mingled with new dread. "She tried to write something in the dressing room." His voice choked as he whispered, "A word starting with *H* . . ."

"She might have been trying to write *HELP*," Jimmy Barrott snapped. "The point is at least we know she wasn't with Kluger."

"But what was she doing in a dress shop?" Jack O'Neil asked.

Jimmy Barrott's face registered disbelief. "I know it sounds crazy, but she was buying a wedding dress."

"I've got to talk to that woman," Mike said.

"She and her assistant are going to be here as fast as a squad car can deliver them," Jimmy Barrott told him. He pointed to the table. "There's a good chance they can pick out the guy your wife was with from those pictures."

Clarence Gerber was astonished to see the change in the way things looked on the approach to Howville. In his day it had been really rustic, with mountains and the hidden lakes. It never developed like most of the towns around. Pollution had set in years ago. Waste from factories had wrecked the swimming and fishing. But he wasn't prepared for the absolute desolation of the area. Houses were rotting away like they'd been abandoned forever. Junk and wrecked cars were piles of rust in the gullies off the road. Wonder why a fellow like Donny Rubel would stick himself out here? Clarence thought.

Memories long buried came back to him. Timber Lane wasn't directly off the highway. He should take that fork down the road a mile or two, go about five miles, then make a right on a dirt road that turned into Timber Lane.

213]

Clarence was pleased with the sunny day, pleased that his eleven-year-old car was behaving so well. He'd just had the oil changed and even though it puffed a little on hills, "just like me," he'd say, it was a good heavy automobile. Not like the pieces of tin they call cars today and stick with price tags that in his day would have bought a mansion.

Brenda's sisters had arrived before he'd even had a cup of coffee. They all were glad to see him on his way, all full of the talk of that fellow who was nailing pictures of his missing wife all over the county. Clarence tried to picture Brenda missing. He chuckled. They'd never sue him for disturbing the peace hammering her picture around.

He found the fork in the road. Stay to the right, he told himself. The sign for Timber Lane might be gone, but he'd know it when he saw it. The toaster was beside him on the seat. He'd remembered to bring a blank sheet of paper and an envelope. If Donny wasn't home, he'd write a note. Maybe when he came back to pick up the toaster, Donny and he could have a nice visit. Donny sure must get lonely living around here. Didn't seem like there was a soul for miles around.

The second screw was on the floor. The third one was beginning to work loose. Kay rotated her weight from side to side as she turned the handle of the screwdriver. She sensed some slack developing in it. Oh God, please don't let it break. How long had he been gone? At least an hour? The phone had rung twice and the caller received the message about the extended vacation, but Donny did not call. She straightened up and brushed the perspiration from her forehead. A lightheadedness warned her that she was nearing exhaustion. Her legs were cramped. Hating to waste the time, she stood up and stretched. She turned and her glance fell on the prom photo on the opposite wall. Sickened, she dropped back into the crouch and with a new burst of energy twisted the handle of the screwdriver. Suddenly it was twirling in her hand. The third screw was free. She pulled it out and for the first time dared to hope that she might really have a chance.

And then she heard it, the sound of a car, the squeal of brakes. No, no, no. Numbly she laid the screwdriver on the floor and folded her hands. Let him see what she was doing. Let him kill her here and now.

At first she thought she was fantasizing. It couldn't be. But it was. Somebody was thumping on the door. An old man's voice was calling, "Hey, anybody home?"

The wailing of the siren in the squad car, the mad dash through red lights made the ten-mile ride from Pleasant-wood to the O'Neil home in Jefferson Township seem an eternity to Vina Howard and her assistant, Edna. *I saw that woman's picture last night, Vina reproached herself silently, and all I worried about was that wallpaper. If only . . .* It should have been obvious that there was something wrong. That fellow was in such a hurry. She insisted on trying on the dress, tried to stall by asking for other dresses. He opened the curtain of the dressing area as though he didn't trust her. And all I thought about was wallpaper.

Jimmy Barrott cut Vina off when she tried to tell all this at the O'Neil home. "Mrs. Howard, please. We believe that whoever abducted Kay Crandell may be in these pictures. Won't you study them now? You're sure he had red hair? Sure he had blue eyes?"

"Absolutely," Vina said. "In fact, didn't we comment that he looked as though he'd just had his hair set?"

Marian Martin got up from the table. "Sit here. I want to go over the list again." The terrible gnawing feeling that she had missed something—why was it exploding inside her?

She walked into the recreation room. Gene Pearson followed her.

Virginia beckoned to her friends. They clustered on a semicircular couch across the room from Marian Martin and Gene Pearson.

Mike stood at the table watching the earnest faces of the two middle-aged women who had seen Kay yesterday. Pleasantwood. He had been there. "What time did you say Kay was in your shop?" he asked Vina.

"Around three o'clock. Maybe quarter past or so."

He had left this house yesterday at three o'clock and driven directly to Pleasantwood. He must have been in that town when Kay was there. The irony made him want to smash the wall with his fists.

Jack O'Neil was stacking the prints after Vina and Edna rejected them. "You couldn't miss him," Vina told Jimmy Barrott. "All you have to do is look for that head of hair." She paused and picked up one picture. "You know, it's funny. There's something about this one . . ."

"What is?" Jimmy Barrott snapped.

"There's something so familiar." Vina bit her lip in irritation. "Oh, I'm wasting time. I know what it is. I'm looking at *his* picture." She pointed into the den where Gene Pearson was going over the reunion list with Marian.

Edna took the picture from her. "I see what you mean, but . . ." Her voice trailed off. She continued to study the picture. "It sounds silly," she said, "but there's something about this man with the beard and dark glasses . . ."

In the den, Marian Martin was studying the list of alumni from a different viewpoint. She was searching for a name that for some reason she'd let slip by. She was just beginning to read the R list when something that Virginia was saying caught her attention.

"Remember how we all wanted to dress like Kay Wesley?

[216

She could have been prom queen when she chaperoned our prom."

The prom, Marian Martin thought. That's what I've been trying to remember. Donny Rubel, that odd, withdrawn boy who had such a crush on Kay. Her fingers raced down the page. He had signed up for the reunion, but she absolutely had not seen him in any of the pictures. That was why his name hadn't jumped out at her.

"Virginia," she asked, "did any of you see Donny Rubel at the reunion?"

Virginia looked at her classmates. "I didn't see him," she said slowly. The others nodded in agreement. "I've heard he has some kind of fix-it business, but he was always a loner," Virginia continued. "I doubt if he bothered with anyone from school after we graduated. I think I'd have noticed him if he showed up for the reunion."

"Donny Rubel," Gene Pearson interrupted. "I'm *sure* I spoke to him. He even talked about his fix-it business. I asked if he'd speak on career day. It was right at the end of the picnic. He was in such a rush, he brushed me off."

"A little heavyset," Marian snapped. "Dark brown hair, brown eyes. Just under six feet tall."

"No. This guy was pretty skinny. He had a beard and damn little hair. In fact I was surprised when he said he graduated only eight years ago. Wait a minute." Gene Pearson stood up, and ran a hand over the stubble of beard on his face. "He's in one of those pictures with me. Let me get it."

As one, Pearson, Marian Martin, Virginia, and her classmates raced from the den into the kitchen. Vina Howard had just grabbed the picture of Pearson and Donny Rubel from her assistant's hand.

"He wore a wig!" Vina shrieked. "That's why we thought his hair looked so set. That's the man who came into my shop."

217]

Marian Martin, Virginia, and her friends stared at the thin, bearded stranger whom none of them had recognized. But Gene Pearson was shouting, "That's Rubel! That's Rubel!"

Jimmy Barrott grabbed the list from Marian's hand. Donny Rubel's address was next to his name. "Timber Lane, Howville," he said. "That's about fifteen miles from here. The squad car is outside," he told Mike. "Let's go."

Clarence Gerber could not believe his ears. A woman's voice inside the house kept shouting at him to go for help, to phone the police, to tell them she was Kay Crandell. But suppose this was some kind of joke or whoever was in there was on drugs or something. Clarence decided to try to take a look inside. But it was impossible to force the doors or shutters open.

"Don't waste time," Kay shouted. "He'll be back any minute. Go for help. He'll kill you if he finds you here."

Clarence gave one last pull at the shutter on the front window. It was bolted from the inside. "Kay Crandell," he said aloud, now realizing why the name was familiar. That was the woman Brenda and her sisters were talking about this morning, the one whose husband was putting up posters. He'd better get to the police fast. Totally forgetting the toaster he had set down on the porch, Clarence got back in his car and tried to coax speed from the aging engine as it wheezed and groaned up the twisting, bumpy dirt road.

Kay heard the car pull away. *Let him be in time, let him be in time.* How far was it to a phone? How long would it be before the police would get here? Ten minutes? Fifteen? Half an hour? It might be too late. The fourth screw was still tightly in place. She could never work it free. But maybe. With three screws missing, she was able to use the screwdriver to force a corner of the metal plate away from the

[218

wall. She began to work the chain into the opening until she could grasp it in both hands. She arched her back, straightened her arms, and dragged the chain with her until she was rewarded by a crunching, ripping sound; then she toppled backward as the metal plate separated from the wall, a chunk of aging plaster still clinging to it.

Kay stood up, feeling the thin trickle of blood where her head had grazed a corner of the couch. The metal plate was heavy. She grasped it under one arm, looped the chain around her wrist, and started for the door.

The familiar sound of the van driving into the clearing assaulted her ears.

The excitement building in Donny had reached fever pitch. He'd gotten rid of every single job. He'd explained to all his customers that he was getting married and taking a long vacation. They'd looked surprised, then said how pleased they were for him and they'd sure miss him. Said let us know when you come back.

He'd never come back. Everywhere he went, he kept seeing Kay's pictures. Mike Crandell was looking all over for her. Donny felt for the gun in the inside pocket of his jacket. He'd kill Mike and Kay and himself before he'd lose her.

But he didn't want to think about that. It was going to be fine. He had taken care of everything. He and Kay would get married in a few minutes and have their wedding brunch. He'd bought champagne and some stuff from the deli and a coconut cake that looked a little like a wedding cake. Then they'd go away. By tonight they'd be in Pennsylvania. He knew some good camping grounds. He fretted that he hadn't had time to buy a wedding nightgown for Kay. But the one she'd been wearing was real pretty.

He reached the fork in the road. Another ten minutes. He

hoped Kay had memorized the wedding service. A June bride. He wished he'd thought of buying her flowers. He'd make it up to her. "Your husband will take care of you, Kay," he said aloud. The sun was so bright that even with the dark glasses he began to squint. Happy is the bride that the sun shines on today. He thought of Kay's sun-streaked hair. Tonight her head would be lying on his shoulder. Her arms would be around him. She'd be telling him how much she loved him.

He heard before he saw the old car approaching. He had to pull to one side to let it pass. He got a glimpse of straggly white hair, of some skinny little guy bent over the wheel. He had posted big NO TRESPASSING signs at the last bend on the road to his place, and anyhow nobody would bother going near a boarded-up house. Even so, Donny felt his body tingle with anger. He didn't want people snooping around.

Recklessly he pressed his foot on the accelerator. The van bounced along the twisted road. Straggly white hair. That car. He'd seen it before. As he brought the van to a halt, Donny remembered yesterday's phone call. *Clarence Gerber*. That was the guy in the car.

He jumped out of the van and started to run toward the house, then saw the toaster on the porch. He remembered the intense way Gerber was driving, like he was trying to make the car go faster. *Gerber was going for the police.*

Donny jumped back into the van. He'd catch up with Gerber. That old wreck he was driving couldn't go more than forty miles an hour. He'd run him off the road. And then . . . Donny started the van, his mouth a thin, unforgiving line. And then he'd come back here and take care of Kay, who he knew now had betrayed him.

Mike sat beside Jimmy Barrott in the back of the squad car, listening as the siren wailed and screeched. Kay is fifteen miles away, twelve miles away, eight miles away. "God, please if You exist and I know You do, anything You want of me, I swear I'll do it. Please. Please," he thought.

The landscape had changed sharply. Suddenly they were no longer in pretty suburban towns with well-kept lawns and budding rosebushes. The highway was surrounded by junk-filled gullies. The traffic had almost disappeared.

Jimmy Barrott was studying a county road map. "I bet there hasn't been a street sign around here for twenty years," he muttered. "We'll hit a fork in the road in about a mile," he barked to the patrolman at the wheel. "Veer to the right."

They were almost at the fork when the driver jammed on the brakes to avoid hitting an old man who was swaying in the middle of the road, whose blood-encrusted hair clung to his head. In the gully below they could see a car burst into flames. Jimmy flung open the door, jumped out, and lifted the old man into the squad car.

Clarence Gerber gasped, "He ran me off the road. Donny Rubel. He's got Kay Crandell."

With total disbelief, Kay heard the screeching of the tires as the van roared back down the road. Donny must have seen the car the old man was driving, must have suspected something. Don't let Donny hurt him, she pleaded to a God who seemed silent and far away. She hobbled to the door, pushed back the bolts, yanked the door open. If that old man was able to make it to the phone, she had a chance. She might be able to hide in the woods until help came. There was no use trying to run away. She could hardly move with the weight she was dragging. Some instinct made her pull the door closed behind her. If Donny searched the house, it would give her a few additional minutes.

221]

Where should she try to hide? The brilliant sun was high in the sky, mercilessly finding its way into every opening between the branches of the shaggy, overgrown trees. He would be sure that she'd try for the road. She stumbled toward the woods on the other side of the clearing and headed for a cluster of maple trees. She had barely reached them when the van raced up the road again and stopped. She watched as, gun drawn, Donny walked with deliberate, precise steps toward the house.

"Trust me. I know where I'm going," Clarence Gerber told Jimmy Barrott, his voice uneven and quivering. "I was there five minutes ago."

"The map says—" Jimmy Barrott clearly thought that Gerber was confused.

"Forget the map," Mike ordered. "Do it his way."

"It's kind of a shortcut," Clarence told them. It was hard to talk. He was feeling kind of dizzy. He could hardly believe it had happened. One minute he was driving, fast as he could push his good old car, the next he was being cut off, was being forced to the right. He'd barely had a glimpse of Donny Rubel's van before he'd felt his wheels go off the road. Any other car and he'd have been killed. But he'd hung on to the wheel for dear life until the car stopped turning over. He'd smelled the gas, and knew he had to get out fast. The driver's door was pinned to the ground, but he'd managed to push open the passenger door and then climb up the gully. "Down here," he told the driver. "Listen to me, will you? Now that next right, by the No Trespassing sign. His place is in a clearing a couple hundred yards down."

Mike watched as Jimmy Barrott and the policemen drew their guns. *Kay, be there for me, be there. Be alive. Please.*

[222

The squad car burst into the clearing and came to a stop behind Donny Rubel's fix-it van.

Kay watched as Donny opened the door and kicked it aside. She could almost feel his fury when he realized she was gone. The cabin was less than thirty yards from the clump of trees where she was hiding. *Let him start looking on the road,* she begged.

An instant later, he was framed in the doorway, looking around wildly, the gun pointed straight in front of him. She hugged her arms against her sides. If he ever looked this way, the white eyelet dress would show through the leaves and branches. Any movement would cause the chain to rattle.

She heard the sound of the approaching vehicle at the same moment she saw Donny jump back into the house. But he did not close the door. Instead he stood, waiting. The car pulled in behind the van. Kay saw the flashing red dome. A police car. Be careful, she thought, be careful. He doesn't care whom he kills. She watched as two uniformed police-men emerged from the car. They had parked on the side of the cabin. The windows were boarded up. There was no way they could see Donny, who was now stepping out onto the porch, a reckless caricature of a smile on his face. The back door of the squad car opened. Two men got out. *Mike. Mike was here.* The policemen had drawn their guns. They were moving cautiously against the side of the house. Mike was with them. Donny was tiptoeing across the porch. He would shoot when they turned the corner. He didn't care if he died. *He would kill Mike!*

The clearing was utterly still. Even the squawks of the bluejays and the buzzing of the flies had stopped. Kay had a fleeting sense of the ending of the world. Mike had moved forward. He was only a few feet from the corner of the porch where Donny waited.

Kay stepped from behind the tree. "I'm here, Donny," she called.

She saw him running toward her, tried to press against the tree, felt the bullet graze her forehead, heard the sound of other guns exploding, saw Donny crumple onto the ground. Then Mike was running toward her. Sobbing with joy, Kay stumbled toward the clearing, and into the arms that were rushing to enfold her.

Jimmy Barrott was not a sentimental man, but his eyes were suspiciously moist as he watched Kay and Mike, silhouetted against the trees, holding each other as if they'd never let go.

One of the policemen was bending over Donny Rubel. "He's gone," he told Jimmy.

The other cop had wrapped a bandage around Clarence Gerber's head. "You're a tough one," he told Clarence. "Mostly lacerations as far as I can see. We'll get you to a hospital."

Clarence was absorbing every detail to tell Brenda and her sisters. The way Kay Crandell had tried to draw Donny Rubel's fire, the way Donny had run toward her, shooting at her. The way that young couple were holding on to each other, now crying in each other's arms. He looked around so that later he could describe the cabin. The women would want to know every detail. His glance spotted something on the porch and he hurried over to claim it. Even though he was a hero, it would be just like Brenda to remind him that he had forgotten to bring the toaster home.

LUCKY
DAY

I t was a chilly Wednesday in November. Nora walked quickly, grateful that the subway was only two blocks away. She and Jack had been lucky to get an apartment in the Claridge House when it opened six years ago. With the way prices had skyrocketed for new tenants, they'd never be able to afford one in that building now. And its location on Eighty-seventh and Third made it accessible to subways and buses. Cabs too. But cabs weren't included in their budget.

She wished she'd worn something heavier than the jacket she'd gotten at the wrap party of the last film she'd worked on. But with the name of the film emblazoned on the breast pocket, it was a visible reminder of the fact that she did have solid acting experience.

She stopped at the corner. The light was green, but the traffic was turning, and it was worth anyone's life to attempt to cross. Next week was Thanksgiving. Between Thanksgiving and Christmas, Manhattan would be one long parking lot. She tried not to think that now Jack wouldn't have the Christmas bonus from Merrill Lynch. Over breakfast he'd just admitted that he'd been part of the cutback at Merrill Lynch but was starting a new job today. *Another* new job.

She darted across the street as the light turned red, barely escaping the gypsy cab that charged across the intersection. The driver shouted after her, "You won't keep your looks if you get splattered, honey." Nora spun around. He was giving her the finger. In a reflex action she returned it and then was ashamed of herself. She rushed down the block ignoring window displays, stepping around the sleeping bag lady who was sprawled against a storefront.

She was about to plunge down the subway stairs when she heard her name called. "Hey, Nora, don't you say hello?" Behind the newspaper stand, Bill Regan, his leathery face creased in a smile that revealed overly bright false teeth, reached out a folded copy of the *Times* to her. "You're daydreaming," he accused.

"I guess I am." She and Bill had struck up an acquaintance over their daily morning encounter. A retired deliveryman, Bill filled his days by helping out the blind newsdealer in the morning rush time and then working as a messenger. "Keeps me busy," he'd explained to Nora. "Ever since May died, it's just too lonesome home. Gives me something to do. I meet a lot of nice people and get a chance to gab. May always said I was a great gabber."

DOUBLE VISION

Jimmy Cleary crouched in the bushes outside Caroline's garden apartment in Princeton. His thick brown hair fell on his forehead and he pushed it back with the studied gesture that had become a mannerism. The May evening was unseasonably raw and chilly. Even so, perspiration soaked his sweat suit. He moistened his lips with the tip of his tongue. His whole body tingled with nervous exhilaration.

Five years ago tonight he had made the blunder of a lifetime. He had killed the wrong girl. He, the best actor in the entire world, had fouled up his ultimate scene. Now he was going to rectify that error. This time there would be no mistakes.

The back door of Caroline's apartment opened onto the parking lot. For the last few nights he'd been studying the area. Last night he'd unscrewed the light bulb outside her apartment, so now the back entrance was in deep shadows. It was 8:15; time to go in.

From his pocket he took out a spikelike tool, inserted it in the keyhole, and twisted it until he heard the click of the cylinder. With gloved hands he turned the knob and opened the door just wide enough to slip in. He closed and relocked it. There was an inside chain that she probably fastened at night. That was fine. Tonight she'd lock the two of them in. It gave Jimmy distinct pleasure to contemplate Caroline carefully securing the place. It would be like the ghost story that ended, "Now, we're locked in for the night."

He was in the kitchen, which opened directly from an archway into the living room. Last night he'd hidden outside the kitchen window and observed Caroline. There were plants on the sill, so the shade didn't go all the way down. At ten o'clock, she came out of the bedroom wearing red-and-white-striped pajamas. While she watched the news, she exercised, bending from the waist so that her blond hair flew from shoulder to shoulder.

She went back to her bedroom where she probably read for a while because the light stayed on for about an hour. He could just as easily have finished her then, but his sense of drama wanted him to wait for the exact anniversary.

The only light came from the outside streetlamps, but there weren't many places to hide in the apartment. He could fit under her bed, which had a velvet dust ruffle. It was an interesting idea: He could wait there, while she read, got sleepy, turned off the light; wait until she stopped moving and her breath became even. Then he could silently ease his

[256

body out, kneel beside her, watch her the way he had watched the other girl, and then wake her up. But before he decided, he'd check other possibilities.

When he opened the door of the bedroom closet, a light went on automatically. Jimmy caught a glimpse of an almost full traveling bag. Quickly he closed the door. There was no place to hide here.

Imagine a woman who has less than two hours to live. Does she sense it? Does she go about her normal routine? These were the hypothetical questions Cory Zola had thrown at the acting class one night. Cory was a famous teacher who only took on students he thought had the potential to become stars. He put me in his private class the first time I auditioned for him, Jimmy reminded himself now. He knows talent.

There was no place to hide in the living room. The front door, however, opened directly into it, and there was a closet at a right angle. The closet door was open a couple of inches. Swiftly he moved over to inspect it.

This closet didn't have an automatic light. He pulled a pencil-thin flashlight from his pocket and shone the beam on the interior, which was unexpectedly deep. A heavy dress bag, encased in voluminous layers of plastic, hung at the front. This was the reason the door wasn't closed. It would have squashed the dress. He'd bet anything it was her wedding gown. Last night when he'd followed her, she'd stopped at a bridal shop and stayed nearly half an hour, probably for a final fitting. Maybe they'd bury her in this dress.

The cascade of plastic created a perfect hiding place. Jimmy stepped into the closet, slid between two winter coats and pulled them together. Suppose Caroline went into this closet and found him? The worst that could happen would be that he couldn't kill her exactly as he'd planned. But those traveling bags in the other closet were almost full. She probably was just about packed. He knew she was flying to St. Paul in the morning. She was getting married next week. She *thought* she was getting married next week.

Jimmy eased out of the closet. At five o'clock, in his rented car, he'd been waiting for Caroline outside the State House in Trenton. She'd worked late. He'd followed her to the restaurant where she met Wexford. He'd stood outside, and didn't leave until, through the window, he'd seen them order. Then he came directly here. She wouldn't be back for another hour at least. He helped himself to a can of soda from the refrigerator and settled on the couch. It was time to prepare himself for the third act.

It had begun five and a half years ago, that last semester at Rawlings College of Fine Arts in Providence. He'd been in the theater program studying acting. Caroline had majored in directing. He'd been in a couple of the plays she directed. As a junior he'd played Biff in *Death of a Salesman*. He'd been so fantastic that half the school started calling him Biff.

Jimmy sipped the soda. In memory he was back at college on the set of the senior play. He had the lead. The president of the college had invited an old friend, a Paramount producer, as his guest for opening night, and the word was out that the producer was looking for new talent. From the beginning he and Caroline hadn't seen eye to eye on his interpretation of the part. Then two weeks before opening night, she'd taken the part from him and given it to Brian Kent. He could still see her, her blond hair in a Psyche knot, her plaid shirt tucked inside her jeans, her earnest, worried look. "You're just not quite right, Jimmy. But I think you'd be perfect as the second lead, the brother."

Second lead. The brother had about six lines. He'd

[258

wanted to plead, to beg, but had known it was useless. When Caroline Marshall made a casting change she couldn't be budged. And he'd known in his gut that somehow being the lead in that play was crucial to his career. In that split second he'd made up his mind to kill her, and right away started performing. He'd laughed, a lighthearted, chagrined chuckle, and said, "Caroline, I've been working up the courage to tell you I'm so far behind in term papers, I can't even think about acting."

She'd fallen for it. And looked relieved. The Paramount producer had come. He'd invited Brian Kent to the Coast to test for a new series. The rest, as we say in Hollywood, Jimmy thought, was history. After nearly five years, the series was still in the top-ten ratings, and Brian Kent had just signed to do a movie for three million bucks.

Two weeks after graduation Jimmy had gone to St. Paul. Caroline's family's home was practically a mansion, but he'd quickly found that the side door was unlocked. He'd made his way along the downstairs floor, up the wide, sweeping staircase, past the master-bedroom suite. The door was ajar. The bed was empty. Then he'd opened the next bedroom door and seen her: lying there asleep. He could still see the outlines of her room, the brass four-poster bed, the silky sheen of the soft, expensive percale sheets. He remembered how he'd bent over her as she lay there curled up in bed, her blond hair gleaming on the pillowcase. He'd whispered, "Caroline," and she'd opened her eyes, looked at him, and said "No."

He'd thrown his arms over her and covered her mouth with his hands. She'd listened, her eyes panicking, while he whispered that he was going to kill her, that if she hadn't taken the lead from him, he'd have been seen by the Paramount producer instead of Brian Kent. Finally he'd said,

259]

"You're not going to direct anything anymore, Caroline. You've got a new role. You're the victim."

She'd tried to pull away from him, but he yanked her back and twisted the cord around her neck. Her eyes had widened, blazing out at him. Her hands had lifted, palms outstretched begging him, then had fallen limp on the sheet.

The next morning he couldn't wait to read the newspapers. "Daughter of Prominent St. Paul Banker Slain." He remembered how he'd laughed, then cried with frustration when he read the first few sentences. *The body of 21-year-old Lisa Marshall was found by her twin sister this morning.*

Lisa Marshall. Twin sister.

The story continued: *The young woman had been strangled. The twins were alone in the family home. Police have been unable to question Caroline Marshall. At the sight of her sister's body, she went into profound shock and is under heavy sedation.*

He'd tell Caroline about that later on tonight. All these years in Los Angeles he'd had a subscription to the Minneapolis-St. Paul papers, watching for any news about the case. Then he read that Caroline was engaged and would be married on May 30—next week. Caroline Marshall, who was a lawyer on the staff of the Attorney General in Trenton, New Jersey, was marrying an associate professor from Princeton University, Dr. Sean Wexford. Wexford had been a graduate student when Jimmy was at Rawlings. Jimmy had him for a psychology course. He wondered when Caroline and Wexford got together. They weren't going around when Caroline was a student at Rawlings. He was sure of that.

Jimmy shook his head. He took the empty soda can out to the kitchen and tossed it in the wastebasket. Caroline might be coming along anytime now. He went into the bathroom and winced at the noisy flush of the toilet. Then with infinite care he stepped into the closet and pulled the winter coats around him. He felt for the length of cord in the pocket of his sweat suit. It was cut from the same roll of heavy fishing tackle he'd used on her sister. He was ready.

"Cappuccino, darling?" Sean smiled across the candlelit table. Caroline's dark blue eyes were pensive with that look of absolute sadness that sometimes came into them. Understandable tonight. It was the anniversary of the last night she'd spent with Lisa.

To try to distract her, he said, "I felt like a bull in a china shop when I picked up your gown this afternoon."

Caroline raised her eyebrows. "You didn't look at it? That's bad luck."

"They didn't let me get near it. The saleslady kept apologizing that they couldn't send it."

"I've been rushing around so much this last month I've lost weight. They had to take it in."

"You're too thin. We'll have to fatten you up in Italy. Pasta three times a day."

"I can hardly wait." Caroline smiled across the table. She loved the bigness of Sean, the way his sandy hair always looked a bit disheveled, the humor in his gray eyes. "My mother phoned this morning. She's still worried that my dress doesn't have sleeves. She reminded me twice that the joke in Minnesota is, 'Which day was summer?' "

"I volunteer to keep you warm. Your dress is in the front closet. By the way, I'd better give you back your extra keys."

"Keep them. If I forget anything, you can bring it out with you next week."

When they left the restaurant Caroline followed him to the roomy Victorian house that would be theirs when they returned from the honeymoon. She was leaving her car in the second garage while they were away. Sean drove his car into the driveway, parked it, and got into hers. She slid over and he drove her home, his arm around her.

Jimmy was proud that even after an hour of standing still, he felt fine. That was because he was in shape from the gym and all the dancing lessons.

He'd spent the past five years studying, knocking on doors, trying to see casting people, getting close and then shut out. To get a good agent, you needed to show you'd had some good roles. To get sent to the good casting people, you needed a hotshot agent. And sometimes he'd hear the ultimate killer: "You're a Brian Kent type, and that isn't helping you."

The memory infuriated Jimmy, and he shook his head. And all of this after his mother had persuaded his father to stake him to a year of what he called "trying to act."

Jimmy felt the old anger again. His father had never liked what he did. When Jimmy was so great in *Death of a Salesman,* had his father been proud? No. He wanted to cheer for a son who was the quarterback, a Heisman Trophy contender.

Jimmy hadn't bothered to ask for more when the money from his father ran out. Every month or so his mother sent him whatever she could squeeze from the house money. The old man might have plenty, but he sure was tight. But boy, would he have loved it if James Junior had been the one to sign Brian Kent's three-million-dollar contract last week. "That's my boy," he'd be yelling.

That's the way the scene would have been played if five years ago Caroline hadn't yanked him from the part and given it to Brian Kent.

Jimmy stiffened. There was a sound of voices at the front

[262

door. Caroline. *She wasn't alone.* A man's voice. Jimmy shrank against the wall. As the door opened and the light was snapped on, he glanced down and froze. The light filtered into the closet. He was sure he couldn't be seen, but the tips of his beat-up running shoes, pointing outward, screamed their presence.

Caroline glanced around the living room as the light went on. Tonight, for some reason, the apartment seemed different, alien. But of course that was only because it was tonight. Lisa's anniversary. She put her arms around Sean and he gently kneaded the back of her neck. "You do know that all evening you've been miles away."

"I always hang on your every word." It was an attempt at lightheartedness that failed. Her voice broke.

"Caroline, I don't want you to be alone tonight. Let me stay with you. Look, I know why you want to be by yourself, and I understand. Go into the bedroom. I'll stretch out on the couch."

Caroline tried to smile. "No, I'm really okay." She wrapped her arms around his neck. "Just hold me tight for one minute and then get out of here," she said. "I'm setting the alarm for six-thirty. I'm better off doing final packing in the morning. You know me. Sharp in the A.M. Fade in the P.M."

"I hadn't noticed." Sean's lips caressed her neck, her forehead, found her lips. He held her, feeling the tension in her slender body.

Tonight she had told him, "Once the anniversary is over, I'm really okay. It's just that the couple of days before, it's as though Lisa is with me. It's a feeling that builds and builds. Like today. But I know it will be fine tomorrow, and I'll go home and get ready for the wedding and be happy."

Reluctantly, Sean released Caroline from his arms. She looked so tired now, and oddly that made her look so

263]

young. Twenty-six, and at this moment she could have passed for one of the kids in his freshman class. He told her that. "But you're much prettier than any of them," he concluded. "It's going to be awfully nice to wake up and look at you first thing in the morning for the rest of my life."

Jimmy Cleary's body was soaked with perspiration. Suppose she let Wexford spend the night here. They'd surely see him in the morning when Caroline took the wedding dress from the closet. They were wrapped up in each other less than a foot from where he was standing. Suppose one of them smelled the perspiration from his body. But Wexford was leaving.

"I'll be here at seven, love," he told Caroline.

And you'll find her the way she found her sister, Jimmy thought. That's how you'll envision her in the morning for the rest of your life.

Caroline bolted the door behind Sean. For an instant she was tempted to reopen it immediately, call out to him, tell him yes, stay with me. I don't want to be alone. But I'm not alone, she thought as she took her hand from the knob. Lisa is so close to me tonight. Lisa. Lisa.

She went into the bedroom and undressed quickly. A hot shower helped to relieve some of the tension she felt in the muscles of her neck and back. She remembered the way Sean's hands had kneaded those muscles. I love him so much, she thought. Her red-and-white-striped pajamas were on the hook on the bathroom door. She'd been shopping for lingerie and nightgowns in a Madison Avenue boutique when she'd spotted them. "If you like them, better make up your mind fast," the salesgirl had said. "We only got in one pair in red. They're comfortable and awfully cute."

One pair. That had decided Caroline. One of the hardest things in these past five years was to break the habit of

[264

buying *two* of everything. For years if she saw something she liked, she'd automatically buy two. Lisa had done the same thing. They were exactly the same size, same height, same weight. Even their parents had trouble telling them apart. When they were juniors in high school, Mother had urged them to buy different gowns for the prom. They'd shopped separately in different stores and arrived home with exactly the same blue and white dotted-swiss gown.

The next year, they'd tearfully agreed with their parents and the school psychologist that they'd be doing themselves a favor if they attended different colleges and did not discuss being an identical twin. "Being close is wonderful," the psychologist had said, "but you've got to think of yourselves as individuals. You're not going to grow to your full capacity unless you give yourselves and each other space."

Caroline had gone to Rawlings, Lisa to Southern Cal. In college it secretly delighted Caroline that people thought she had inscribed her own picture, "To my best friend." They'd even graduated on the same day. Mother had gone to be with Lisa. Dad had come to Caroline's commencement.

Caroline went into the living room, remembered to fasten the chain on the back door, turned on the television, and halfheartedly began bending from side to side. A commercial for life insurance came on. "Isn't it a comfort to know that your family will be taken care of after you're gone?" Caroline snapped off the television. Turning off the living-room light, she rushed into the bedroom and slipped under the covers. Lying on her side, she pulled her legs against her body and buried her face in her hands.

Sean Wexford could not shake off the feeling that he should have flatly refused to leave Caroline. He sat in the car for a few minutes looking at her door. But she needed to be alone. Shaking his head, Sean reached for the car keys.

On the drive home his emotions seesawed between his concern for Caroline and anticipation that a week from tomorrow they'd be married. How astonished he'd been last year when he'd seen her jogging ahead of him on the Princeton campus. She'd been in only one of his classes in Rawlings. In those days he'd been working so hard on his doctoral thesis, he hadn't even thought about dating. That morning a year ago, she'd told him about going to Columbia Law School, clerking for a New Jersey Superior Court judge, and then going to work in the Attorney General's office in Trenton. And, Sean thought, as he steered the car into his driveway, over that first cup of coffee we both knew what was happening to us. He parked Caroline's car behind his own and went into the house smiling at the realization that soon their cars would always be together in the driveway.

Jimmy Cleary was surprised that Caroline had turned off the television so abruptly. He thought again of the questions Cory Zola had thrown at the acting class: *Imagine a woman who has less than two hours to live. Does she sense it? Does she go about her normal routine?* Caroline might be sensing danger. When he was back in class, he'd bring up that question again. "In my opinion," he would say, "there is a quickening of the spirit as it prepares to leave the body." He had a feeling that Zola would find his insight profound.

Jimmy felt a cramp in his leg. He wasn't used to standing perfectly still for so long, but he could do it for as long as necessary. If Caroline's intuition was warning her of danger, she'd be listening for even the smallest sound. These garden-apartment walls weren't thick. One scream and someone might hear her. He was glad she'd left the bedroom door open. He wouldn't have to worry about the door creaking when he went to her.

[266

Jimmy closed his eyes. He wanted to duplicate the exact stance he'd been in when he woke her sister. One knee on the floor beside the bed, his arms ready to wrap around her, his hands in position to clamp over her mouth. Actually he'd knelt for a minute or two before he awakened the other girl. He probably wouldn't chance that luxury now. Caroline would be sleeping lightly. Her spirit would be pounding at her to beware.

Beware. A beautiful word. A word to whisper from the stage. He would have a stage career now. Broadway. Not nearly the pay you got for a film, but prestige. His name on the marquee.

Caroline was his jinx, and she was about to be removed.

Caroline lay curled up in bed, shivering. The soft down comforter could not stop the trembling. She was afraid. So terribly afraid. Why? "Lisa," she whispered, "Lisa, was this the way you felt? Did you wake up? Did you know what was happening to you?" *Did I hear you cry out that night and go back to sleep?*

She still didn't know. It was only an impression, a blurred, dreamy image that came to her in the weeks after Lisa's death. She and Sean had talked it through. "I think I might have heard her. Maybe if I had forced myself awake . . ."

Sean had made her understand that her reaction was typical of families of victims. The "if only" syndrome. In this last year, through him and with him, she'd begun to experience peace, a healing. Except for now.

Caroline turned in the bed and forced herself to stretch out her legs and arms. "Irrational anxiety and profound sadness are symptoms of depression," she had read. Sadness, okay, she thought. It is the anniversary, but I won't give in to the anxiety. Think of the happy times with Lisa. That last evening.

267]

Mother and Dad had left for a bankers' seminar in San Francisco. She and Lisa had ordered pizza with everything on it, drunk wine, and talked their heads off. Lisa's decision to go to law school. Caroline had taken the law-school admittance exams too but still wasn't sure what she wanted to do.

"I really loved being in the theater group," she'd told Lisa. "I'm not a good actress but I can sense good acting. I think I could make a pretty fair director. The play went over well, and Brian Kent, who I just knew was right for the lead, was picked up by a producer. Still, if I get a law degree maybe we can open an office and tell people they're getting double their money's worth."

They'd gone to bed about eleven o'clock. Their rooms adjoined. Usually they left the door open, but Lisa wanted to watch a television show and Caroline was sleepy, so they blew kisses and Caroline closed the door. If only I'd left it open, she thought. I would surely have heard her if she'd had a chance to cry out.

The next morning, she hadn't waked up until after eight. She remembered sitting up, stretching, thinking how good it felt to have college behind her. As a graduation present, she and Lisa had been given a trip to Europe that summer.

Caroline remembered how she'd jumped out of bed, deciding to get coffee and juice and bring it up on a tray to Lisa. She squeezed fresh juice while the coffee perked, then put the glasses and cups and coffeepot on a tray and went up the stairs.

Lisa's door was open a crack. She'd kicked it open and called, "Wake up, my girl. We've got a tennis date in an hour."

And then she'd seen Lisa. Her head slumped unnaturally, the cord biting her neck, her eyes wide open and filled with

[268

fear, her palms extended as though trying to push something back. Caroline had dropped the tray, splashing her legs with the coffee, had managed to stumble to the phone and dial 911 and then scream, scream until her throat broke into a harsh, guttural sound. She awakened in the hospital three days later. She was told that the police found her lying beside Lisa, Lisa's head on her shoulder.

The only clue, the muddied partial print of a running shoe just inside the side door. "And then," as the chief of detectives told them later, "he, or she, was polite enough to scrape the rest of the mud off on the mat."

If only they had found Lisa's murderer, Caroline thought as she lay in the darkness. The detectives all believed that it was someone who had known Lisa. There was no attempt at robbery. No attempt to rape. They'd exhaustively questioned Lisa's friends, her dates at college. There was one young man in her class who had been obsessed by her. He'd remained a strong suspect, but the police could never prove he was in St. Paul that night.

They'd looked into mistaken identity, especially when they learned that neither girl had told her college friends she had an identical twin. "At first we didn't tell because we promised not to. It became a game with us," Caroline said.

"How about friends from college visiting your home?"

"We just didn't bring college friends home. We were glad to have time together during holidays and school breaks."

Oh, Lisa, Caroline thought now. If I only knew why. If I only could have helped you that night. She was not sleepy but was suddenly weary.

At last her eyelids began closing on their own. Oh, Lisa, she thought, I wanted you to have happiness like mine too. If only I could make it up to you.

The window was open a few inches from the bottom. Protective side locks kept it from being raised higher. Now a sharp gust of wind made the shade rattle. Caroline jumped up, realized what had happened, and forced herself to lie back against the pillows. Stop it, she told herself, stop it. Deliberately she closed her eyes and after a while fell into a light dream-filled sleep, a sleep in which Lisa was trying to call her, trying to warn her.

It was time. Jimmy Cleary could sense it. The rustling of the sheets had stopped. There was absolutely no sound coming from the bedroom. He slipped between the garments that had concealed him and eased aside the bag containing Caroline's gown. The hinges gave off a faint rubbing noise when he pushed the closet door open, but there was no reaction from inside the bedroom. He made his way across the living room to the side of the bedroom door. Caroline had a night-light plugged into one of the sockets, and it threw off just enough light so that he could tell she was sleeping restlessly. Her breathing was even but shallow. Several times she turned her head from side to side as though she was protesting something.

Jimmy felt in his pocket for the cord. It was strangely satisfying to know it came from the same roll of tackle he'd used on the sister. This was even the same jogging suit he'd worn five years ago and the same running shoes. He'd known it was a little risky to keep them, just in case the cops ever questioned him, but he'd never been able to throw them away. Instead he'd put them with other stuff in a storage space he rented where nobody asked questions. Of course he'd used a different name.

He tiptoed to the side of Caroline's bed and knelt down. He was able to savor a full minute of watching her before

[270

her eyes fluttered open and his hands snapped around her mouth.

Sean watched the ten o'clock news, realized he had absolutely no sleep in him, and opened a book he'd been wanting to read. A few minutes later he tossed it aside impatiently. Something was wrong. He could feel it as tangibly as though he could see smoke pouring from the next room and know that there was a fire blazing in the house. He'd phone Caroline. See how she was doing. On the other hand, maybe she'd managed to get to sleep. He walked over to the liquor cabinet and poured a generous amount of scotch into a tumbler. A few sips helped him to realize that he was probably acting like a nervous old biddy.

Caroline opened her eyes as she heard her name whispered. It's a nightmare, she thought, I've been dreaming. She started to cry out, then felt a hand clasped on her mouth, a hard, muscular hand that squeezed her cheekbones, that clamped her lips together, that half covered her nostrils. She gasped, fighting for breath. The hand slid down a fraction of an inch and she was able to breathe. She tried to pull away, but now the man was holding her with his other arm. His face was close to hers. "Caroline," he whispered, "I've come to correct my mistake."

The night-light sent eerie shadows onto the bed. That voice. She'd heard it before. The outline of his bold forehead, the square jaw. The powerful shoulders. Who?

"Caroline, the hotshot director."

Now she recognized the voice. Jimmy Cleary. Jimmy Cleary, and in that same instant she knew why. Like a scene from a movie, the moment when she'd told Jimmy he simply wasn't right for the part flashed through

271]

Caroline's mind. He'd taken it so well. Too well. She hadn't wanted to know he was acting. It had been easier to pretend that he agreed with her decision. *And he killed Lisa when he wanted to kill me. It's my fault.* A moan slipped past her lips, disappeared against his palm. *My fault. My fault.*

And then she heard Lisa's voice as clearly as though Lisa was whispering in her ear, telling secrets again, the way they had as children. *It's not your fault, but it's your fault if you let him kill again. Don't let this happen to Mother and Dad. Don't let it happen to Sean. Grow old for me. Have babies. Name one after me. You've got to live. Listen to me. Tell him he didn't make a mistake. Tell him you hated me too. I'll help you.*

Jimmy Cleary's breath was hot on her cheek. He was talking about the part, about Brian Kent being signed up by the producer, about Brian's new contract. "I'm going to kill you exactly the way I killed your sister. An actor keeps at his role until he has it perfect. You want to hear the last thing I said to your sister?" He lifted his hand a fraction so she could mouth an answer.

Tell him you're me.

For a split second Caroline was six again. She and Lisa were playing on the foundation of a house being built near theirs. Lisa, always more daring, always surefooted, was leading the way over the piles of cinder block. "Don't be a scaredy-cat," she'd urged. "Just follow me."

She heard herself whisper, "I'd love to hear all about it. I want to know how she died, so I can laugh. You did murder Caroline. I'm Lisa."

She felt the hand slap her mouth with savage force.

Someone had rewritten the script. Furiously, Jimmy dug his fingers into her cheekbones. Whose cheekbones? Caroline's? If he'd already killed her, why hadn't his luck changed? Without moving the arm that lay over her chest, he reached into the breast pocket of his sweat suit for the cord. Get it over with, he told himself. If they're both dead, you'll be sure you got Caroline.

But it was like being on stage in the third act without knowing how the play ended. If the actor didn't know the climax, how could you expect the audience to feel any tension? Because there was an audience, an invisible audience named fate. He had to be sure. "If you try to scream, you won't even get so far as a yelp," he told her. "That's all your sister got out."

She *had* heard Lisa that night.

"So nod if you promise not to scream. I'll talk to you. Maybe if you convince me, I'll let you live. Wexford wants to look at you first thing in the morning for the rest of his life, doesn't he? I heard him say so."

Jimmy Cleary had been here when they came in. Caroline felt darkness close over her.

Do as he says! Don't you dare pass out. Lisa's bossy voice. "The Duchess has spoken," Caroline used to tell her, and they'd laugh together.

Jimmy angled the arm that lay across Caroline's body, yanked the cord around her neck, and tied it in a slipknot. It was twice the length of the section he'd used last time. It had occurred to him that this time he'd make a double knot, a grand final gesture as he exited from the spotlight of death.

The extra length gave him the ability to manipulate her. Calmly he told her to get out of bed, that he was hungry—he wanted her to fix him a sandwich and coffee—that he'd be holding the end of the cord and would pull it till she strangled if she raised her voice or tried anything funny.

Do as he says.

Obediently Caroline sat up as Jimmy lifted the weight of his arm from across her body. Her feet touched the cool

273]

wood of the floor. Automatically she fumbled for her slippers. I may be dead in seconds and I worry about bare feet, she thought. As she bent forward the cord bit into her neck. "No . . . please." She heard the panic in her voice.

"Shut up!" She felt Jimmy Cleary's hands on her neck, loosening the cord. "Don't move so fast and don't raise your voice again."

Side by side they walked through the living room and into the kitchen. His hand rested on the back of her neck. His fingers gripped the cord. Even loosened, she could feel its pressure, like a band of steel. In her mind she could see the grayish stripe embedded in Lisa's throat. For the first time she began to remember the rest of that morning. She'd dialed 911 and begun to scream. Then she'd dropped the receiver. Lisa's body was almost on the edge of the bed as though in that last moment she'd tried to escape. Her skin was so blue, I was thinking she was cold, I had to warm her, Caroline recalled as she opened the refrigerator door. I ran around the bed and got in and put my arms around her and began to talk to her and I tried to get the cord from around her neck and then I felt as though I was falling.

Now the cord was around her neck. In the morning would Sean find her as she had found Lisa?

No. It mustn't happen. Make the sandwich. Make him coffee. Act as though you two are playing a great scene. Tell him how bossy I was. Come on. Take all the good things and turn them around. Blame me the way he's blaming you.

Caroline looked inside the refrigerator and had a swift feeling of gratitude that she'd put off emptying it. She'd always kept sandwich makings for Sean on hand; the cleaning woman was coming in the morning to take them home. She pulled out ham and cheese and turkey, lettuce, mayonnaise, and mustard. She remembered that at school when

[274

the cast went out for a late snack Jimmy Cleary always ordered a hero.

How would I have known that? Ask him what he wants.

She looked up. The only light came from the refrigerator but her eyes were adjusting to the darkness. She could clearly see the unmistakable square jaw that toughened Jimmy Cleary's face, and the anger and confusion in his expression. Her mouth dry with fear, she whispered, "What kind of sandwich do you want? Turkey? Ham? I've got whole wheat bread or Italian rolls."

She could sense that she passed the first test.

"Everything. The works on a roll."

She felt the cord loosen slightly. She put the kettle on to boil. She made the sandwich swiftly, piling turkey and ham on top of cheese, spreading the lettuce, gobbing mayonnaise and mustard across the roll.

He made her sit next to him at the table. She poured coffee for herself, forced herself to sip. The cord was biting into her neck. She moved her hand to loosen it.

"Don't touch that." He released it slightly.

"Thank you." She watched him wolf the sandwich.

Talk to him. You've got to convince him before it's too late.

"I think you told me your name but I didn't really get it."

He swallowed the last bit of sandwich. "On the marquee it's James Cleary. My agent and my friends call me Jimmy."

He was gulping the coffee. How could she make him believe her, trust her? From where she was sitting Caroline could see the outline of the front closet. It had been almost closed before. That was where he must have been hiding. Sean had wanted to stay with her. If only she had let him stay. In those first couple of years after Lisa's death, there had been times when it seemed too much of a struggle to get

275]

through the day. Only the harsh demands of law school had kept her from sinking into suicidal depression. Now she could see Sean's face, so inexpressibly dear. *I want to live,* she thought. *I want the rest of my life.*

Jimmy Cleary felt better. He hadn't realized how hungry he was. In a way this was better than last time. Now he was acting out a cat-and-mouse scene. Now he was the judge. Was this Caroline? Maybe he hadn't made a mistake last time. But if he'd wasted Caroline, why hadn't the jinx been lifted? He finished the coffee. His fingers curled around the end of the cord, drawing it a hairbreadth tighter. Reaching over, he turned on the table lamp. He wanted to be able to study her face. "So tell me," he said easily. "Why should I believe you? And if I believe you, why should I let you live?"

Sean undressed and showered. In the bathroom mirror he looked at himself intently. He'd be thirty-four in ten days. Caroline would be twenty-seven the next day. They'd celebrate their birthdays in Venice. It would be good to sit in St. Mark's Square with her, to sip wine and hear the sweet sounds of the violins and watch the gondolas glide by. It was an image that had occurred to him several times in the past few weeks. Tonight it was as though he was drawing a blank. That picture simply wouldn't form.

He *had* to talk to Caroline. Wrapping a thick bath towel around him, he went to the bedside phone. It was nearly midnight. Even so, he dialed her number. The blazes with making excuses, he thought. *I'll just tell her that I love her.*

"It's not easy to be a twin." Caroline tilted her head so she could look directly into Jimmy Cleary's face. "My sister and I fought a lot. I used to call her the Duchess. She was so bossy. Even when we were little, she'd do things and blame me. I ended up hating her. That's why we went to colleges at opposite ends of the continent. I wanted to get away from her. I was her shadow, her mirror image, a nonperson. That last night she wanted to watch television and her set was broken, so she made me change rooms. When I found her that morning, I guess I just collapsed. But you see, even my mother and father didn't realize the mistake."

Caroline widened her eyes. She dropped her voice, making it intimate, confidential. "You're an actor, Jimmy. You can understand. When I came to they were calling me Caroline. You know the first words my mother said when I woke up were 'Oh, Caroline, we thank God it wasn't you.' "

Very good. You're getting to him.

She was six again. They were playing on the foundation. Lisa was running faster and faster. Caroline had looked down and gotten dizzy. But she'd still tried to keep up with her.

Jimmy was enjoying himself. He felt like a casting agent telling a hopeful to give him a cold reading. "So just like that you decided to be Caroline. How did you get away with it? Caroline went to Rawlings. What happened when Caroline's friends from Rawlings showed up?"

Caroline finished her own coffee. She could see the glints of madness in Jimmy Cleary's eyes. "It really wasn't hard. Shock. That was the excuse. I pretended not to remember lots of people we both knew. The doctors called it psychological amnesia. Everyone was very understanding."

Either she was a darn good actress or she was telling the truth. Jimmy was intrigued. He started to feel some of his anger fading. This girl was different from Caroline. Softer. Nicer. He felt a kinship with her, a regretful kinship. No matter what, he couldn't let her live. The only trouble was that if he had killed Caroline, if she wasn't lying—and he

277]

still wasn't sure—why hadn't the jinx been lifted five years ago?

Those cute red-and-white pajamas she was wearing. He laid his hand on her arm, then withdrew it. He had a sudden thought. "How about Wexford? How come you got together with him?"

"We just bumped into each other. I heard him call 'Caroline,' and I knew it was someone I was supposed to know. He told me his name as soon as he caught up with me jogging and in the next breath said something about having me in class, so I just faked it."

Remind Jimmy that Sean didn't bother with the real Caroline at Rawlings. Point out that he fell for you right away.

Jimmy shifted restlessly. Caroline said, "I can't tell you how many times Sean has said that I'm a much nicer person now. That's because I'm not the same person. Don't you love it? I'm glad you're sharing my secret, Jimmy. For the last five years you've been my secret benefactor, and at last I'm getting to know you. Would you like more coffee?"

Was she trying to snow him? Did she mean it? He touched her elbow. "More coffee sounds fine." He stood behind her, slightly to the side, as she turned the heat under the kettle. A very pretty girl. But he realized he couldn't let her live. He'd finish the coffee, bring her back into the bedroom and kill her. First he'd explain to her about the jinx. He glanced at the clock. It was 12:30. He'd killed the other sister at 12:40, so the timing was perfect. An image came into his mind of how the other girl had reached out her hands as though she wanted to claw him, how her eyes had blazed and bulged. Sometimes he dreamed about that. In the daytime the memory made him feel good. At night it made him break into a sweat.

The phone rang.

[278

Caroline's hand gripped the handle of the kettle convulsively. She knew it would be Sean. Other nights when he'd sensed that she was terribly down and probably not sleeping, he'd phoned.

Convince Jimmy you've got to answer the telephone. You've got to let Sean know that you need him.

The phone rang a second, a third time.

Sweat glistened on Jimmy's forehead and upper lip. "Forget it," he said.

"Jimmy, I'm sure it's Sean. If I don't answer he'll think there's something wrong. I don't want him here. I want to talk to you."

Jimmy considered. If that was Wexford she was probably telling the truth. The phone rang again. It was attached to an answering machine. Jimmy pushed the button that made the conversation audible, picked up the receiver and handed it to her. He tightened the cord so that it bit into her throat.

Caroline knew she could not allow her voice to sound shaky. "Hello." She managed to sound sleepy and was rewarded by a slight relaxing of the pressure on her neck.

"Caroline, honey, you were asleep. I'm sorry. I was worried that you were feeling pretty low. I know what tonight means to you."

"No, I'm glad you called. I wasn't really asleep. I was just starting to drift off." *What can I tell him?* Caroline wondered desperately.

The dress. Your wedding dress.

"It's kind of late," she heard Sean say. "Did you finish packing tonight after all?"

Jimmy tapped her shoulder and nodded.

"Yes. I felt wide awake, so I finished it."

Jimmy was looking impatient. He signaled for her to cut it short. Caroline bit her lip. If she didn't carry this off, it was the end. "Sean, I love you for calling and I'm really fine. I'll

279]

be ready at seven-thirty. Just one thing. When they packed my dress, did you remember to ask them to be sure to put lots of tissue in the sleeves so they wouldn't wrinkle?" She thought, don't let Sean give me away.

Sean felt his fingers holding the receiver go clammy. The dress. Caroline's dress did not have sleeves. And there was something else. Her voice had a hollow sound. She wasn't in bed. She was on the kitchen phone and the conference button was on. She wasn't alone. With a supreme effort he kept his voice steady. "Honey, I can swear on a stack of bibles that the saleslady said something about that. I think your mother had called to remind her too. Now listen, get some sleep. I'll see you in the morning and remember, I love you." He managed to put the receiver down without letting it bang, then dropped the towel and pulled his sweat suit from the closet. The keys to Caroline's apartment were on the dresser with his car keys. Should he take the time to call the police? The phone in his car. He'd call them while he was on the way. Dear God, he thought, please . . .

Sean had understood. Caroline replaced the receiver and looked at Jimmy. "You did a good job," he told her. "And you know, I'm starting to believe you." He led her back into the bedroom and forced her to lie down. He laid his arm across her, exactly as he had held down the sister. Then he explained what his teacher, Cory Zola, had told him about the jinx. "We were doing a dueling scene in class last week, and I guess I was pretty mad. I cut the other student. Zola really got upset with me. I tried to explain that I'd been thinking about this jinx someone put on me and how it's spoiling everything. He told me to stay away from class until I'd gotten rid of it. So, even if I believe you that I got Caroline last time, I still have to get rid of that feeling because I can't

[280

go back to class until I'm free of it. And in my book, Lisa—that's the real name, huh?—you inherited it."

His eyes glittered. The expression was vacant, cold. He is mad, Caroline thought. It will take Sean fifteen minutes to get here. Three minutes gone. Twelve minutes more. Lisa, help me.

Brian Kent is the jinx. Strangers on a Train.

Her mouth was so dry. His face was so near hers. She could smell the perspiration that was dripping from his body. She felt his fingers begin to pull the cord. She managed to sound matter-of-fact. "Killing me won't solve anything. Brian Kent is the jinx, not me. If he's out of the way, you'll have your chance. And if I kill him you'll have just as big a hold on me as I have on you."

The astonished sucking in of his breath gave her hope. She touched his hand. "Stop fooling with that cord, Jimmy, and listen to me for two minutes. Let me sit up." Again the memory of playing follow-the-leader on the foundation of that new house ran through her mind. At one point they'd come to a gaping space left for a window. Lisa had jumped over. Caroline, a few steps behind her, had hesitated, closed her eyes, and jumped, barely clearing the opening. She was taking a jump now. If she failed, it was all over. Sean was coming. She knew it. She had to stay alive for the next eleven minutes.

Jimmy released his arm, allowing her to sit up. She drew her legs against her body and locked her hands around her knees. The cord was digging against her neck muscles but she didn't dare ask him to ease it. "Jimmy, you told me that your big problem is that you're too much like Brian Kent. Suppose something happened to Brian? They'd need to have a replacement. So, become him. Replace him the way I became Caroline. He has a sudden accident, they'll be frantic to find someone to step into that movie. Why shouldn't it be you?"

Jimmy shook the sweat from his forehead. She was suggesting a new interpretation of the role Brian was playing in his life. He'd always concentrated on becoming a star, becoming bigger than Brian, surpassing him, getting a better table in the restaurants, watching him fade. Never once had he thought about Brian just disappearing from the scene. And even if he killed this girl, this Lisa, because now he believed she was Lisa, Brian Kent would still be signing contracts, posing for spreads in *People* magazine. And worse, agents would still be telling him that he was a Brian Kent type.

Did he believe her? With her tongue, Caroline tried to moisten her lips. They were so dry it was hard to talk. "If you kill me now, they'll find you. Jimmy, the cops aren't dumb. They always questioned whether or not the wrong twin was killed."

He was listening.

"Jimmy, we can bring off *Strangers on a Train*. You remember the plot. Two people exchange murders. There's no motive. The difference is, we'll carry it off. You've already done your part. You got Caroline out of the way for me. Now let me get rid of Brian Kent for you."

Strangers on a Train. Jimmy had done a scene from that movie in class. He'd been great. Cory Zola had said, "Jimmy, you're a natural." His eyes flickered over her face. Look at her, smiling at him. She was a cool one. If she'd gotten away with convincing her family she was Caroline, she might be capable of setting up Brian Kent and pulling it off. But what insurance did he have that she wouldn't scream for the cops the minute he left her? He asked her that.

"Why, Jimmy, you have the best insurance in the world.

[282

You know I'm Lisa. They never checked Caroline's finger-prints against our birth records. You could give me away. Do you know what that would do to my parents, to Sean? Do you think they'd ever forgive me?" She looked directly into Jimmy's eyes, awaiting his judgment.

Sean ran from the house, then bit his lip in wild frustra-tion. Caroline's car was blocking his. He wanted to be able to phone the police on the way. He ran back into the house, grabbed her car keys, pulled her car out of the way and got into his own. As he backed with furious speed onto the road, he ripped the car phone off its cradle and dialed 911.

Jimmy was experiencing a dazzling sense of rebirth. How many times in L.A. had he seen Brian Kent drive by in that Porsche of his? They'd gone to school together for four years, but Brian never gave him more than a cool nod if they bumped into each other. How much better if Brian didn't exist. And Lisa—she was Lisa, he was convinced of that—was right. He would have a hold on her. Deliberately he released his grip on the cord but did not remove it from her neck. "Let's say I believe you. How would you get him?"

Caroline fought to keep back the lightheaded sensation that came with hope. What could she tell him?

You'll go to the Coast. Look up Brian.

Desperately she searched for a plausible plot. Again she was six, skimming over the foundation. The gaping spaces between the cinder blocks were getting wider.

Poison. Poison.

"Sean has a friend, a professor who specializes in the history of medicine. Last week at dinner, he was talking about how many absolutely undetectable poisons there are. He described one of them, exactly how to prepare it from things you have in your medicine chest. A few drops is all

283]

it takes. Next month when I come back from my honey-moon, I have to go to California to depose a witness. I'll call Brian. After all, I—I mean Caroline gave him his big break. Right?"

Be careful.

She had slipped. But Jimmy didn't seem to notice. He was listening intently. The perspiration had caused his hair to curl so that it lay in damp ringlets on his fore-head. She didn't remember that his hair was that curly. He must have had a body wave. Now it was cut exactly like the recent picture she'd seen of Brian Kent. "I'm sure he'd be glad to see me," she continued. As though stretching her legs from cramping, she eased them over the side of the bed.

His hand reached for and encircled the end of the cord. She slipped her hand over his. "Jimmy, there's a poison that takes a week, ten days to act. The symptoms don't even begin for three or four days. Even if there's an inquiry, who would connect the fact that Brian had coffee with an old college friend, who just married a Princeton professor, with a murderer? It's the perfect scenario."

Jimmy realized he was nodding in assent. The night had turned into a dream, a dream that would start his whole life all over. He could trust her. With dazzling clarity he ac-cepted the truth of what she had pointed out to him. As long as Brian Kent was alive, he, who was the greatest actor in the world, would go unnoticed. The night-light in the bed-room became a footlight. The darkened living room was the theater where the audience was sitting. He was standing on stage. The audience was clapping its approval. He savored the moment, then chucked Caroline—no, Lisa—under the chin. "I do believe you," he whispered. "'When exactly are you coming to California?"

Hang on. You're almost safe.

[284

They were running faster and faster over the foundation. She couldn't keep up. Caroline heard her voice crack as she answered, "The second week in July."

Jimmy's remaining doubts vanished. Kent was due to start his new movie the first of August. If he was dead by then, they'd be frantic looking for a replacement.

He stood up and pulled Caroline to her feet. "Let me get that thing off your neck. Just remember it's right here in my pocket in case I ever need it again. I'm leaving now. We've got a deal. But if you don't keep your part of the bargain, some night when your professor is away or some afternoon when you stop for a red light, I'll be there."

Caroline felt the cord loosen, felt him pull it over her head. Hysterical sobs of relief were breaking in her throat. "It's a deal," she managed to say.

He dug his fingers into her shoulders and kissed her on the mouth. "I don't seal agreements with handshakes," he said. "Too bad I haven't got more time. I could go for you." His caricature of a smile became a bemused, wide-toothed grin. "I feel like the jinx is lifted already. Come on." He walked her to the back door. He reached up his hand to unfasten the chain.

Caroline caught a glimpse of the clock on the kitchen wall. It was twelve minutes since Sean had phoned. In the next thirty seconds Jimmy would be gone and she could chain and barricade the door. In the next few minutes Sean would be there.

Again the memory of being six, running on the foundation. She had glanced down. It was eight or ten feet to the ground. Jutting pieces of broken concrete were lying there. Lisa had made the last jump over a wide space left for a door . . .

Jimmy opened the door. She could feel the cool rush of night air on her face. He turned to her. "I know you never

285]

had the chance to see me perform, but I am a truly great actor."

"I know you're a great actor," Caroline heard herself say. "After *Death of a Salesman*, didn't everyone in school call you Biff?"

On the foundation she had hesitated that one moment before she made the final jump after Lisa. She had lost momentum. She had tumbled and her forehead had smashed against the concrete. With sickening fear she knew she had once again failed to follow Lisa.

The door slammed shut. For a split second she and Jimmy stared at each other. "Lisa couldn't have known that," Jimmy whispered. "You've been lying to me. You *are* Caroline." His hands lunged for her neck. She tried to scream as she backed away from him, turned and stumbled toward the front door. But only a low moan came from her lips.

Sean raced through the quiet streets. The 911 operator was asking him his name, where he was calling from, what was the nature of the emergency. "Get a squad car to eighty-one Priscilla Lane, apartment one-A," he shouted. "Never mind how I know there's something wrong. Get a car there."

"And what is the nature of the emergency?" the operator repeated.

Jimmy's hand slammed onto the front door as she tried to turn the lock. Caroline ducked past him and ran around the club chair. In the shadowy light she caught a glimpse of herself in the mirror over the couch, his looming presence behind her. His breath was hot on her neck. If she could only live for a minute more, Sean would be here. Before she could complete the thought, Jimmy had vaulted over the club

[286

chair. He was in front of her. She saw the cord in his hands. He spun her around. She felt her hair pulled back, the cord on her neck, saw their reflection in the mirror over the couch. She dropped to her knees and the cord tightened. She tried to crawl away from him, felt him leaning over her. "It's all over, Caroline. It's really your turn to be the victim."

Sean turned into Caroline's street. The brakes screeched as he jammed them on in front of her house. From a distance he could hear sirens. He ran to the door and tried the knob. With one fist he pounded on the door while he groped in his pocket for her keys. He remembered that the damn security lock had not been installed properly. You had to pull the door toward you before it would turn. In his anxiety, he could not match up the cylinder and the lock. It took three turns of the key before the lock released. Then the other key for the regular lock. Please . . .

She was on her knees, clawing at the cord. It was choking her. She could hear Sean pounding on the door, calling her. So close, so close. Her eyes widened as the cord cut off her breath. Waves of blackness were rolling over her. Lisa . . . Lisa . . . I tried.

Don't pull away. Lean backward. Lean backward, I tell you.

In a final effort to save her life, Caroline forced herself to bend backward, to slide her body toward Jimmy instead of pulling away from him. For an instant the pressure on her throat eased. She gulped in one breath before the cord began to tighten again.

Jimmy shut out the sounds of the pounding and shouting. Nothing in the whole world mattered except to kill this woman who had ruined his career. Nothing.

The key turned. Sean slammed the door open. His gaze

fell on the mirror over the couch, and the blood drained from his face.

Her eyes were blazing, bulging, her mouth was open and gaping, her palms extended, her fingernails like claws. A bulky figure in a sweat suit was bending over her, strangling her with a cord. For an instant Sean was rooted, unable to move. Then the intruder looked up. Their eyes met in the mirror. As Sean watched, in that one second, still unable to move, he saw the horrified expression that came into the other man's face, watched him drop the cord from his hands, throw his arms over his face.

"Stay away from me!" Jimmy screamed. "Don't come any nearer. Stay away."

Sean spun around. Caroline was on the floor, clawing at the cord that was choking her. Sean dove across the room, butted the man who had been attacking her. The force of the blow sent Jimmy back against the window. The sound of shattering glass mingled with his screams and the wail of sirens as patrol cars screeched to a halt.

Caroline felt hands yanking at the cord. She heard a low moaning sound come from her throat. Then the cord released and a rush of air filled her lungs. Darkness, sweet, welcome darkness, enveloped her.

When she awoke, she was lying on the couch, an icy cloth around her neck. Sean was sitting by her, chafing her hands. The room was filled with policemen. "Jimmy?" her voice was a harsh croaking sound.

"They took him away. Oh, my darling." Sean lifted her up, wrapped her in his arms, laid her head against his chest, smoothed her hair.

"Why did he start screaming?" she whispered. "What happened? In another few seconds I'd have been dead."

"He saw the same thing I did. You were reflected in the mirror over the couch. He's completely nuts. He thought

[288

that he was seeing Lisa. He thought she was coming for revenge."

Sean would not leave her. After the policemen were gone, he lay beside her on the roomy couch, pulled the afghan over them and held her close. "Try to get some sleep." Safe in his arms, beyond exhaustion, she did manage to drift off.

At 6:30 he woke her up. "You'd better start getting ready," he told her. "If you're sure you're okay, I'll run home and get showered and dressed." Brilliant sunlight spilled through the room.

Five years ago this morning, she had walked into Lisa's room and found her. This morning, she had awakened in Sean's arms. She reached up and held his face in her hands, loving the faint stubble on his cheeks. "I'm all right. Really."

When Sean left, she went into the bedroom. Deliberately she stared at the bed, remembering how it had felt to open her eyes and see Jimmy Cleary. She showered, letting the hot water run for long minutes over her body, her hair, wanting all trace of his presence to be washed away. She dressed in a khaki-colored jumpsuit, cinching a braided belt around her waist. As she brushed her hair, she saw the reddish-purple welt around her neck. Quickly she turned away.

It was as though time were in abeyance, waiting for her to complete what must be completed. She packed her suitcase, set it with her handbag near the door. Then she did what she knew she had to do.

She knelt on the floor just as she had been kneeling when Jimmy Cleary tried to strangle her. She arched her body backward and stared at the mirror. It was as she had expected. The bottom of the mirror was a fraction of an inch above her hairline. There was no way she could

289]

have been reflected there. Jimmy had been right: He had seen Lisa.

"Lisa, Lisa, thank you," she whispered. There was no feeling of an answer. Lisa was gone, as Caroline had known she would be gone. For the last time the thought that she had been the cause of Lisa's death filled her consciousness and then was vanquished. It had been an act of fate, and she would not insult Lisa's memory by dwelling on it. She stood up, and now she was reflected in the mirror. Tenderly she raised her fingertips to her lips and blew a kiss. "Good-bye. I love you," she said aloud.

In the street she heard a car pull up. Sean's car. Caroline hurried to the door, flung it open, pushed out her suitcase and purse, reached for the plastic-wrapped garment bag that enveloped her wedding gown, and carrying it cradled in her arms, slammed the door behind her and ran to meet him.

THE LOST ANGEL

It snowed the night before Christmas Eve, a steady stream of small pellets that whipped through the air, settled on bare branches, bunched on rooftops. By dawn the storm began to let up and an uncertain sun broke through the clouds.

At six o'clock, Susan Ahearn got out of bed, turned up the thermostat, and made coffee. Shivering, she closed her hands over the cup. She always felt so cold; it was probably all the weight she had lost since Jamie disappeared.

One hundred and ten pounds wasn't enough to cover her five feet eight inches; her eyes the same blue-green as Jamie's seemed too big for her face; her cheekbones had become prominent; even her chestnut hair had darkened to a deep brown that accentuated the pale, drawn look that was now habitual.

She felt infinitely older than twenty-eight; three months ago that important birthday had been spent following one more blind lead. The child discovered in a Wisconsin foster home had not been Jamie. She hurried back under the covers while warm air whistled and grumbled through the isolated house twenty-two miles west of Chicago.

The bedroom had an oddly unfinished appearance. There were no pictures on the walls, no curtains on the windows, no carpets or rugs on the pine floors. Sealed boxes were stacked haphazardly in the corner by the closet. Jamie had disappeared just before they were to leave this house.

It had been a long night. Most of it she had spent awake, trying to overcome the fear that was her constant companion. Suppose she never found Jamie? Suppose Jamie became one of those children who simply disappeared? Now to stave off the emptiness of the house, the bereft moaning of the wind, the rattling of the windows, Susan began to pretend.

"You're an early bird," she said.

She envisioned Jamie in her red-and-white flannel night-gown padding across the room and climbing into bed with her. "Your feet are freezing. . . ."

"I know. Grandma would say I'll catch my death. Grandma always says that. You say Grandma is gloomy. Tell me the Christmas story."

"Don't quote Grandma to me. Her sense of humor isn't terrific." Her arms around Jamie. Tucking the blankets around her. "Now about New York on Christmas Eve. After our ride through Central Park in the horse and car-

[292

riage, we'll have lunch at the Plaza. That's a big, beautiful hotel. And right across the street . . ."

"We'll look in the toy store . . ."

"The most famous toy store in the world. It's called F A O Schwarz. It has trains and dolls and puppets and books and everything."

"I can pick out three presents . . ."

"I thought it was two. Okay, we'll make it three."

"And then we'll visit the baby Jesus in St. Pat's . . ."

"It's really St. Patrick's Cathedral, but we Irish are a friendly group. Everyone calls it St. Pat's. . . ."

"Tell me about the tree . . . and the windows like fairyland. . . ."

Susan gulped the last of the coffee over the lump in her throat. The phone began to ring and she tried to quell the wild leap of hope as she reached for it. Jamie! Let it be Jamie!

It was her mother calling from Florida. The heartsick tone that had become her mother's normal speaking voice since Jamie's disappearance was especially marked today. Determinedly, Susan forced her voice to sound positive. "No, Mother. No word. Of course I would have phoned you. . . . It's difficult for all of us. No, I'm sure I want to stay here. Don't forget she did phone once . . . For God's sake, Mother, no, I don't think she's dead. Give me a break. Jeff is her father. In his way he loves her. . . ."

She hung up in tears, biting her lip to keep from dissolving into angry hysterics, all the monsters unleashed. Even her mother did not know how bad it really was.

So far, six indictments had been issued for Jeff's arrest. The entrepreneur she thought she had married was really an international jewel thief. The reason for this remote house in this remote suburb was because it had made a good hiding place for him. She'd learned the truth last spring when FBI agents had come to arrest Jeff just after he had left on one

293]

of his "business trips." He never returned, so she'd put the house up for sale. She was making arrangements to move to New York—the four years she'd spent in college there had been the happiest of her life. Then a few weeks after his disappearance Jeff went to Jamie's nursery school and took her away. That was seven months ago.

On the drive to work Susan could not rid herself of the fear her mother's call had triggered. *Do you think Jamie is dead?* Jeff was absolutely irresponsible. When Jamie was six months old, he'd left her alone in the house to go out for cigarettes. When she was two years old, he didn't notice that she'd waded out in water over her head. A lifeguard had saved her. How could he possibly be taking care of her now? Why had he *wanted* her?

The real-estate office was festive with Christmas decorations. They were a nice group, the sixteen people she worked with, and Susan appreciated the hopeful glances they offered her each morning. All of them wanted to hear good news about Jamie. Today, nobody was interested in doing much work, but she kept busy by reviewing papers for future closings. Everything she handled was a reminder. The Wilkes—a couple buying their first home because they were expecting a baby; the Conways selling their big house to move nearer to their grandchildren. As she finished talking to Mrs. Conway, she felt the familiar tears welling in her eyes and turned her head.

Joan Rogers, the agent at the next desk, was reading a magazine. With a stab of pain Susan saw the title of the article: "Children Aren't Always Angels on Christmas Day." Whimsical photographs of children in white robes and halos dotted the page.

Susan stared, then reached over and frantically grabbed the magazine from Joan's hand. The angel in the upper right-hand corner. A little girl. Hair so blond it was almost white. But the eyes. The mouth. The rounded curve of the cheek. "Jamie," Susan whispered. She pulled open her desk drawer, fumbled through its contents and found a Magic Marker. With trembling fingers she covered the bright hair of the child in the photograph with the warm brown tone of the pen and watched as the angel's image became identical with the framed picture on her desk.

Jamie looked thoughtfully out the window of the bedroom at the cold winter scene outside and tried not to listen to the quarreling voices. Daddy and Tina were mad at each other again. Someone in the apartment building had shown Daddy her picture in the magazine. Daddy was yelling, "What are you trying to pull? We'll all land in jail. How many other times did she pose?"

They'd come to New York at the end of the summer, and Daddy started to take a lot of trips without them. Tina said she was bored and might as well do a little modeling. But the woman she went to said, "I don't need any more of your type, but I can use the little girl."

Posing for the picture of the angel was easy. They'd asked her to think about something nice, so she'd thought about Christmas Eve and how Mommy and she had planned to spend it in New York this year. Now she was in New York and she was near every single place she and Mommy had planned to go—but it wasn't the same at all with Daddy and Tina.

"I asked you how many times she posed!" Daddy yelled.

"Twice, three times," Tina shouted.

That was a fib. She had gone to the studio lots of times when Daddy was away. But when he was in New York, Tina "booked her out."

Now Tina was saying, "What do you expect me to do while you're gone? Read Dr. Seuss and play jacks?"

On the street below people were hurrying as though they were cold. It had snowed during the night, but this snow melted under the wheels of the cars and turned into dirty piles of slush. It was only from the corner of her eye that she could see Central Park where the snow was as pretty as it was supposed to be.

Jamie swallowed over the lump in her throat. She knew that the baby Jesus came on the night of Christmas Eve. Every single day she had prayed that this year when God brought the baby Jesus, he would bring Mommy too. But Daddy told her that Mommy was still very sick. And tonight they were going to get on a plane again and fly to someplace else. It sounded like bananas. No. It was ba-ha-mas.

"Jamie!"

Tina's voice was so angry when she called her. She knew Tina didn't like her. She was always telling Daddy, "She's your kid."

Daddy was sitting at the table in his bathrobe. The magazine with her picture was thrown on the floor and he was reading the newspaper. Usually he said, "Good morning, Princess," but today he didn't even notice her when she kissed him. Daddy wasn't ever mean to her. The only time he'd slapped her was when she tried to phone Mommy. She'd just heard Mommy's voice on the phone saying "Please leave a message" when Daddy caught her. She managed to say, "I hope you're getting better, Mommy, I miss you," before Daddy slammed down the phone and slapped her. After that he locked the phone whenever he and Tina weren't right there. Daddy said that Mommy was so sick, she would hurt herself trying to talk. But Mommy didn't sound sick when she said "Please leave a message."

Jamie sat down at the table where cornflakes and orange juice were waiting. That was all Tina ever did put on the table for her.

[296

Daddy was frowning and he sounded mad when he read out loud, "The servants think the shorter of the two thieves may have been a woman." Then Daddy said, "I told you that outfit was a giveaway."

Tina leaned over his shoulder. Her robe was open and she was popping out of her nightgown. Her hair was all messy and she blew smoke rings while she read: "*May be an inside job.* What more do you want?"

"Just as well we're leaving," Daddy said. "We've overworked this town.

Jamie thought of all the apartments they had gone to see. "Do we have to go to ba-ha-mas?" she asked. It sounded so far away. Farther and farther away from Mommy. "I liked the apartment yesterday," she urged. She toyed with the cornflakes, turning the spoon around in them. "Remember you told that lady that you thought it was just what you were looking for?"

Tina laughed. "Well, in a way it was, kiddo."

"Keep quiet." Daddy sounded so cross. Jamie remembered how yesterday the woman who showed them the apartment had said what a beautiful family they were. Daddy and Tina were all dressed up in the clothes they wore when they looked at apartments, and Tina's hair was pulled back in a bun and she didn't have much makeup on.

After breakfast Tina and Daddy went into their bedroom. Jamie decided to put on the purple pants and striped long-sleeved shirt she'd been wearing the day Daddy had come to school to say Mommy was sick and he had to take her right home. Even though they were getting small, she liked them better than any of her new clothes. She remembered when Mommy had bought them.

She brushed her hair and was always surprised to see how funny it looked now. It was exactly the color of Tina's hair and when they were out Daddy made her call Tina

297]

"Mother." She knew Tina wasn't her mother, but she'd always called Mommy *Mommy,* so it didn't bother her too much. It was a different name for a different person.

When she went back into the living room, Daddy and Tina were dressed to go out. Daddy was carrying a briefcase that looked heavy. "I won't be sorry to leave this place tonight," he was saying. Jamie didn't like it here either. She knew it was nice to live only a block from Central Park, but this apartment was dark and messy and the furniture was old and the rug had a tear in it. Daddy kept telling the people who showed them their apartments how anxious they were to have a really fine New York residence.

"Tina and I are going out for a while," Daddy told her. "I'll double-lock the door so you'll be safe. You read or watch television. Later on, Tina will take you shopping for summer clothes for the Bahamas and you can pick out a couple of Christmas presents. Won't that be fun?"

Jamie managed to smile back at him as her eyes flickered over to the telephone. *Daddy had forgotten to put the lock on it. When they left she was going to call Mommy again. She wanted to talk to Mommy about Christmas. Daddy wouldn't know.*

She waited a few minutes to be sure they were gone. Then she picked up the receiver. She had made herself say the number every single night before she went to sleep so she wouldn't forget it. She even knew that you had to dial "1" first. Saying the numbers out loud, she dialed as she said, "One . . . three one two-five four—"

The key turned in the door. She heard Daddy curse and she dropped the phone even before he grabbed it from her. He listened, heard the dial tone, then put the receiver down and snapped the lock around it before he said, "If it weren't Christmas Eve, I'd smack you one."

He was gone again. Jamie hunched in the big chair, wrapped her arms around her legs, and laid her head on her knees. She knew she was too big to cry. She was almost four and a half. Even so, she had to bite her lip to keep it from trembling. But after a minute she was able to play the pretend game.

Mommy was with her and they were going to have their special Christmas Eve. First they would go for a ride through Central Park. The horses would jingle because they had bells on. Then they would have lunch at the big hotel. Fretfully she realized she couldn't remember the name of the hotel. She frowned, trying so hard to make it come back. She could see the hotel in her mind. She had made Daddy show her where it was. *She could so remember.* The Plaza. After lunch, they'd go right across the street into the toy store. F A O Swarzzz. . . . She'd pick out two toys. No, Jamie thought, Mommy said I could pick out three toys. "We'll walk down Fifth Avenue to visit the baby Jesus and then . . ."

Tina said she was such a pest always asking where everything was. But now she knew exactly how to go to Fifth Avenue from here and how to find all the places she and Mommy planned to see together. Mommy had gone to school in New York. But that was a long time ago. . . . Maybe Mommy would have forgotten how to find places, but Jamie knew. Her eyes closed, she slipped her hand in Mommy's and said, "The big, beautiful tree is right down there. . . ."

The phone number of the magazine was on the masthead. Susan's fingers flew on the dial: 212 . . . Oblivious that the others in the office were gathering at her desk, she waited as the phone continued to ring. *Don't let them be closed today, don't let them be closed.*

299]

The operator who finally answered tried to be helpful. "I'm sorry, but there's just about nobody here. A child model? That information would be in the accounting department and that's closed. Can you call on the twenty-sixth?"

In a torrent of words Susan told her about Jamie. "You've absolutely got to help me. How do you pay a child who poses? Don't you have an address?"

The operator cut in. "Hold on. There's got to be a way to find out."

Minutes passed. Susan clutched the receiver, dimly aware that someone was gripping her shoulders. Joan, dear Joan, who had happened to be reading that article.

When the operator came back on, she was triumphant. "I reached one of the editors at home. The children we used for that article were from the Lehman Model Agency. Here's the number."

Susan was put through to Dora Lehman. In the background she could hear the sounds of a Christmas party. Lehman's strident but friendly voice said, "Sure, Jamie's one of my kids. Sure, she's around. She did a great job last week."

"She's in New York!" Susan cried out. Dimly she was aware of the cheers that went up behind her.

Dora Lehman did not have an address for Jamie. "That Tina character used to pick up Jamie's checks here. But I do have a phone number. I was only to use it if a really big job came in. Tina said to pretend it was a wrong number if her husband answered."

Susan scribbled the number, wild with impatience, and managed not to hang up as the Lehman woman urged her to drop in with Jamie when she got to New York.

Joan stopped her from dialing. "You'll only tip them off.

We've got to get the New York police. They can trace the address. You get yourself booked on a plane."

After all the months of waiting, to be able to *do* something. Someone looked up the flight schedules. The next plane she could catch was leaving O'Hare at noon. But when she tried to make a reservation the clerk almost laughed. "There isn't an empty seat on a plane leaving Chicago today," she said. Pleading finally got her to a vice president. "You get out here," he told her. "We'll get you on that flight even if we have to bump the pilot."

Joan finished talking to the police in New York just as Susan hung up the phone. It took Susan a moment to realize that Joan's face was somber, that the excitement had disappeared from her eyes. "Jeff was just arrested for a robbery he and that woman—Tina—he's living with committed last night. A neighbor thinks she saw Jamie and the woman come by in a cab as he was being put in a squad car. If Tina knows that Jeff is in custody, God knows where she'll disappear with Jamie.'

Daddy and Tina weren't gone long. Jamie could tell time, and both hands were on eleven when they got back. Tina said to put her coat on because they were going to Bloomingdale's.

It wasn't fun to shop with Tina. Jamie could tell that even the lady who sold them the clothes was surprised that Tina didn't act as though she cared what she bought. She said, "Oh, she needs a couple of bathing suits, and some shorts and shirts. That should do for her."

Then they went to the toy department. "Your father said you can pick out a couple of things," Tina told her.

She didn't really want anything. The dolls with their shiny button eyes and frilly dresses didn't look nearly as nice as the

Minnie Mouse rag doll she always used to sleep with at home. But Tina looked so mad when she said she didn't want anything that she pointed to some books and asked for them.

They took a cab back to the apartment, but when the driver pulled up to the curb, Tina started to act funny. There were two police cars parked there and Jamie saw Daddy walking between two policemen. She started to point to him, but Tina pinched Jamie's knee and said to the driver, "I forgot something. Take us back to Bloomingdale's, please."

Jamie shrank back on the seat. Daddy had talked about the police this morning. Was Daddy in trouble? She didn't dare ask Tina. Tina's mouth had the mean look and the fingers she'd used to pinch Jamie's knee were still in the air ready to snap down again.

Back in Bloomingdale's, Tina shopped only for herself. She bought a suitcase, a dress, a coat and hat, and big dark glasses. When Tina paid for everything, she cut off all the tags and told the saleswoman she'd decided to wear her new clothes right away.

When they left Bloomingdale's she looked like a different person. Her white mink jacket and leather pants were in the suitcase. The new coat was black like the one she wore when they looked at apartments; the hat covered all of her hair, and the dark glasses were so big you could hardly see her face.

Jamie was so hungry. All day she'd had only some corn-flakes and the orange juice. The street was crowded. People went by carrying bundles. Some of them looked worried and tired. Others looked happy. There was a Santa Claus on the corner and people were dropping money into the box next to him.

Near the corner she saw a hot dog and soda cart with an

[302

umbrella over it. Timidly Jamie tugged at Tina's sleeve. "Could I have . . . Is it all right if I have . . . ?" For some reason there was a big knot in her throat. She was so hungry. She didn't know why Daddy was with the policemen and she knew Tina didn't like her.

Tina had been trying to signal a cab. "You're a pest," she said. "All right. Make it snappy."

Jamie asked for a hot dog with mustard and a Coke. The cab came up before the man added mustard, and Tina said, "Hurry up! Skip the mustard."

In the cab, Jamie tried to eat carefully so there wouldn't be any crumbs. The driver turned and said to Tina, "I know the kid can't read. How about you?"

"Oh, sorry, I didn't notice." Tina pointed to the sign. "That says you can't eat in this cab. Wait till we get to the Port Authority."

The Port Authority was a big, big building with so many people. They got on a long line. Tina kept looking around as though she was scared of something. When they reached the counter, she asked about buses to Boston. The man said there was one at two-twenty they could make. Then a policeman started to walk toward them. Tina turned her face away and said under breath, "Oh my God."

Jamie wondered if the policeman was going to make them go in a car the way they took Daddy. But he didn't come near them at all. Instead he started talking to two men who were yelling at each other. Mommy used to tell her that policemen were her friends, but she knew that in New York it was different, because Daddy and Tina were both afraid of them.

Tina brought her to where some people were sitting in a row of chairs. One old lady was asleep with her hand over her suitcase. Tina said, "Now, Jamie, you wait right here for me. I have to go on an errand and it may take a long time.

Finish your hot dog and Coke and don't talk to anyone. If anyone talks to you, say you're with that lady."

Jamie was glad to sit down and have a chance to eat. The hot dog was cold and she wished it had mustard on it, but even so it tasted good. She watched Tina go back up the escalator.

She waited a long, long time. After a while, her eyes got heavy and she began to fall asleep. When she woke up, there were so many people hurrying past as though they were late for something. The old lady she was sitting next to was shaking her. "Are you alone?" She looked worried.

"No. Tina is coming right back." It was hard to talk. She was still so sleepy.

"Have you been here long?"

Jamie wasn't sure, so she said again, "Tina is coming right back."

"All right, then. I have to catch my bus. Don't talk to anyone until Tina gets back." The old lady picked up her suitcase as though it was heavy and began to go away.

Jamie had to go to the bathroom. Tina would be mad if she didn't wait for her, but she just couldn't not go to the bathroom. She wondered where the bathroom was and how she could find it if she couldn't ask anyone. Then she heard the woman on the chair behind her say to her friend, "Let's go to the john before we leave."

Jamie knew that meant they were going to the bathroom. Tina always talked about the john. She picked up the package with her new clothes and books and followed closely so it looked like she was with them.

In the bathroom there were so many people and some of them had kids, so it was easy to go in and out of one of the stalls without anyone paying attention. She washed her hands and left the messy bathroom as fast as she could. For the first time she noticed the big clock on the wall. The little

[304

hand was on four. The big hand on one. That meant it was five after four. The man at the counter had told Tina the next bus was at two-twenty.

Jamie stopped, realizing Tina hadn't meant to take her on that bus at all. . . . Tina wasn't coming back.

Jamie knew that if she stayed here a policeman would start talking to her. She didn't know where to go. Daddy wasn't home and Tina had gone away. Maybe if she phoned Mommy, even if Mommy was sick, she'd send someone. But she didn't have any money. She wanted so much to see Mommy. She knew she was going to start crying. It was Christmas Eve and she and Mommy were supposed to be together.

The big doors at the end of the room—people were going in and out of them. That must be the way out to the street. The package was heavy. The string on the box cut through her mittens. She knew what she could do. The apartment was on Fifty-eighth Street and Seventh Avenue. That was the address Tina and Daddy always gave to the driver in a cab. If she could find the apartment, she could walk one block more to Central Park. From there she knew where the Plaza was. She would play the pretend game. She would pretend that Mommy was with her and they had had a carriage ride in Central Park and lunch at the Plaza. Then she'd go into the toy store across the street from the Plaza, just as she and Mommy had planned. She'd walk down Fifth Avenue and visit the baby Jesus and see the big tree and the Lord and Taylor windows.

She was out on the street. It was getting dark and the wind bit her cheeks. Her head felt cold without a hat. A man in a gray sweater and white apron was selling newspapers. She didn't want him to know she was alone so she pointed to a woman holding a baby and struggling to open a stroller.

"We have to go to Fifty-eighth Street and Seventh Avenue," she told the man.

"You've got a long walk," he said. He waved his hand. "It's eighteen blocks up that way and one block over that way."

Jamie waited till he was making change for someone before she darted across the street and began to make her way up Eighth Avenue, a tiny figure in a pink snow jacket, the cap of white-gold hair framing her face.

The plane was late departing and took an hour and forty minutes to LaGuardia Airport. It was three o'clock when she landed. Susan ran through the terminal, trying to close her ears to the joyful welcomes other deplaning passengers were receiving.

As the cab snaked through the traffic on the Fifty-ninth Street Bridge, she tried not to remember that this was the day she and Jamie had planned to spend in New York. It was cold and overcast and the driver told her it was supposed to snow again. The sun visor was covered with pictures of his family. "I'm gonna pack it in after this run and get home to the kids. You got any kids?"

At the police station, a Lieutenant Garrigan was waiting in his office.

"Have you found Jamie?"

"No, but I can assure you we're covering all the airports and bus stations." He showed her a mug shot. "Is this your former husband, Jeff Randall?"

'Is that what he's calling himself?"

"In New York, he's Jeff Randall. In Boston, Washington, Chicago, and a dozen other cities, he's someone else. It seems that he and his girl friend have been posing as wealthy out-of-towners looking for a co-op in New York. Having the little girl with them has made the act more convincing.

[306

He was carrying airline tickets—they were planning to fly to Nassau this evening."

Susan saw the compassion in his eyes. "Can I speak to Jeff?" she asked.

He hadn't changed in the last year. The same wavy brown hair, the same guileless blue eyes, the same ready smile, the same concerned, protective manner. "Susan, it's good to see you. You're looking very well. Thinner, but it's becoming."

They might have been old friends bumping into each other unexpectedly. "Where would this woman take Jamie?" Susan asked. She clenched her hands, afraid she would hammer his face with her fists.

"What are you talking about?"

They were sitting across from each other in the small, crowded office. Jeff's nonchalant air made it seem as though the handcuffs on his wrists were a mirage. The policemen on either side of him might have been statues, so totally was he ignoring them. The lieutenant was still behind his desk, the compassion gone from his eyes. "You're liable to be spending enough years in prison without adding a kidnapping charge," he said. "I would imagine your former wife might drop that complaint if your little girl is found immediately."

He would not answer any questions, not even when Susan's control snapped and she screamed at him, "I'll kill you if anything happens to her." She bit her hand to hold back the racking sobs as they took Jeff away.

The lieutenant brought her to a waiting room. It had a leather bench and some old magazines. Someone brought her coffee. Susan tried to pray but could not find any words. Only one thought echoed in her mind, insistent. "I want Jamie. I want Jamie."

At ten after four, Lieutenant Garrigan told her that a clerk in the Port Authority remembered that a woman with a child resembling Jamie's description had bought tickets on the two-twenty bus to Boston. They were wiring ahead to have it checked at one of the rest stops. At four-thirty, it was determined that they were not on the bus. At a quarter of five, Tina was picked up at Newark Airport as she tried to board a plane to Los Angeles.

Lieutenant Garrigan tried to sound optimistic as he told Susan what they had learned. "Tina left Jamie sitting in the waiting room of the Port Authority Terminal. One of the transit cops is still on duty. He remembers seeing a child answering her description leave with two women."

"They could have taken her anywhere," Susan whispered. "What kind of people wouldn't take a lost child to the police?"

"Some women will take a lost child home first and ask their husbands what to do," the lieutenant said. "Believe me, you're a lot better off if that's what's happened. It means she's safe. I wouldn't want to think Jamie is wandering around Manhattan alone today. There are an awful lot of weirdos on the streets during the holidays. They try to spot kids who have gotten separated from adults."

He must have seen the terror on Susan's face because he added quickly, "We're going to try to get an appeal on the radio stations and have her picture on the evening news. That Tina woman says Jamie knows the address of the apartment and the telephone number. We've got an officer in the apartment in case anyone calls. Maybe you'd like to wait there. It's just a few blocks away. I'll send you in a squad car."

A young cop was watching television in the living room. Susan walked through the apartment, noticing a dish with a few dried cornflakes on the dinette table, the coloring books stacked beside it. The smaller bedroom . . . The bed was unmade, the imprint of a head on the pillow. Jamie had slept here last night. The nightgown folded over the chair.

[308

She picked it up and hugged it against her as though somehow Jamie would materialize. Jamie had been here only hours ago, but the sense of her presence was not in this room.

Susan felt her lungs closing, her lips quivering, hysteria rising in her chest. She walked over to the window, opened it and drank in the fresh air. Glancing down, she could see the traffic on Seventh Avenue. To the left, Central Park South was lined with horses and carriages. Her eyes blurred as she saw a family turn from Seventh Avenue onto Central Park South. The mother and father were ahead. Their three children trailed behind, the two boys shoving each other, a little girl close on their heels.

Christmas Eve. She and Jamie were supposed to be here together. They were going to have their special day. A sudden, irrational thought flashed through Susan's mind—Suppose Jamie wasn't with those women after all. . . . Suppose she was alone.

The policeman, his attention thoroughly diverted from the television, took down the places she named. "I'll call the lieutenant," he promised. "We'll comb Fifth Avenue for her."

Susan grabbed her coat. "So will I."

Jamie's feet were so tired. She had walked and walked and walked. At first she counted every block, but then she saw that the signs on the corners showed the numbers. Forty-three, forty-four. She didn't like walking here. There weren't any pretty store windows and the ladies who were leaning against the buildings or in doorways dressed like Tina.

She was very careful to walk near mothers and fathers and other kids. Mommy had told her about that. "If you're ever lost, always go to someone with children." But she didn't

309]

want to talk to any of these people. She wanted to play the pretend game.

She knew when she reached Fifty-eighth Street. She could tell by the stores. That was the place where they got pizza. That was the stand where Daddy bought newspapers. The apartment was on this block.

A man came up to her and took her hand. She tried to pull away but could not. "You're alone, aren't you, darling?" he whispered.

He wouldn't let go of her hand. He was smiling, but somehow he looked scary. It was hard to see his eyes because they were narrow. He was wearing a dirty jacket and his pants kind of hung on him. She knew she shouldn't tell him she was alone.

"No," she said quickly. "Mommy and I are hungry." She pointed into the pizza shop and a lady who was buying pizza looked out and kind of smiled.

The man dropped her hand. "I thought you needed help."

Jamie waited till he walked across the street and then she began to run down the block. When she was three buildings away, she saw a police car pull up to the apartment house. For just a minute she was scared that they had come to get her too. But then a woman got out and ran in the building and the car drove away. She rubbed the back of her hand across her eyes. It was so babyish to cry.

When she got to the apartment house, she kept her head down. She didn't want anyone to see her and maybe stop her and take her to jail too. But the box was so heavy. As she passed the building, she stopped for a minute and put the box behind the stone flower boxes. Maybe she could just leave it here for a while. Anyhow, even if someone took it, she wouldn't need a bathing suit or shorts. She wasn't going to ba-ha-mas.

It was so much easier to walk without the box. She turned

[310

at the corner and looked back. The man in the dirty jacket was following her. That scared her a little. She was glad that some people walked past her, a mother and a father and two boys. She hurried to get close to them. The group came to the corner and turned right. She knew that was the way she was supposed to go. Central Park was across the street. She watched as some people got out of one of the carriages. Right now she could start to play the pretend game.

Susan hurried along Central Park South, going from one to the other of the drivers in the hansom cabs. The harnesses of the horses were entwined with ribbons and bells. The carriages were brightened with red and green lights.

The drivers wanted to help. They all studied the picture of Jamie in the magazine. "Pretty little girl . . . She looks like an angel." They all promised to keep an eye out for her. At the Plaza, Susan spoke to the doorman, to the desk clerks, to the hostess in the Palm Court. The lobby was ablaze with holiday decorations. The Palm Court restaurant in the center of the lobby was crowded with well-dressed people sipping cocktails, late shoppers wearily enjoying tea and delicate sandwiches.

Susan held the magazine open to Jamie's picture. Over and over she asked, "Have you seen her?"

She caught a glimpse of herself in the mirror near the elevators. The dampness had caused her hair to curl around her face and shoulders. Her face was so pale, but it was the face Jamie would have when she grew up. If she grew up.

No one at the Plaza remembered seeing a child alone. F A O Schwarz was her next stop. The toy store was filled with last-minute shoppers snapping up teddy bears and games and dolls. No one remembered seeing an unaccompanied child. She went to the second floor. A clerk studied the picture thoughtfully. "I can't be sure. I'm much too busy. But there was a little girl who asked to hold a Minnie Mouse rag doll. Her father wanted to buy it for her, but she said no. I thought it was peculiar. Yes, indeed, there's a striking resemblance to this child."

"But she was with her father," Susan murmured, adding, "Thank you," and turned away too quickly to hear the clerk say that she *thought* of course it was her father.

The clerk stared after Susan as she got on the escaltor. Come to think of it, what child who obviously wants a doll doesn't let her father buy it for her? And there'd been something creepy about that guy. Ignoring an insistent customer, the clerk ran from behind the counter to catch Susan. Too late—Susan had already disappeared.

Seeing the Minnie Mouse doll had made Jamie want to cry and cry. But she couldn't let that man buy her a present. She knew that. She was scared that he was still following her.

Outside the toy store the streets weren't quite as crowded now. She guessed everybody was going home. On one of the corners people were singing Christmas carols. She stopped and listened to them. She knew the man who was following her had stopped too. The women singers had bonnets on instead of hats. One of them smiled at her when the song was finished. Jamie smiled back, and the woman said, "Little girl, you're not alone, are you?" it wasn't really fibbing because she was pretending she was with Mommy. Jamie said, "Mommy's with me. She's right over there." She pointed at the crowd of people looking in the windows of a store and hurried toward them.

In St. Patrick's Cathedral she stopped and gazed around. Finally she found the manger. There were a lot of people standing around it, but the baby Jesus wasn't in the crib. A man was putting new candles in holders and Jamie heard a lady ask where the statue of the Infant was. "It's placed during Midnight Mass," he told her.

Jamie managed to find a place right in front of the crib. She whispered the prayer she had been saying for so long. "When You come tonight, bring Mommy too. Please."

There were so many people coming into the church. The organ began to play. She loved the sound of it. It would be good to sit here awhile where it was nice and warm, and rest. But somehow just telling the lady who was singing that Mommy was with her made it seem so real. She'd go to the tree now and then to the Lord and Taylor windows. After that if the man was still following her, maybe she would ask him what she should do. Maybe if he liked her enough to keep following her, he really did want to take care of her.

Susan's eyes scanned the faces of the children as she passed. One little girl made her catch her breath, the golden hair, a red jacket. But it wasn't Jamie. Every few blocks, there were volunteers dressed as Santa Claus collecting for charity. To each one of them she showed Jamie's picture. A Salvation Army choir was singing on the corner of Fifty-third Street. One of them had seen a little girl who certainly looked like Jamie. But the child had said she was with her mother.

Lieutenant Garrigan caught up with her just as she was about to go into the cathedral. He was in a squad car. Susan saw the pity in his eyes as he glanced at the picture she was holding.

"I'm afraid you're wasting your time, Susan," he said. "A Trailways bus driver said two women and a small girl were on his four-ten run out of the Port Authority. That jibes with the time the transit cop saw them leave."

Susan's lips were rubbery. "Where did they go?"

"He let them off on Pascack Road in Washington Town-

313]

ship, New Jersey. The police there are cooperating fully. I still think we have a chance of a phone call from those women . . . if they took her. CBS has agreed to let you make a special appeal just before the seven o'clock news. But we'll have to hurry."

"Could we drive down Fifth to Lord and Taylor's?" Susan asked. "I don't know—I just have this feeling . . ."

At her insistence the squad car drove slowly. Susan's head turned from side to side as she tried to see the passersby on both sides of the street. Tonelessly she told how a salesclerk had seen a child like Jamie but that child was with her father; a Salvation Army caroler had seen a child like Jamie who was with her mother.

She insisted that they stop in front of Lord and Taylor's. People were patiently lining up to walk past the fairyland displays. "I just think that if Jamie was in New York and remembered . . ." She bit her lip. She knew that Lieutenant Garrigan thought she was being foolish.

The little girl in the blue and green snowsuit. About Jamie's size. No. The child almost hidden behind the stocky man. She studied her eagerly, then shook her head.

Lieutenant Garrigan touched her sleeve. "I honestly think the best thing you can do for Jamie is to broadcast the appeal on television."

Reluctantly Susan agreed.

Jamie watched the ice skaters. They were skimming around the rink in front of the Christmas tree, like dolls come to life. Before her daddy took her away, Mommy and she had gone ice-skating at a pond near their house. . . . Mommy had given her beginner's ice skates.

The tree was so tall that she wondered how they had been able to put the lights on it. Last year Mommy had stood on

[314

a ladder to trim their tree and Jamie had handed her the ornaments.

Jamie rested her chin on her hands. She could just see over the railing to look down at the rink. In her mind she began to talk to Mommy. "Can we go ice-skating here next year? Will my skates still fit? Or maybe I can give them away and get bigger ones?" She could just see Mommy smiling and saying, "Sure, pumpkin." Or maybe she'd joke and say, "No, I think we'll squish your feet into your old skates."

Jamie turned away from the tree. She had just one more place to see, the Lord and Taylor's windows. The man and woman next to her were holding hands. She tugged at the woman's arm. "My mother asked me to ask you how far it is to Lord and Taylor's."

Twelve more blocks. That was a lot. But she had to finish the pretend game. It was starting to snow harder. She slipped her hands into her sleeves and bent her head so the snow wouldn't get in her eyes. She didn't look to see if the man was still following her—she knew he was. But as long as she walked next to other people he didn't come too close.

The squad car pulled up to the CBS studios at Fifty-seventh Street near Eleventh Avenue. Lieutenant Garrigan went inside with her. They were sent upstairs and a production assistant talked with Susan. "We're going to call this segment 'The Lost Angel.' We'll do a close-up of Jamie's picture, and then you can make a special appeal."

Susan waited in the corner of the television studio. Something seemed to be bursting inside her. It was as though she could hear Jamie's voice calling her. Lieutenant Garrigan was waiting with her. She grabbed his arm. "Tell them to show the picture. Let someone else make the appeal. I've got to go back."

315]

A sharp "sshhh" made her realize that her voice was rising, that it might be picked up by the microphones. She shook the lieutenant's sleeve. "Please, I've got to go back."

Jamie waited on the line to walk in front of the windows at Lord and Taylor's. They were as beautiful as Mommy had promised, like paintings from her fairy-tale books except that the figures moved and bent and waved. She found herself waving back. They were pretend people. It was almost as though they understood the pretend game. "Next year," Jamie whispered, "Mommy and I will come back together." She wanted to stay here, to keep watching the beautiful figures bend and turn and smile, but someone kept saying, "Please keep moving. Thank you."

The trouble was, the pretend game was over. She had been everywhere she and Mommy had planned to go. Now she didn't know what to do. Her forehead was wet with snow and she brushed her hair back. She could feel the cold wet air on her head.

She didn't want to stop looking in the windows. She squeezed herself against the rope so that people could pass her. "You're lost, aren't you, dear?" She looked up. It was the man who had been following her. He was talking so low she could hardly hear him. "If you know where you live, I could take you home," he whispered.

A bubble of hope grew in Jamie's chest. "Would you please phone my mother?" she asked. "I know the number."

"Of course. Let's go right now." He reached for her hand.

"Please keep moving," the voice said again.

"Come on," the man whispered. "We have to go."

There was something hurting Jamie. It was more than being tired and cold and hungry. She was scared. She clung to the edge of the windows, stared at the doll figures, and

[316

whispered her baby Jesus prayer. "Please, please let Mommy come now."

The squad car pulled up. "I know you think I'm crazy," Susan said. Her voice trailed off as she studied the still-dense crowd around the windows. The snow was starting to fall heavily and people were pulling coat collars up and scarves and hoods forward. There were a number of children in the line, but it was impossible to see their faces because they were facing the store windows. She was opening the door when she heard Lieutenant Garrigan say to the driver, "Sam, do you see who's on that line? It's that stinking child molester who didn't show up for trial. Come on!"

Shocked, Susan watched as they dashed across the side-walk, pushed through the line, grabbed the arms of a skinny man in a dirty jacket, and hurried him back toward the squad car.

And then she saw her. The small figure who did not turn around with the rest of the astonished bystanders, the small figure with the cap of unfamiliar white-gold hair that curved around the familiar cheek and neck.

Dazedly, Susan walked toward Jamie. Her hungry arms stretched out, she bent over and listened as Jamie continued to beg, "Please, please let Mommy come now."

Susan sank to her knees. "Jamie," she whispered.

Jamie thought she was still playing the pretend game. "Jamie."

It wasn't pretend. Jamie spun around and felt arms close around her. *Mommy.* It was *Mommy.* She locked her arms around Mommy's neck. She dug her head into Mommy's shoulder. Mommy was hugging her so tight. Mommy was rocking her. Mommy was saying her name over and over. "Jamie. Jamie." Mommy was crying. And around them

317]

people were smiling and cheering and clapping. And in the fairyland windows, the beautiful dolls were bowing and waving.

Jamie patted Mommy's cheek. "I knew you'd come," she whispered.